THE BAGHDAD SHUFFLE

A Novel

by
Josh Bates

© 2025, Josh Bates

All rights reserved. No part of this publication may be reproduced, stored in a retrieval system, or transmitted in any form by any process—electronic, mechanical, photocopying, recording, or otherwise—without the prior written permission of the copyright owner. The scanning, uploading, and distribution of this book via the Internet or via any other means without permission of the copyright owner is illegal and punishable by law.

Library and Archives Canada Cataloguing in Publication
Bates, Josh, author
The Baghdad Shuffle / Josh Bates

Issued in print and electronic formats.

ISBN: 978-1-998501-48-9 (paperback)
ISBN: 978-1-998501-49-6 (ebook)

Cover Design: COVER ARTIST
Interior Design: Richa Bargotra

Double Dagger Books
Toronto, Ontario, Canada
www.doubledagger.ca

This is a work of fiction. Names, characters, businesses, places, events and incidents are either the products of the author's imagination or used in a fictitious manner.

Part One

The Sand Box

1

Our Lady of Sorrows Cathedral
Baghdad, Iraq – Saturday, 12 April 2003

Dig the Mercedes. Shot to fuck and still running. German engineering for the win.

The driver tried to crawl out of the vehicle. He didn't make it. Torso on the blacktop, legs in the pedal well. He clutched a stained white towel in his hand, the universal 'don't shoot!' signal for Iraqi motorists. The towel didn't work. Dude got zapped good and proper. The driver's gut-shots oozed. The guy in the passenger seat was already dead. He'd been ear-holed by a round that scattered his dome all over the upholstery.

Corporal Benitez yelled over the hum of the generators, "Sir, the nuns won't take these guys."

"Whaddya mean the nuns won't take 'em? They actually said that?" I don't make a habit of questioning the boys, but the notion of nuns refusing to provide medical treatment seemed preposterous, even here in crazy town.

"That's what's up, Sir. The nuns won't let us bring these guys inside the church. They must be some evil motherfuckers if the nuns ain't playing."

"Well, that's mighty Christian of them."

What had already been a fucked-up day just got worse. Providing security for this half-assed, jury-rigged hospital wasn't my idea of time well spent. Since rolling into Baghdad three days ago, we'd been stuck with these bullshit protection gigs. We should be out hunting down the rest of the senior regime guys. Saddam, Tariq Azziz, Ibrahim al-Duri. Those mustachioed bastards whose mugs were made famous on the DIA's 'deck of cards.' Or maybe we should get out there and beat the bushes for the ever-elusive Weapons of Mass Destruction. Give the suits in DC the win they'd been slobbering for. Anything would be better than babysitting a bunch of salty-ass nuns that spent most of their nights patching up the same assholes we shot during the day.

The driver looked salvageable. Maybe. I had Doc Strickland take a look. Doc gave the driver a once-over with eyes that said 'why bother?'

Doc said, "Sir, this dude's alive but circling quick. He caught a tight burst. I count two rounds to the gut and one that I think clipped his lung."

The driver confirmed Doc's diagnosis with a heavy, wet wheeze. Fucker hacked up enough blood to fill a Gatorade bottle. There was still a glimmer of life left in his unfocused eyes. But not much. Homeboy was in the final countdown.

Doc checked his bag of goodies. "I'm not going to waste any of the QUIK CLOT on him. At this point it wouldn't do much good and I don't want to use what little I have left in case our boys need it later."

"Fair enough. I'd like to keep him alive long enough for the interrogators but not if it means depleting your goodie bag," I replied.

The driver looked like he might have some intel value. His moustache, car, and clothes screamed 'regime.' But keeping him alive long enough for interrogation would be tricky. We needed to move him to another medical facility stat. I looked up to see Benny escorting an older Iraqi man towards the Benz.

Benny hollered again over the generators, "Sir, there's a guy here says he knows a real hospital a couple of blocks away that will take these two."

The old man stepped forward so I could clock him in the light of our battery-powered camp lantern. He was wearing dusty black slacks, a beige windbreaker, and a pair of oversized, Henry Kissinger glasses. The get-up made him look like a cross between a community college professor and a pedophile. He held the ubiquitous white handkerchief in one hand and pulled his jacket open with the other. The old fella was going to great lengths to show Benny he was unarmed. I stepped to Benny's 7 o'clock. I didn't want to obstruct the field of fire if the old-timer got buggy and Benny had to give him the good news.

I said, "Evening, Sir. Do you know another hospital that will take these men?" I assumed he spoke English since he'd already spoken to Benny.

"Fortunately, I do, Lieutenant." The accent was Brit. He pronounced it 'left-tenant.' I wasn't wearing rank insignia and the boys never called me 'lieutenant.'

"Well, Sir, here's the situation. This car just pulled up to our checkpoint and as you can see, the occupants are not doing so well. Apparently, the nuns decided these guys aren't worthy of their Christian charity and they've refused to treat them. More precisely, they won't treat the guy that's still alive. Would you be willing to take the wounded man to another hospital?"

"I can be of assistance Left-tenant. *Al-Yarmouk* Hospital is nearby. However, I must insist that you put them in your vehicle and follow me. It would be unsafe for me to be seen with them in my car."

The sound of machine gun fire in the distance provided a momentary distraction. I counted three distinct bursts. The machine gunner was disciplined. Each burst timed to the singsong "die motherfucker die" refrain taught at the School of Infantry. It didn't sound close enough to warrant our attention just yet.

I glanced at Benny, then Doc. They both vibed 'this is bullshit.' They were right to be suspicious. The hospital scenario had set-up written all over it. Better than even odds that if we followed this guy he'd roll us into an ambush. I couldn't confirm that the hospital existed. It certainly wasn't annotated on any of our maps. Still, there was something unsavory about leaving the dead guy and his wounded buddy on the steps of the church. Dead Iraqi storage was not a priority at Our Lady of Sorrows. Dumping the these guys on consecrated ground would be a dick move.

I decided to gamble. "Ox! You and Blanky get your crews and saddle up!"

Corporal Kyle 'Ox' Oxford was kicked back in the .50 caliber machinegun turret of our truck, chain-smoking Miamis while he cleaned his sidearm. Ox's handle was more than an obvious abbreviation of his surname. Dude was built like a draught animal. He was also a surgeon with the .50. One of those rare men bred for combat. Hanging out at the church all night was depriving Ox the opportunity to add to his kill tally. A little trip across town would be just the thing to cheer him up.

I turned to Benny who looked disappointed. He rightly suspected he was getting left behind at the church.

I said, "I'm going to take Ox and Blanky and we're gonna follow this guy to the other hospital. Not sure it'll do the wounded guy any good, but it's worth a try in case he lives long enough to tell us what particular breed of bad man he represents and where his homeboys might be holed up. I need you guys to pat 'em down for pocket litter while we gear up."

Rifling through the Mercedes guys' pockets was a bloody, sticky affair. Benny stepped off to ask Doc Strickland for some latex gloves. Not one to pass up an opportunity to fuck with his Marines, Doc claimed he didn't have enough gloves to go around. Doc told Benny they would have to use their bare hands to dig through the gore. Benny's eyes went ice cold. Doc backtracked and quickly dug out his reserve stash of latex.

Benny dug through the dead passenger's pockets. The guy didn't have any personal effects on him. Not even one of those cheap plastic wallets with the stock photos of movie stars (Kate Winslet in her *Titanic* garb seemed to be a favorite) that were standard issue in the Iraqi Army. From what was left of the guy's head he looked to be in his late 20s or maybe early 30s. He was definitely a 'military-age male.' Probably one of the thousands of Iraqi Army joes that had ditched the uniform for civvies over the past couple of weeks. There weren't any weapons in the Benz. If these two were military or regime lackeys, they were either confident or desperate enough to roll slick. Either way, the lack of hardware piqued my interest.

The Marines worked the rest of Mercedes. They tore through the glove compartment, seatbacks, headliner, trunk. The car was clean. No registration, no water bottles, no license plates. Not even a cigarette butt or hint of ash. The lack of cigs was super suspicious. I'd yet to meet a rag that wasn't nicotine powered. Iraqis rivaled the French in competitive smoking.

Benny managed to prop the wounded driver into a seated position and hurriedly pawed through the man's pockets for anything of intel value. Like his dead passenger, the driver's pockets were clean. No wallet, no smokes, no lighter. Not even a set of keys other than the one still in the ignition.

"Benny, grab his legs," I said. I under-hooked the driver's arms in something approximating a fireman's drag.

We hoisted the dying man into the gun truck. He groaned once and passed out. I was about to have Ox help Benny load the dead passenger into the truck when I changed my mind. "Benny, do you still have that carboard stencil that says 'Danger: Keep Away' in Arabic?"

'Yeah, Boss, it's in my truck."

"OK, here's what I want you to do,' I said. "Drag this dead fucker to that little service road that leads to the back of the church. I know your boys are covering that approach, but the standoff down that connecting alley is for shit. Prop his corpse up at the entrance to the alley and use the stencil and the cardboard from a MRE box to make a warning sign. Put the sign in his lap and lean him against the vehicle barrier. There should be some spray paint in Doc's truck. Use some of the glow sticks so it's legible in the dark. I want the locals to know they're risking their lives if they cruise down that road."

Benny grunted an acknowledgement and walked off to find the stencil. He was obviously still pissed that he was on corpse duty while his platoon commander was fixing to head out into the wild. It was actually his fault. Benny was one of the most competent non-commissioned officers in the Battalion, which meant any time we did split ops he was my first choice to leave in charge of the stay-behinds.

It was time to get this show on the road. "Ox, I'm going to head over and talk to this old-timer real quick. While I distract him, go plant one of those infrared strobe lights on his ride, somewhere he won't find it. I want to be able to track this guy if he tries to fuck us."

Ox gave me a thumbs up. He already had an IR strobe prepped with adhesive. I hustled over to the old man.

"Mr. — uh, what's your name?" I asked.

"Fuad."

"OK, Fuad, we're just about ready to roll."

I pulled out a map and spread it across the hood of the truck to distract Fuad. Ox recognized the signal and slunk off into the shadows. Within seconds he'd discreetly mounted the IR strobe to the undercarriage of Fuad's Chevy Caprice.

"So, we're here." I fingered a spot on the map. "Can you show me where the hospital is located?"

"Left-tenant, we need to hurry if we're going to save that man. Please, just follow me."

Fuad had a point. The Mercedes driver was fading fast. It was looking less likely he'd live long enough to chat with the interrogators. I decided to hold off contacting the 'gators until we had a better idea of Mr. Gut-shot's lifespan.

I tried to lock eyes with Fuad. The reflection of the lantern in his giant glasses obscured his features. The lens distortion made it tough to get a read on the guy.

I said, "Ok Fuad. We'll follow you. But just so you know, if we get ambushed, I'm gonna shoot you first."

Fuad didn't reply. He speed-walked to the Chevy, U-turned, and gunned it away from the church. I hopped behind the wheel of the gun truck. Technically, officers won't supposed to drive tactical vehicles, but I couldn't justify wasting a talented gunner on chauffer duties.

Ox took his position in the turret. He had the warlord swagger down cold. I envied his ease behind the gun. If we were headed into an ambush, having Ox behind the .50 would dramatically increase our chance of survival.

The lack of electricity gave the city a jaundiced pallor. Pale yellow buildings in a brown sky. Twilight was the trickiest time of day. The Iraqis fortunate enough to own generators didn't fire up their lamps until it was completely dark. It was too dark for naked eyeballs, but still too light for night vision goggles. The lack of exterior lighting along the streets made distances and shadows harder to gauge. If we did get hit, picking out targets would be tough.

Fortunately, Fuad had been truthful about the proximity of the hospital. I counted eleven blocks south and five blocks west from the church before the hospital peeked into view.

A few hundred meters out I spotted a long string of green lights that were looped around a semicircular driveway. The illuminated approach allowed ambulances easy access to the emergency room, but it also provided enemy gunners a good sight picture if we lingered too long.

I clocked the surroundings as we approached the driveway. The hospital was hemmed in on both sides by three-story apartment buildings. The apartments had dark, evenly spaced windows arrayed across the upper floors. The windows gaped like eye sockets in a stack of sand-colored skulls. The overall aesthetic was fucking creepy. Worse yet, the apartment buildings allowed for more overhead firing positions than we could realistically cover with two gun trucks.

I told Ox to keep his eyes on the roofs. As if he needed to be told. Ox could spot and react to threats faster than anyone in the game. Still, we didn't have a lot of room to maneuver. Taking fire from above would be problematic.

Fuad pulled up in front of the hospital's receiving area. I radioed Blanky to have him pull his truck to the far side of the driveway. I wanted Fuad boxed in. If we got hit at the hospital, I wanted to punch Fuad's ticket before we bailed out.

An orderly scurried out of the hospital and ran up to Fuad's Chevy. Fuad barked a couple of commands in Arabic. The orderly hustled over to help unload the patient. I helped the orderly pull the Mercedes driver from the truck. As soon as we laid him on the deck it was clear he'd died in transit. The orderly checked for a pulse and then looked back at Fuad and shook his head. I felt a wetness on my upper thighs. I'd soiled my 'cleanest' pair of cammie trousers with the dead man's blood.

"Well, Fuad, we tried. Sorry he didn't make it," I said.

"Don't be sorry, Left-tenant. He was not a good man. He is… or I should say was, *Mukhabarat*. He was one of Saddam's intelligence officers."

"I guess that explains the Mercedes. But if he was a bad guy then why didn't you tell me back at the church?"

Before Fuad could answer, Ox shuffled in his turret.

"Boss, we've got company. Two shooters, nine o'clock," Ox said.

Sure enough, two shapes darted through the shadows about 100 meters out. I horse-collared Fuad and dragged him down behind the gun truck. I indexed the barrel of my 9mm to Fuad's throat. "What the fuck are you playing at, Fuad?"

"Left-tenant… please! I am just trying to help. I wish you no harm." Fuad was pleading. His forehead popped sweat. His breath reeked of fear. If Fuad had planned this little caper, he was one hell of an actor.

I shouted at Ox to see if he had a bead on the gunmen. The .50 cal barked in response. True to form, Ox cut the strings on the lead gunman with a single burst. The silhouette broke in half next to a parked car.

A second gunman sprinted for cover. Ox and Blanky opened up with controlled bursts. The .50 cal rounds sparked and chewed. The car rocked on its suspension. A tracer round caught the second gunman at the knee. His lower leg spun off into the gutter like a bowling pin clipped on a 7-10 split. His pantleg caught fire from the tracer. If he was lucky, his trousers might burn long enough to cauterize the stump. Regardless, his dancing days were over.

"We better bounce, Boss. Those guys were obviously just recon. The rockets and heavy guns are sure to follow." Ox's assessment was delivered with a calmness I certainly didn't feel.

I pushed Fuad into the back of the truck. Ox stood in the turret and repositioned himself so he could pin Fuad to the seat with his boot. I flexi-cuffed Fuad's wrists and ankles and tossed him into the back seat. Ox could stomp his ass from the turret if required. It dawned on me Fuad might not survive a stomp from Ox, but I didn't have time to make other arrangements. I flashed the 'moving out' signal to Blanky's truck and sped out of the driveway. I looked back at the hospital in the sideview mirror. The orderly was gone. He'd left the body of the Mercedes driver on the curb.

The gunmen that moved on us at the hospital would have a backup crew positioned along the egress route. They'd try and set another ambush to catch us on our way back to the church. I didn't know who they were. Saddam's *Fedayeen?* Iranian gun thugs? Dudes just looking to party? It didn't really matter. There were still plenty of bucks looking to take a shot at the title. One thing I did know for certain is that they'd be waiting for us. I radioed Blanky and ordered him to tuck in behind us. Our only option at this point was to drive fast, shoot straight, and pray hard.

———

We cranked through the city. The church was still blocks away. Blanky hollered over the radio that we were being followed. Ox shouted down through the gun turret, confirming the tail. In the sideview mirror I saw an SUV gaining on Blanky's truck. I stole a glance at Fuad. The old fella was sweating like a kiddie diddler in gen pop.

Blanky let off a short burst from his .50 cal that missed the SUV, tracer rounds skidded off the pavement at sharp angles. The SUV accelerated and locked up with Blanky's rear bumper. At such close range, the depression stop on the .50 cal prevented Blanky from lowering the barrel enough to engage the Toyota. A pair of arms holding an AK-47 appeared out the SUV's passenger side window. The muzzle flashed. A wild burst scratched across Blanky's bumper. With the .50 cal out of action, Blanky drew his 9mm and dumped all fifteen rounds across the SUV's windshield. The arms in the window dropped the AK onto the street. The SUV braked hard and swerved down a small alley.

I shouted a little louder than I intended into the radio, "What's happening, Blanky?"

"I dumped em, Sir. They broke off into an alley," Blanky said.

"Ox, you have a visual?" I tapped Ox's leg to get his attention.

"Negative," said Ox. "They disappeared down a side-street. I coulda waxed those fools if Blanky had gotten out of the way." Ox was pissed he'd just been cock-blocked from adding to his body count.

Now I was convinced Fuad wasn't acting. Those dudes in the SUV weren't part of anything he'd cooked up. Bumper-locking a gun truck was a suicide play. Nothing about Fuad indicated he was ready to check out.

———

We made it back to the church. Blanky's truck took a couple of rounds but there was no tire or mechanical damage. Blanky's assault pack didn't fare so well. He strapped it to the back of the truck. His last pair of clean skivvies got shredded by the AK burst. Poor Blanky would be freeballin' for a stretch.

I pulled Fuad out of the truck. It was time we had a heart-to-heart. I grabbed him by the neck and forced him to do the Baghdad Shuffle across the lot with his arms and legs still cuffed. We found a little room that the nuns used as an office. I sat between Fuad and the door. Fuad needed to understand his path to freedom ran through me.

"Take a seat, Fuad. Let's jump right to it. What the fuck was that all about?"

Fuad eased himself into the chair and removed his glasses. It was an awkward movement with his wrists still bound together. He wiped the specs with the cuff of his windbreaker.

"Left-tenant, I swear I had nothing to do with those men at the hospital," Fuad said. "I was simply trying to help you find treatment for the wounded man."

"I'm not sure I believe you," I said. "But put that aside for now. Tell me who you are. What do you do? Where do you live? What were you doing out on the street at this hour? How did you know those men were *Mukhabarat*? Start talking, Fuad."

"Many questions, Left-tenant, I will try and answer in order. My name is Fuad. I am a history professor at the university here in Baghdad. I was on my way home from visiting a sick friend who lives near the church. I saw the driver of the Mercedes lying on the street and your men did not seem to be doing anything to help him… so I approached and offered my services."

Red flags galore. This asshole was dissembling. "You didn't answer my other question. How did you know those two were *Mukhabarat*?"

"Iraqis know these things. Those men, and the regime they represent, are objects of fear in this country. We tend to memorize the identities of those we fear so we can better avoid them."

"So, you actually recognized those two? Who are they? What department did they work for? Why are they still in the city? What are they planning?"

"I do not know those men. But I know the type. Their car was the first indicator. As you noted back at the hospital, only Saddam's men drive Mercedes. Also, did you notice the driver was wearing cowboy boots? I can assure you, Left-tenant, there is no domestic market for cowboy boots here in Iraq. That man had surely been abroad."

The contrast of the British accent with the guttural punctuation of Arabic words like 'Iraq,' which Fuad pronounced 'Ur-ruk," was off-putting. It was like listening to a German call play-by-play on a baseball game. Fuad was obviously a man who lived in many different worlds. I wasn't happy he'd shown up in mine.

Before I could follow-up, Benny popped his head into the room. Worried that Fuad might hear him, he leaned close to my ear and whispered, "Sir, Battalion needs us back at the Country Club. A time-sensitive mission. They said another unit would cover down here at the church. They need us back ASAP."

The Country Club was the nickname for our Battalion's current headquarters. It was a spa retreat for senior *Ba'athists* back in the day. The compound consisted of several large banquet halls with tennis courts and an indoor pool. The entire spread was tightly nestled along the eastern bank of the Tigris. The neighborhood was markedly upscale for such a busted-ass city.

I welcomed the thought of spending the night inside the Battalion perimeter after dealing with whatever this next mission entailed. The extra manpower at the Country Club would afford us more sleep. However, I was conflicted about leaving the nuns before our relief arrived. The nuns were a soft target. The nutjobs prowling Baghdad right now wouldn't harbor the slightest reservation about offing church folk… especially Christians. The church didn't have anything worth stealing, but the nuns would still be easy prey. Nobody wants nun-blood on their conscience.

What to do about Fuad? I was convinced he hadn't orchestrated that caper at the hospital, but he was still playing an angle I couldn't decipher. Like maybe he wanted me to bring him in. Fuck it. I decided to release him back into the wild and see how it shook out. 'Fuck it' always wins.

"OK, Fuad, it's your lucky day. You're free to go," I said.

Fuad looked genuinely confused. "I thought you didn't believe me when I told you I had nothing to do with the incident at the hospital?"

"I'm still not sure I believe anything you've told me. But I have bigger fish to fry right now and I don't feel like carting your ass around the city. Beat it. Get the fuck out of here."

Fuad's confusion turned to worry. I cut his cuffs and escorted him out of the church. Fuad walked off, pausing once to look inside the Mercedes. By the time I'd returned to the gun truck, he was long gone.

2

Rusafa District
Baghdad, Iraq – Saturday, 12 April 2003

We didn't make it back to the Country Club. I caught a call from Battalion. We got tasked with a new mission in-stride. The intel bubbas heard chatter that a bank was about to get hit. Soon. Likely within the hour. Local crews were making a play to snatch up whatever treasure Saddam's boys missed before they hightailed it out of the city.

We raced to the bank in a long, staggered column. The sound of red-lined tachometers and howling transmissions drowned out the radio buzz. I scanned the column to make sure all our gun trucks were still accounted for. All the trucks were up, bristling with weapons and hyper-caffeinated Marines. A low-budget *Mad Max* outtake.

We were too late. The heist was in full swing by the time we arrived. The bank was on fire. Automatic weapons sang the 'Cordite Blues.' A call and response dirge of gunfire and death. Bodies littered the street. A Red Crescent ambulance burned in the parking lot, black skeletons still aflame in the stretcher bay.

I set the platoon into a hasty perimeter and dismounted. Four Marines hustled to cover the far side of the bank. I spotted seven gunmen tooled up in black. Balaclavas, leather jackets, combat fatigues–call it 'Strongarm Chic.' The gunmen stacked outside the vault room. One dude broke out of the stack and fired a rocket propelled grenade into the exterior wall. The wall crumbled, exposing the vault. I yelled at the Marines to start shooting. The boys were way ahead of me. The Marine to my right dropped two of the crew before I'd even drawn a sight picture. The bank robber at the front of the stack ran hard for the blown-out wall. I put a round through his upper back as he dove. A little puff of smoke jumped off his shoulder blade as he disappeared behind the debris.

With three of their crew down, the other four heist-men broke off in separate directions. Two disappeared around the corner to my left. I heard Ox clapping with the .50 cal. Half a beat later, Ox hollered over the radio that he'd zapped the pair. I broke off to chase the other two at a dead sprint. They angled through a maze of blacked-out streets behind the bank. Both runners fired on the move. Green tracers skipped off the street in front of me. I dove for cover behind a blasted-out taxi. I risked a quick turkey-peep over the hood and noted one of the two remaining runners was down. He was turtled, his body cantilevered on a large backpack. His arms and legs cut the air as he scrambled for purchase on the concrete. His partner ran up and shot the prone bastard in the forehead.

The shooter ripped off his balaclava and wiped the sweat out of his eyes. He struggled to free the dead man's pack. The deadweight made it a chore. A car raced past. The headlights caught the shooter in profile. His face was scarred and shiny with sweat. Scarface didn't see me. I fumbled a reload. Scarface snatched his dead partner's backpack and disappeared.

The gunfire ceased. A backup platoon from another battalion arrived. Their platoon commander said they'd help establish a cordon to keep the crowd in check. I instructed Doc Strickland to set up casualty collection points for the dead and wounded.

I inspected the body of the guy Scarface plugged. He was clean. No ID, no pocket litter, no surprise. There was nothing left to take back to the intel guys.

Back at the bank, Doc was busy managing the casualty-collection effort. The bodies of the heist-men were already stacked. There was a larger pile of dead civilians in the bank parking lot.

Locals started to gather across the street. They wailed and shouted. A couple of young Iraqi guys tried to break through the cordon to inspect the dead. They scanned the bodies in a frenzy, looking for familiar faces. Marines from the cordon platoon formed a wall to keep the distraught locals corralled. I walked into the bank. Ox was kicking around inside the blown-out vault, surveying the damage.

"Ox, any wounded in the vault?" I asked.

"No, Sir, it's empty," Ox replied.

"Damn. I plugged one of 'em. Got that fucker in the back. I saw the round impact his shoulder."

"Well hell, good for you, Sir. I'll be sure to let you know if we find him in the rubble. Make sure you get a souvenir from your first confirmed kill." Ox sported a Cheshire grin. He thrived on the mayhem. He was going to have a hard time adjusting to life back in the World.

"Uh… ok, Ox. Thanks for that… I guess. You find anything in the vault? Any dinar, American dollars, Krugerrands, gold, diamonds? Anything to indicate what those boys were after?"

"Negative, Sir. There's a few small bills scattered around. All dinars. Nothing like what the intel guys thought was in here."

I surveyed the vault room. Ox was right. There didn't seem to be anything worth taking.

Ox lit up a Miami and gestured towards the debris. "Doesn't seem like much of a score for all this craziness. You ever heard of bank robbers using an RPG? That's some wild-west shit."

The destruction jazzed Ox. The rubble, the smoke, the blood, Ox was impressed with the whole she-bang. No doubt he was already weighing the pros and cons of pulling his own RPG-aided bank caper back home in Iowa.

"But here's what doesn't make much sense, Boss. It looks like these guys hit the offices first, then came back outside the bank and tried to breach the vault from the outside," Ox said.

For not having ever received any formal investigative training, Ox's powers of observation impressed me. He'd pieced all this together after walking through the bank for five minutes.

"Were there vaults in the offices?" I asked.

"Yes, Sir, or at least in one of them. There was a wall-mounted safe that they'd blown open. Nothing left inside. Just a few scraps of charred paper on the ground underneath the vault."

"Did you bag any of those scraps?"

"Yes, Sir, got 'em right here." Ox pulled a plastic Ziploc bag out of his cargo pocket and handed it over.

The scraps were badly burned. One page was slightly less damaged than the others. There were a few digits printed along the edge that were still legible. But that was about it. I couldn't decipher any readable text or other info. The Intel bubbas would really earn their keep if they unraveled this one.

I told Ox to bag and tag anything that looked legible. The crowd across the street had already doubled in the five minutes I was inside the vault room. The wails of the women rattled my fillings. I hustled back to the truck and picked up the radio handset. I needed to check-in with Battalion to figure out the next step.

The crowd swelled. The noise drowned out the voice on the other end of my radio. A chorus of new cries pierced the cacophony. Startled, I looked back towards the parking lot.

A mangy dog chowed down on one of the bodies in the casualty pile. Not a good look for the newly 'liberated' Iraq.

———

The bank-caper debrief took forever. Major Miller, my Company Commander, was down south in Babylon for a special planning session at Division Headquarters. That meant there was no buffer between the Battalion Commander and me when it came time to answer the tough questions. The Old Man was particularly unhappy that a French TV crew broadcast footage of the aftermath within minutes of us leaving the scene. I tried to offer some consolation by noting that the Marines seen in the broadcast were from another battalion. I was also quick to throw out that we'd greased most of the heist-crew before they accessed the vault room.

My attempts to assuage the Old Man were unsuccessful. He was salty. An expression that most would mistake for boredom was how the Old Man broadcast his disappointment. Which, to be fair, was not unreasonable. The optics were not good. Dozens of citizens killed or wounded, massive fire damage, stray dogs munching on dead bodies. It was tough to put a positive spin on that shit no matter how many bad guys we stacked. There was also the lingering issue of Scarface getting away with his colleague's backpack. Whatever was in the pack must've been damn important for Scarface to clip his own guy. I didn't want the platoon to take any more heat for the bank, so I decided not to mention the backpack during the debrief.

After the Old Man dismissed me, I tracked down the Battalion intelligence officer, a Captain named Derrick Vandershot. I didn't like the guy. The Marines fucking hated him. He cultivated the 'I have a secret' persona to annoying perfection. Despite acting like a douche most of the time, Vandershot did have some moves. I'd seen him leverage other intelligence units with better toys. He got us all sorts of high-speed technical collection that most battalions would never receive. So, on rare occasions, my reluctance to endure Vandershot's dickhead personality could be outweighed by his professional competence. I'd have to trust him with our findings in the vault room if I had any hope of getting some answers. I pulled Vandershot aside and showed him the papers Ox had bagged. Vandershot studied the charred scraps and clued-in on the row of numbers still legible in the margin. He said the numbers looked like the serials used to record wire transfers. It was all esoteric shit. None of his off-the-cuff analysis meant anything to me. Fortunately, Vandershot's curiosity was piqued.

"I'll contact Treasury and have their analysts take a look," Vandershot said.

"Treasury?" I replied, not knowing what the fuck he was talking about.

"Yeah, as in the Treasury Department."

"Uh, sure. Whatever."

Vandershot broke contact without another word. Apparently he had better shit to do than explain the nuances of the Federal Government's analytical brain trust to a straight-leg grunt.

3

Al-Muthana Neighborhood
Baghdad, Iraq – Tuesday, 15 April 2003

Night patrols. All night, every night. Rambling through the city looking to scrap was good for the platoon's morale, but the lack of sleep was starting to take a toll. Tonight's adventure involved surveillance in Baghdad's east end. Captain Vandershot and his intel crew identified an abandoned *souk* that served as an assembly area for *Badr Corps* paramilitaries. The *Badr* boys were the new kids on the block. They'd joined the party fresh from Iran. The surveillance Op felt like a longshot. I couldn't fathom that the locals would be stupid enough to funnel their Iranian homeboys through the same location night after night. But we didn't have any other 'actionable intel' so the *souk* would have to suffice. This type of 'operation by default' was becoming standard practice. The chain of command didn't really know what to do now that Baghdad had fallen. I sure as hell wouldn't admit it to the boys, but we were making shit up on the fly. I had a feeling we weren't the only ones. If the suits back in DC had anything resembling a plan, they'd yet to share it with those of us out here in the streets.

After scanning the deserted market for what seemed like the five hundredth time that night, we finally got some motion. A low-slung sedan coasted into the *souk* in neutral. The driver had killed the lights a couple of blocks out. The car slow-rolled to the curb and stopped.

I grabbed the radio handset. "Benny, what's up with that car?"

"I count a single occupant. Looks like an IR strobe flashing under the car. The driver just got out and popped the trunk," Benny replied.

The car was difficult to make out in the dark. The driver had parked it in the far corner of the *souk* near a squat, single-story building with a big picture window, some sort of café in better times. The driver stood by the open trunk, waiting like he expected someone. A couple beats later the low murmur of voices floated down the street.

"Benny, you hearing this?"

"Roger, looks to be three men approaching the car from the north."

"Any of them armed?"

"I don't see any weapons. Wait… they're talking to the driver. He's showing them something in the trunk."

I pulled down my NVGs to get a better look at these clowns. As soon as my eyes adjusted to the green and black world of the goggles, I noticed the infrared strobe light pulsing underneath the car. I looked closer. Bingo — it was Fuad's car. I adjusted my goggles to get a better fix on the driver. Yep, it was Fuad. There was no good reason a college professor would be out here in the dead of night. Running the streets at this hour was asking to get killed. Fuad was definitely on the make.

"Benny, let's jam these fools. Foot mobile on my mark. I'll be coming in with Blanky on your left." I whispered up to Ox that we were moving out and gave the go-order over the radio.

We closed on the sedan fast. Within seconds we'd hemmed in the four shadowy figures between the car and the café. They had nowhere to run.

"*Tawaqquf!* Freeze! Don't move!" I yelled.

The Marines put all four men face down on the deck. Benny and Blanky zip-tied their wrists and patted them down for weapons.

I jumped back on the handheld. "How we looking Ox? Any movement? Anyone stirring?"

"Negative, no movement." Ox had a near-perfect overwatch position. If anyone was looking to dance he'd get the drop on them.

"Let's get these guys into that cafe-looking thing."

I motioned to Benny to move the detainees inside. We didn't have an interpreter. But Fuad spoke English and I wanted some answers.

As I walked towards the café, I peered into the open trunk of Fuad's Chevy. Packed around the spare tire were dozens of bottles of Johnny Walker Black Label. The scotch was stacked neatly in cardboard dividers. It wasn't the cargo I was expecting. Guns, ammo, illicit cash… sure. That all made sense. But scotch? Didn't see that coming. Maybe I'd been too quick to judge. Maybe Fuad wasn't all bad.

"Good evening, Left-tenant. It is good to see you again." Fuad looked sheepish as fuck in his giant Kissinger glasses.

"Well, well, well, if it isn't Professor Fuad. What's with the booze, my man, you guys getting your swerve on?"

"It seems you've caught me in the midst of… let us say… extracurricular activities."

"Extracurricular is one way of putting it. Do you want to explain any further or am I just supposed to guess?"

"Well, Left-tenant, in these uncertain times, my neighbors could do with a little liquid refreshment… to help calm their nerves."

"So, you just arranged to meet these guys out here on the far side of town, in a deserted *souk*, in the middle of the night, to sling some medicinal whiskey? Doesn't seem like a very credible story, Fuad."

I looked back at the other three Iraqis who Benny had put down on their knees. They were still staring intently at the floor. Not one of them had made so much as a peep since they'd been cuffed.

I said, "Why here, Fuad? From what you told me the other night, you don't live anywhere near here."

"You are correct, Left-tenant, I do not. But these men are long-time customers. I have many such customers all over the city."

"Customers? That professor pay must not be cutting it, huh?"

Before Fuad could reply, a long string of heavy machine gun fire rumbled in the distance. The familiar bass-drum pattern was followed by the faint whooshing of rocket propelled grenades, or something much larger.

I keyed the handheld. "Ox, you got a visual on that drama, any tracers?"

"Negative. Sounds like it's a couple klicks to the north," Ox replied.

"Roger. Have O'Reilly's crew take up positions along that main access road to the north of the *souk*. Have them keep eyes on that approach. And hit up Battalion for the latest patrol updates. I need to know if there are any friendlies in the area."

I turned back to Fuad, and pointed towards the gunfire. "Do you know what that's all about?"

Fuad shuffled and wiped at his face with cuffed hands. "I'm afraid not, Left-tenant. But the shooting has increased considerably these past few nights."

"Well, Fuad, it's funny you mention that, because a little birdy told me that you might have some new neighbors in this part of town. You know, the kind of bad guys with beards instead of moustaches. Maybe the kind with 'Persian' accents?"

"As a matter of fact, Left-tenant, I am indeed aware of a certain foreign presence that recently arrived in this very neighborhood. About two hours ago, as I visited some of my other customers, I just so happened to witness some of your Persian friends moving what I assume were weapons into an apartment several kilometers northeast of here."

"Fuad, we've been shooting the shit here for the past five minutes and you *just now* think to tell me you know where some Iranians are stashing weapons? For Christ sakes man, why didn't you start with that!"

"I was simply trying to answer your questions in order."

"Well guess what, Fuad, you're going to take us to that apartment." I turned to Benny and pointed towards the other three men. "Did these three have any identification on them?"

"Negative, Sir. These two had wallets with money but no IDs of any kind." Benny pointed at the Arab kneeling in front of Blanky. "That guy didn't have a wallet, no money, nothing."

The guy with no wallet looked vaguely familiar. It was hard to get a good read in the dark. From what I could make out, his face looked off-kilter. I fancied myself a good judge of a man's capacity for evil based solely on looks. Those 19th century phrenologists were on to something. But this cat's warped face was pure mystery.

I debated what to do with Fuad's friends. There was a good possibility that they knew about the Iranian stash house and that, if I let them go, they'd run off and warn the occupants. But keeping four men under gun all night would burn valuable manpower and we didn't have time to dump them at the Country Club.

"OK, as much as I hate to do it, cut those three loose. We're going to take Fuad with us on a panty raid," I said.

I radioed Ox to let him know we were headed back to the truck with a 'plus one.'

———

Battalion sent a platoon to establish a cordon around the suspected Iranian stash house. The plan—and it wasn't a great one—was to roll on the apartment in our gun trucks. Not ideal, but better than moving on foot through block after block of bandit country. I'd arranged to hit the apartment at 0600. If Iraq had taught me nothing else, it was that no one in this part of the world was at the top of their game that early in the morning.

Battalion greenlit the raid, but it came with a catch. We got saddled with a CNN reporter named Miguel and his cameraman, Eddy, an East London geezer with all the fixings. Miguel looked sleazy in the typical TV reporter mold. Eddy vibed that particular flavor of instability that comes from a lifetime of substance abuse and no-win situations. Worse yet, I couldn't understand a single word out of his mouth. The platoon didn't even rate an Arabic translator, so I reckoned a cockney interpreter was out of the question.

I didn't dig the idea of letting Miguel and Eddy tag along, but I knew better than to push back. Ever since the bank caper, the Old Man was hellbent on wrangling more positive press coverage. The CNN boys were along for the ride whether I liked it or not.

Miguel and Eddy's Toyota Hi-Lux SUV rolled into our assembly area. It had "TV" painted on the door. As if the bad guys gave a shit. Fuckin' wannabe *Mujahedden* would probably use the 'V' as an aiming point. I pushed the platoon into overwatch. Miguel and Eddy jumped out of the Hi-Lux with their video camera and microphones ready to go.

I took another look at the stash house. The façade looked to be of typical Iraqi construction, which meant concrete mixed on the ground, impregnated with all manner of debris. The walls looked like they had the structural integrity of *papier-mache*. The apartment would provide little in the way of cover when the shooting started.

Miguel lurked in my personal space. I warned him and Eddy to stay out of the Marines' way. Miguel offered a half-assed thumbs up. Eddy just stared and wiped his nose obsessively. His beady eyes lacked focus. He looked coked out, which seemed impossible given the setting, but Brits are shady like that. I had a bad feeling Eddy was about to become a major liability.

Fuad sat cramped below Ox's gun turret. I braced him again. "One last time, Professor, tell me exactly what you saw."

Fuad studied Miguel and Eddy for a beat. No doubt he was praying to keep his mug off tonight's Headline News video feed. Fuad came across as the kind of guy who went to great lengths to shun public exposure.

"Just as I told you before, Left-tenant," Fuad said. "I saw three, Farsi-speaking men unloading what looked like weapons crates from a truck parked there on the corner. They carried the crates into the apartment through that door on the left." He pointed with both cuffed hands at an unscreened, aluminum door. "I didn't see anyone else. There wasn't any noticeable activity on the second floor. However, it was dark, so I can't be certain that there aren't other men in the apartment."

It wasn't much in terms of reliable recon, but it would have to do. Benny, O'Reilly, and their teams were already in position on the roof of a derelict building next to the target. On my signal they would jump onto the roof of the stash house, breach the access door to the central stairwell, and clear the joint from top to bottom. Ox and Blanky would maintain their position across the block to hose down any squirters. The other four trucks held the perimeter to deter would-be party crashers. The geometry of fires was fucked, but we didn't have the time or resources to develop a better approach.

Go time. Benny, O'Reilly, and their Marines landed hard on the stash-house roof. O'Reilly kicked in the topside door and disappeared into the stairwell. Shots rattled around inside the apartment. I heard O'Reilly's voice over the handheld. He confirmed a kill. Seconds later a shirtless man carrying an AK-47 ran out the door of the apartment. Ox dumped the guy before he made the curb. New voices echoed down the street. A dark, bearded man with an RPG popped out on the street about 50 meters away. Ox didn't have a clean bead on the bearded guy, so he dismounted with his rifle and sprinted into the street. Ox popped him from the off-hand with a single shot.

"Got him!" Ox yelled.

Miguel directed Eddy towards the street so they could get a better camera angle on Ox's heroics. A second man emerged with a rifle about 100 meters down the street. Ox dropped prone and got off another round. The gunman spun violently and folded into the ground, his shattered arm pinned underneath his torso.

"He's still moving, Boss!" Ox sounded annoyed his first round hadn't sealed the deal.

The gunman reached for his rifle with his good hand. His shattered arm dangled awkwardly. I was amazed the guy still had enough in the tank to stay in the fight. Dumbass should've played dead.

"Hit him again, Ox!" I shouted.

Eddy dropped to a knee a few yards behind Ox, his camera fixed downrange on the wounded man. The shot-up gunman managed to get into a seated position. Ox splattered the guy's melon with a follow-up round. A loud chorus of cheers rang out. Three Marines from the overwatch truck laughed and pointed towards Ox's latest kill. Eddy smiled, his fucked-up British fangs illuminated in the light of his camera's eyepiece.

————

The raid was a bust. O'Reilly bagged a guy in the stairwell and Ox added three more kills to his tally, but there was nothing of note 'stashed' in the stash house. We found a couple of additional AKs but nothing sexy. None of the occupants were Iranian or important regime types. I sized up the dead. They vibed criminal. I pegged 'em as a half-assed strongarm crew that we'd caught between capers. The more I thought about it, the more I wondered if they might have been Fuad's black market competition. It seemed as though Fuad might've just used us to take out his rivals. The old fella had some explaining to do.

With the house secured, I ordered the platoon to mount up. It had been an exceptionally long night and the platoon was running on fumes. I needed to get the boys back to the Country Club for some shut eye. It also seemed high time to put Fuad in the box for a real interrogation.

The Battalion detention cell was set up in the building that housed the Country Club's indoor swimming pool. The pool was empty, which made it a natural choice for interrogations. The 'gators had placed a single rug in the deep end under an array of white lights, like the kind used by construction crews for nighttime road work. The overall aesthetic was pretty sinister, if perhaps a little cheesy in the Bond Villain-mode. I had to get back to the Command Post for the debrief, so I handed Fuad over to the 'gators and gave them a quick rundown of the stash house op. I hoped a few hours in the pool would get Fuad's attention.

My buddy Rick was on Ops Watch, manning radios and updating maps to track the night's action. He could tell I was out of gas, so he sped me through the debrief. As I finished my account of the raid, Rick's boss Major McSorley called me over to the map board.

With a radio handset still stuck to one ear, McSorley said, "Jim hold up a sec."

His use of my first name was non-standard. McSorley's tone rattled my nerves.

McSorley wrapped up his radio conversation and fixed me with bagged eyes. "We're kicking that Fuad guy loose, the Old Man okayed it. But Fuad asked to see you before he leaves."

"What the fuck, Sir? I just dropped him off an hour ago. The interrogators are already done with him?"

"It appears so." McSorley gave me the 'Majors don't need to explain themselves to Lieutenants' face.

"Sir, fuck that guy," I said. "I don't trust him. I think he's some sort of half-assed gangster trying to use us to clear out his competition. Get this, after we jammed him up that first night, we left him at the church. I made him leave his car back at the hospital where we'd been ambushed. But last night we find him out running the streets again and, lo and behold, he's still got his Chevy. The fact that the locals didn't jack his ride means he's got some juice. I say we sweat him again or clip him."

"Clip him? Jesus Christ, I hope you're joking. Or just loopy from lack of sleep. We aren't in the business of executing detainees." McSorley eyeballed me hard. "Just humor me and go see what he wants. The interrogators agree with you. They think he's holding back. We could send him south, let the Army interrogators fuck with him for a while. But if we do that, we won't get anything out of it. Better for us if he's back out on the street making moves, especially if we can keep tabs on him. He might lead us to some bigger fish. Maybe even point us towards some senior regime guys. It's worth keeping him in play. Go figure out a way to stay in touch."

I wanted to 'keep in touch' with Fuad about as much as I wanted to 'stay friends' with my ex-wife. But McSorley had a point. If we sent Fuad south, it was unlikely we'd receive any of the intel from the follow-on interrogations. Maybe we could use Fuad to bait some other bad actors.

McSorley dismissed me. I moseyed off to find Fuad. He was standing next to the vehicle control point. A baby-faced Marine I recognized from the Admin Shop was standing next to Fuad with his rifle at the alert.

I waived to the Marine. "I got him from here, killer."

Baby Face nodded and shuffled off to do whatever it is Admin Marines do.

"You wanted to see me, Fuad?" I asked.

"Yes, thank you, Left-tenant—" Fuad broke into a coughing fit. He took a handkerchief from his windbreaker and covered his mouth. The cloth was dotted with blood.

"You OK, Fuad? You're not going to give me tuberculosis, are you?"

Fuad recovered and stuffed the handkerchief back into his jacket. "I'm fine, thank you. Your medical personnel were very gracious in examining me before the interrogation." Fuad spat once more and gathered himself. "I was hoping that, later this week, you would pay me a visit, at my apartment. I would very much like to introduce you to my family."

This was an unexpected wrinkle. My relationship with Fuad had been anything but cordial to this point. On one hand, McSorley had instructed me to try and maintain contact, but this felt like Fuad engineering something sketchy.

"Uh, sure, Fuad, why not? When did you have in mind?" I asked.

"Perhaps tomorrow night or the night after." Fuad replied.

"Well, I guess it's a date. How do I find you?"

"I will leave a message with the guard manning this checkpoint." Fuad gestured towards the Country Club's vehicle control point.

I stared at Fuad, his eyes remained distorted by the funhouse mirror warp of his gigantic glasses. "You know, Fuad, we've known each other for a few days now and you've never even asked me my name."

"How very rude of me. I hope you accept my sincerest apology, Jim. Or do you prefer Left-tenant Wilde?"

4

"The Country Club"
Baghdad, Iraq – Thursday, 17 April 2003

The entire platoon was gathered in one place for the first time in days. We turned to on weapons maintenance, vehicle maintenance, and sleep. Everyone was zonked. The boys weren't even bitching and moaning. That's always a bad sign. When Marines stop complaining, it's time to start worrying.

After taking care of the weapons and making sure the trucks were good to go, I tried to bed down in the shade. I could feel the black velvet curtain descending. Just before I dozed off, Benny appeared.

"Sir, Ops grabbed me as I was headed out of the CP. The watch just got a call from Baker Company. They need some help," Benny said.

I fought off Mr. Sandman and walked towards the CP. Major McSorley called me over to his makeshift workspace. A large city map dominated the wall. Transparency sheets with grease pencil markings hung from the map like shingles. The overlays made the city seem as indecipherable as if felt in real life.

McSorely said, "Baker-2 is on a foot mobile patrol up here in Saddam City. Some locals approached and asked for help. Apparently, some workers were injured attempting to repair a sewer line. It'll take Baker at least an hour to move that far north on foot."

I knew exactly what was coming.

McSorely continued, "I need you to move out and render assistance. We've been trying to get the locals to start repairing the city for days now. Obviously, losing men on the job site isn't the start to the 'great rebuild' that we're looking for."

The Ops O didn't have to say it, but McSorley's tone implied that after the disaster at the bank our superiors wanted us to do whatever we could to make nice with the locals. I still didn't understand how the brass or the Iraqis could blame us for the bank. It's not like *we* robbed it. Whatever. Hearts and minds here we come.

"Roger, Sir, I've got four trucks still down for maintenance right now, but I'll roll with the other half of the platoon," I said.

"Get out there quick and stay up on comms. Saddam City is a slum. Mostly Shi'a. Any favor we can curry with that lot will help us in the long run."

McSorley flicked his wrist towards the door, a gesture that translated to 'dismissed.' By the time I made the door he was on to the next drama, two radio handsets welded to his ears. A human switchboard. I didn't envy him his job.

———

We found the sewer on the first pass. It wasn't marked on the maps, but it was easy to spot by the mob. Hundreds of Iraqis had crowded around an open storm drain. Women were wailing and slapping themselves in the head. The menfolk jabbered back and forth incessantly. Despite the flurry of activity, no one was doing anything constructive.

The crowd vibed dangerous. I had seen similar mob dynamics at play back in college when I moonlighted as a nightclub security stooge. As the crowd started to spoil, you could actually taste the violence. The air soured. It left a metallic film in your throat.

Benny pushed out a security perimeter. I waded into the crowd and found a slight, bespectacled man who claimed to speak English.

"Sir, can you tell me what happened?" I asked.

Spectacles replied, "Mistah, three man trapped… trapped in hole. All dead."

"All three are dead? How do you know?"

"Yes, Mistah, first man go in hole… bad air… cannot breath. He die. Brother go into hole. Try to save. Brother die. Cousin go. Try to save. Cousin die. All die! All three die!"

Spectacles was getting worked up. The wailing women kicked up their lamentations a notch. I felt a headache brewing.

"OK, OK. We're here to help," I said. "Please help me move these people back. No one else goes in the hole, OK. Please tell them, no one else goes in the hole. We'll rig a safety line."

I could tell Spectacles was picking up less than half of what I was saying. I turned to push my way back to the truck to find some rope. Three coffins crowd-surfed to the edge of the mob, passed forward on outstretched arms. The man next to Spectacles lowered the first coffin to the ground. Within seconds, all three wooden boxes were arranged in a perfect line.

Shouting erupted behind me. I turned just in time to see Corporal O'Reilly bowing up on a big, surly looking Iraqi. The surly guy's face registered pure hate.

O'Reilly fixed a bayonet to his M16. Not a good sign. Shit was about to go sideways.

"Get back! Get back, motherfucker!" O'Reilly shouted.

Before I could give the order to stand down, Surly raised his fists and took a step forward. O'Reilly slashed the man across the chest with his bayonet. Surly recoiled as if he'd been struck by lightning. The crowd surged.

"O'Reilly! What the fuck? Stand down, stand down!" I yelled.

We'd have to start shooting people now. So much for hearts and minds.

O'Reilly turned towards me. His pupils danced. He scanned for threats. The nervous energy belied a marrow-deep exhaustion. We needed to snag those bodies quick and get the fuck out of Dodge. I moved in close.

"Fucking hell, O'Reilly, you gotta maintain your cool!" I yelled. "These people are tripping. Three of their boys just died trying to repair that sewer line over there."

O'Reilly looked me in the eyes. A good sign. At least he was listening.

"What the fuck are we doing here, Sir? These people are fucking insane," O'Reilly said. He shook his head back and forth like he was trying to pull himself out of a nightmare.

"Yeah, yeah, I got it," I said. "This is a complete yard sale, but just stay cool. We're going to retrieve these bodies and then hustle back to the Country Club."

I debated whether to confiscate O'Reilly's pig-sticker. I decided if things really headed south we'd need all the blades we could muster. Even if he was temporarily rattled, O'Malley was still a killer who wasn't afraid to put in the work. I gave him a nod and ran back to the truck. Ox was standing in the .50 cal turret, casually surveying the madness.

"Ox, we still have that old web gear?" I asked.

"Yes, Sir, it's in that ammo can behind the A-gunner's seat."

It wasn't pretty, but I managed to fashion a field-expedient harness out of the old web gear and a bundle of 550 cord. The instructors at the Marine Corps' Mountain Warfare School wouldn't have been amused, but the harness looked like it would support the weight of a couple men. If he was quick about it, a harnessed man could grab hold of a body and get hoisted back up to the surface… preferably before succumbing to the sewer fumes that killed the first three.

I shouldered the harness and pulled Doc Strickland through the crowd. "Doc, if any of these guys are still alive when we get 'em to the surface, do your best to try and revive them. And if they're already dead, just go through the motions. I want you to act like you're moving heaven and earth to try and resuscitate them. The natives are getting restless and we gotta at least *look* like we're helping. You tracking?"

"Copy, Sir… I'll do my best." The look on Doc's face didn't inspire confidence.

I found Spectacles and explained the retrieval plan. After some back and forth with several onlookers, a young ginger-haired guy stepped forward to volunteer as the body snatcher. Ginger tried to duck away as I fitted the harness over his shoulders. Ginger and Spectacles started arguing.

Spectacles switched back to English. "He want rope on arm, not body."

"On his arm? Are you kidding me? How the fuck would that work? That's the worst idea I've ever heard," I said.

I couldn't believe this little ginger-headed fuck wanted us to lower him down by the wrist. I'd rigged a perfectly capable Swiss Seat and this kid wanted us to lasso his arm like a roped calf. I guess you had to be brain damaged to volunteer for the sewer in the first place.

"Fuck it. You guys can figure it out. We're outta here," I said. It wasn't worth risking another death. Especially one that the mob would blame on us. I tossed the harness and the safety line to Ginger and signaled for the Marines to mount up.

When I reached the truck, I saw an older man carrying a long, fishhook-shaped piece of rebar. The crowd parted to make way for the rebar man. The old fella positioned himself on the edge of the sewer opening.

I said, "Ox, are you seeing this? They aren't about to do what I think they're about to do, are they?"

Ox started chuckling. "They are, Sir. That old guy sure as shit just skewered a body out of the hole with that fucking rebar."

I stood on the hood of the truck to get a better look. Ox wasn't lying. The old fella hooked a body with the rebar and, after significant exertion, managed to drag it up the surface. A human sheesh-kebob. A pair of younger guys played 'Johnny on the Spot' and transferred the corpse to one of the waiting coffins. I was genuinely impressed by their efficiency.

———

The trip back through Saddam City was eerily quiet. The streets were empty save the piles of burning garbage that served to replace the nonfunctioning streetlamps. Traffic was nonexistent.

Ox said he wanted some patrolling music. Little Richard's "Long Tall Sally" came blasting out of the boombox behind the driver's seat. To the uninitiated, Little Richard would seem an unlikely choice for a Marine Ox's age. But I knew he favored the track because that was the song Jesse Ventura's character played during the helicopter insertion scene in *Predator*. Ox later admitted Little Richard also featured heavily in another of his favorites, the Dolph Lundgren anti-commie vehicle *Red Scorpion*. So, while the pedigree of Ox's Radio Baghdad playlist dated to the '50s, his selection of the tunes owed more to the legacy of '80s action flicks. Somehow it all made perfect sense in 21st century Iraq.

Saddam City gave off a distinct rot. The sickly-sweet smell of the burning trash reminded me of Tijuana on a hungover Saturday morning. The collision of Little Richard's piano riffs and the scent of the burning trash catalyzed a fever dream inside my skull. I zoned out while splashes of color danced across the inside of my sleep-deprived eyelids. The headache that first began brewing back at the sewer was the only thing keeping me awake… and just barely.

I started talking to shake out of the funk . "Ox, anything suspicious up there?"

"Negative, Sir. All quiet," Ox replied. "I haven't seen a single vehicle since we left the sewer. Haven't even seen anyone on the streets for that matter."

"It's too damn quiet. Feels like something's brewing." I reached back and turned off the boombox. I needed my undivided faculties attuned to the road.

We approached a wide intersection. A taxi with the telltale orange-over-white paint job was parked dead center between the lanes. It was still running.

I titled my head towards the turret. "Ox, you seeing this?"

"Tracking, Boss. There's something on the deck next to the cab," Ox said.

The door of the taxicab was cranked open at a weird angle. A man lay next to the car. His head was propped against the fender. I ordered the other gun trucks to form a hasty perimeter around the intersection. I parked about twenty meters from the taxi and hopped out to investigate. The unconscious taxi driver reeked of alcohol, stale piss, vomit, and tooth decay. Doc Strickland hustled over from Benny's truck and took a knee next to the cabbie.

"He's still breathing, Sir. I'm guessing he just got shit-housed, tried to get out of his car and passed out. I don't see any external injuries." Doc sounded pretty blasé, like he'd seen this movie plenty of times back in the World. It wasn't much of a stretch to substitute the taxi driver for a black-out drunk Marine. Honestly, I'm not sure which scenario would be more dangerous… blacking out on the streets of Saddam City or face-planting outside the bricks back in 29 Palms.

"I guess we should move him out of the street, so he doesn't get run over. Help me lift this fucker," I said.

As Doc and I bent down to lift the cabbie, Benny yelled out from his truck. "Sir, there's a cop over here!"

Benny held the collar of a dark man in a ragged, olive drab police uniform. He sat astride an even raggedier motorcycle that I hadn't heard approach. The cop tried to wave Benny off and ride away, but Benny reached down and turned off the ignition before the cop could kick into first gear. The bike stalled and the cop had to do a little tip-toe dance to keep it upright. The cop finally got the kickstand deployed and settled the bike. He shot eye-daggers at Benny.

"Benny, bring that guy over here," I said.

Benny motioned to the cop to get off the bike and follow him. The cop looked downright homicidal. He also looked familiar.

"Move your ass," Benny growled at the cop and shoved him towards the taxi.

Benny hated cops. Their nationality didn't matter. If they were badged up it was a fair bet that Benny would try and start some shit. The cop was mad-dogging Benny and I was convinced they were about to swing on each other. Either that or Benny would just clip him here in the middle of the street. I prayed it didn't come to the latter. 'Cop Killer' would be a tough callsign to explain back in the World.

I hustled over and stepped between the two men, *"As saluum allakum."*

The cop didn't return my greeting. He kept his dagger-stare on Benny. After a tense couple of seconds, he glanced in my direction.

"No English," the cop said.

"Yeah, OK, whatever," I replied. "Look, I just need you to take this guy to the hospital." I pointed to the unconscious cabbie and pantomimed a patient laying in a hospital bed.

The cop didn't move. He just stared at me and Benny, the scar on his face changing colors. I could smell his hate in the air between us.

I realized I was asking the cop to cart off the taxi driver on his motorcycle. Not an easy feat given that the cabbie was still unconscious and the cop's bike didn't have a sidecar or much extra room in the saddle. But the taxi wouldn't start and I couldn't come up with any alternative modes of transport that didn't involve us driving the guy to the hospital ourselves. I patted the cop's shoulder in a gesture of support and then signaled to the Marines to saddle up.

The cop continued to mad-dog me with his rage-stare. His face bothered me. It was mask-like, molted. His bullshit, tough-guy mustache poked through three layers of grime. Something ran straight down the middle of his features. Sweat rivulet? Scar? I couldn't tell. The whole look bothered me. Dude was a goddamn shapeshifter.

I looked back at the taxi as we drove away. The cop stood perfectly still until the last gun truck rolled past the far side of the intersection. Then he kicked the taxi driver in the ribs and took off on his bike. I had half a mind to go back and tune the cop up for abusing the cabbie but I couldn't be bothered. It was late and the platoon was running on fumes. I needed to get the boys back to the Club for some long overdue shut eye.

———

I racked my brain on the drive back to the Country Club. The cop's face bothered me. By the time we got back inside the wire I was pretty convinced I'd seen him before.

"Ox, that cop look familiar to you?" I asked.

"Sir, you know I'm the last person to ask. All these fucking *hadjis* look alike to me. Besides, I never really look at their faces. I'm too busy watching their hands. Ain't no way in hell one of these Rags gonna get the drop on me."

"Well… I guess that's one of those good news/bad news deals," I said. "The bad news is you're not very helpful when it comes to identifying these shit heads. The good news is you'll never be haunted by the faces of the guys you've killed."

Ox smiled and started cleaning his pistol. "I sleep like a baby, Sir. You don't have to worry about me."

I ripped open a chili mac Meal Ready to Eat. The chow gave off a sharp, sodium scent that set my stomach a-grumble. Before I could get the first spoonful down my gullet a grizzled-looking Sergeant from the Ops Shop appeared. I could tell the Marine was in a hurry as he speed-hobbled my direction on blown-out knees. The Sergeant informed me that I was wanted in the CP. I stashed the chili mac and walked towards whatever fresh hell awaited in the head shed. Major McSorley waved me over to a field desk where a Marine Chief Warrant Officer typed furiously on a small, ruggedized laptop.

"Jim, welcome back," McSorley said. His jaw was clenched, a tell that usually meant he was about to deliver bad news. Couple that with the use of my first name and it was a fair bet life was about to suck. "Sounds like the sewer was a disaster."

"You have no idea, Sir," I said. "Three repairmen were dead by the time we got there. The natives were getting pretty restless, so we bounced." I was praying that McSorley hadn't gotten wind of O'Reilly's little bayonet clinic.

"Yeah… probably a good call to get out of there," McSorley said. "You'll have to tell me about it later. In the meantime, your boy Fuad left a message with the guards. He wants you to meet him at his apartment tonight at 2100." McSorley gestured towards the Chief Warrant Officer seated at the field desk. "This is Chief Warrant Officer Souza from the Human Intelligence Exploitation Team, he's going with you to Fuad's tonight."

Souza finished typing whatever it was he was fixated on and looked up with a salesman's smile. He was handsome in the swarthy way young midwestern girls might label exotic. A bit too well-groomed to have been slumming it with the grunts very long. Without bothering to stand, he offered his hand. "Steve Souza, nice to meet ya."

"Jim Wilde. Welcome to the show," I said.

I was immediately suspicious of Souza. First, the HUMINT Exploitation Team, or 'HET,' assigned to our Battalion were all reservists. That meant they were one step above place kickers and one rung below gingers on the scale of human evolution. In my almost four years in the Corps, I had yet to meet a reservist that was worth the care and feeding. Second, I'd heard through the grapevine that all the guys assigned to this particular HET just happened to be cops back in the real world. I didn't share Benny's hatred for cops. I just distrusted them, especially in combat. Third, Human Intelligence Marines were known to be divas. They often worked alone or in small cliques. They always assumed an air of self-important, super-spy assholery that rankled the grunts. At first blush, this Souza cat didn't appear to be an exception.

I studied Souza while McSorely talked. I sensed he'd already anticipated I'd be displeased with the set-up. After all, no one likes straphangers. Infantry guys least of all. But Souza had a way of maintaining his expression that made it hard to figure any angles he might be playing on the side. Was that just part of the super-spy, diva act? Maybe.

After McSorely wrapped his spiel, Souza cut right to the chase. "My colleague debriefed Fuad a couple days ago when you brought him in. We think he's Iraqi Intelligence. Fuad's almost certainly not his real name, but we don't have any verifiable bio data on the guy. No one fitting his description has hit the blotter and he didn't come in here with anything worth holding him on. That said, we need to dig in to get this guy to play ball. He could be a key link to tracking down some of the senior regime officials that are still in the wind."

I nodded. "I agree. Fuad's definitely shady. I told your boys that the other night when we dropped him off. I sure as fuck don't trust the guy."

McSorley interjected, "Here's the map Fuad left at the VCP with the directions to his apartment." McSorley handed me a piece of folded card stock. "Chief Warrant Officer Souza traced the map route in Falcon View and it seems to match up. The good news is he lives nearby. You won't have to waste a lot of time in transit."

I looked at the cheap Timex hooked to my flak vest. It was already 2000. I reckoned it was 50/50 whether I'd have enough time to finish my chili mac *and* take a shit before we had to leave for our date with Fuad.

———

Battalion mandated that no tactical vehicles were allowed outside the Country Club alone, so I had Benny and his boys follow us to Fuad's apartment. Fuad's digs consisted of a narrow, two-story walkup set several blocks back from a main thoroughfare. Most of the locals were bedded down for the night to save on generator fuel. The neighborhood was clenched asshole tight and just as dark. Fortunately, the weather had turned unseasonably cool, which meant less folks hanging out on their rooftops. I didn't like the idea of Fuad's neighbors being able to shoot down at Ox and Benny while I was inside with Souza.

I wanted to get a feel for what Souza might already know about Fuad. I wasn't sure he'd share much, but it was a good opportunity to feel him out. I chatted him up as we walked towards the apartment.

"Fuad must be a player if he's cool with us meeting with him out in the open like this… at his house no less," I said.

"Yeah, he's definitely got some suction. We're just not sure with whom," Souza replied.

I could tell by his tone that Souza wasn't going to offer anything else on the subject without a lot of prying on my part. I decided to throw him a bone.

"It doesn't track," I said. "Fuad having us meet him here. Something about it doesn't jive. That first night he was afraid to be seen with those wounded guys in his car. Now he's inviting infidels to his house. If you ask me, this fucker's on the make."

Souza side-eyed me. "Agreed. Let's roll with it and see if we can figure out his play. I've dealt with shady bastards my entire adult life and there's no one-size-fits-all approach to figuring motive. In fact, don't worry about motive. Out here that shit's a waste of time. Just stay focused on his behavior. We'll compare notes when we get back to the hooch tonight."

The fact that Souza was soliciting my involvement caught me by surprise. I was waiting for him to pull the 'let me do the talking' card. I started to warm to him just a tad.

When we got to the apartment, Souza stepped aside, as if he anticipated someone might try to shoot him through the door. He knocked on the thin aluminum screen with the butt of his MAGLITE. It was a cop move. That little maneuver confirmed the rumors. Souza was fuzz back in the World.

The door opened after the first knock and Fuad quickly ushered us indoors. Fuad wore a heavy cable-knit sweater. Something about the fit of the sweater looked odd. I couldn't be sure, but it looked like Fuad might be strapped. I thought I could make out the faint outline of a pistol grip along his flank. I'd regret having to shoot the old guy in front of his family, but no way in hell I was letting Fuad get the jump. If he thought he'd invite us in just to do us dirty, he thought wrong. Dead wrong. Two seconds in Fuad's house and I was already prepping for gunplay. Baghdad had that effect. Paranoia was part of the landscape.

The apartment was modestly appointed. Simple furniture. Old paint on the walls. Tidy floors with a couple of worn but expensive-looking rugs. The overall presentation was clean and inviting. In contrast to the gun truck I'd lived in for the past 90 days, it was downright cozy. I got the impression that Fuad actually lived here. That implied Fuad trusted us to a degree that I certainly didn't reciprocate.

Fuad beckoned us to take a seat on a small faux-leather couch. Souza and I sat knee-to-knee. The extra girth of our flak vests made the couch a tight fit. I noticed two women enter from the darkened stairwell that led to the second floor.

"Gentlemen, I'd like to introduce you to my wife Zahra and my daughter Adila," Fuad said. He smiled. A proud patriarch.

In an effort to appear gracious, I stood up and put my hand over my heart. I issued a perfunctory "*As saluum allekum*, my name is Jim," and bowed slightly, first in the direction of the wife, then towards the daughter. After an awkward pause, Souza got to his feet and offered a similar greeting. Souza didn't offer his name.

"Would you care for tea?" Zahra asked with a British affectation similar to Fuad's. The offer was directed to both of us, but Zahra never broke eye contact with me. There was a tautness at the edge of her shapely cheekbones that dragged the corner of her sad eyes downward. The sadness was incongruent with the soothing tone of her voice. I recognized her brand of sorrow right away. It was the byproduct of a very particular strain of stress. Zahra was a woman hellbent on maintaining social propriety in the face of an extremely uncertain future. I'd seen the exact same tension in my mom's face in the months after my stepdad was killed. Zahra and Adila both smiled meekly and disappeared into the kitchen. The ladies' brief appearance automatically dampened my edginess.

Fuad said, "Please be seated, gentlemen. The ladies will prepare the tea and rejoin us in a moment."

I found it strange that Fuad didn't ask Souza for his name. Fuad didn't seem the least bit surprised that I'd shown up at his house with a 'plus one.' It was as if he already knew *who* or *what* Souza was.

I gave Souza a sideways glance. To my surprise, he kept his mouth shut. Maybe his cop instincts were strong enough to let him know when to let the other guy do the talking.

Zahra and Adila returned with the tea service. I stole a glance at both women. Despite a conscious effort not to, my gaze lingered on Adila. Neither woman wore a *hijab*. Both mother and daughter were blessed with thick, raven-black hair. Adila's features were a little more angular and severe than I normally found attractive, but I was still drawn to her. She was like a less-striking version of a supermodel who, in person, looks much more cartoonish than they do in photographs.

The thing I noticed most acutely was Adila's scent. As she bent down to pour the tea I caught a whiff of citrus. It took every last bit of willpower not to audibly inhale. I'd lived with the ammonia-reek of exhausted, unwashed male bodies for months. It was jarring how feminine and inviting Adila smelled. Her scent also made me acutely aware of how offensive my own odor must have been in this small, warm apartment. I was still wearing trousers encrusted with the Mercedes' driver's blood. I hadn't showered in over 100 days. I hadn't been laid in probably double that. Meeting Adila like this seemed unfair.

The first cup of tea was all small talk. Suspiciously devoid of familial details, but pleasant nonetheless. I managed a sidebar conversation with Adila while Souza and Fuad chatted at my elbow.

"Your English is perfect," I said.

Adila smiled at the compliment but somehow looked sadder. "Thank you. I lived in the UK for several years. I graduated from the London School of Economics not long ago."

It was an interesting revelation. Overseas education wasn't the domain of the Iraqi proletariat. The family's regime connections started to feel more concrete.

"I miss London," said Adila. Her face grew sadder, wistful. "I miss my friends there. God willing, I'll return one day."

Zahra shifted closer to her daughter. I caught the move as a subtle warning to Adila to be mindful of her surroundings. To remember who she was talking to. To keep the details and revelations about future ambitions in check.

I tried to lighten the mood. "I bet they miss you too. Smart, beautiful women are in short supply. Especially in London."

Adila blushed. Zahra leaned in even closer to her daughter. I was worried I might have pushed too far. The flirt was intentional, but more direct than I'd intended. I needed to watch myself. Fuad's brood was pretty cosmopolitan by Iraqi standards, but I didn't want to test my luck. As I was about to break eye contact, Adila threw me a smile. If nothing else, she seemed entertained. That made me happy. Zahra hawkeyed me but she let the comment pass. I didn't get an overtly hostile vibe, just a concerned mama bear keeping watch over the infidel in bloody pants chatting up her pretty daughter. I'd survived round one.

As I chatted with Adila I kept one ear on the conversation between Souza and Fuad. Souza attempted to elicit a few specifics, but Fuad deflected. It was obvious both men were well-versed in verbal judo. I sensed Souza was frustrated with Fuad's evasiveness, but he did a good job not showing it.

Fuad and Souza fired up cigarettes. The already warm apartment got a little stuffy as the tendrils of Miami smoke started to lace around the couch. For reasons I couldn't articulate, I didn't want to smoke in front of Adila.

Souza cleared his throat. "Fuad, how long have you lived here?"

"Several years. We moved to Baghdad when I began my professorship at the University."

"Where did you live before?"

"Many places. My career as an academic necessitated a fair amount of travel."

The corners of Souza's mouth tightened involuntarily. It was a small tell but it was obvious he was frustrated with Fuad's noncommittal answers. I tried to maintain my focus on Zahra and Adila but it was difficult not to pick up Souza's gestures.

I could feel every one of Souza's micro-reactions as we were crammed nut-to-butt on the too-small couch.

Souza took a long drag of his cigarette to compose himself. "Are professorships controlled by the state? Were you a government employee while at the University?"

"There is very little separation between what you would consider state and private education. Or, I should say, there was. Things will be different now God willing."

I side-eyed Souza. He looked resigned. He wasn't getting anywhere with Fuad. I'd listened to Souza pump the old timer for damn near 30 minutes and I couldn't identify a single thing we'd learned from this visit that we hadn't known going in.

I had to give it to Fuad. He was a cool customer. He wasn't addicted to talk like most of his peers. Arab patriarchs always slanted towards gregariousness and verbosity even in serious situations. Fuad didn't run those patterns. He oozed circumspection. Perhaps that's why the next part of the conversation came as such a shock.

The ladies served a second cup and disappeared into a back room. Fuad changed gears. It was like watching a Formula One driver speed shift. I could hear the verbal gears change but my eyes couldn't detect the effort.

Without preamble Fuad launched into a wild tale. The highlights dropped as follows: 1) The UN Oil-for-Food Program kicked off in the 1990s after Saddam's crew took an ass-whooping in DESERT STORM. The idea was to allow Iraq to sell a limited amount of oil through UN-sanctioned intermediaries. In theory Iraq could leverage the oil profits to fund imports of foodstuffs and other humanitarian supplies to keep a hungry and heavily sanctioned country from going full Donner Party; 2) Saddam started skimming the Oil-for-Food profits right off the bat. A cabal of Eurotrash and Levantine organized crime families infiltrated the program and kicked back large infusions of hard currency and embargoed goods to Saddam's crew in exchange for off-the-books oil deliveries; 3) Saddam's intelligence service, the *Mukhabarat*, transferred the skim to a slew of foreign locales to hide the cash from UN auditors. The transfers were made through existing *hawala* networks in the Middle East, Europe, and the United States. Like an underground Western Union, *Hawaladars* used a system of ciphers in lieu of traditional wire transfer records. Western intelligence services had a bitch of a time tracking these transfers; 4) As the invasion loomed, Fuad went rogue and compiled an index of the *hawala* network that included physical locations of the *hawaladars*, including those operating in the US, the amounts transferred, and the identities of the former Regime officials involved.

Fuad's story implied that he was, as Souza suspected, an officer in the *Mukhabarat*. History professors didn't run in those circles. Despite the inferred Intelligence Service revelation, there were more pressing questions in play. Souza leaned forward on the couch, intent on finally nailing down some details. He immediately asked Fuad to run back through the whole she-bang. I recognized Souza's ploy as the old 'repeat and control.' My uncle Mitch was a LAPD Robbery-Homicide detective back in the day. From the time I was 12 he made a point of dropping cop lessons on me, little bits of advice on how to handle the criminal element. The 'repeat and control' featured regularly in Mitch's curriculum. Humans aren't so great at adhering to fictitious timelines. To paraphrase Uncle Mitch, 'chronology is the arch-enemy of the lie.' Fuad humored Souza and ran back through the whole story, A-to-Z. As far as I could tell, the timelines matched. The details cohered. It seemed legit.

Then Fuad got down to business. "Gentlemen, this is my offer. I will provide the *hawala* index for asylum."

I didn't see this one coming. Heavy silence. Fuad and Souza transitioned form verbal to visual judo. Shifty eyes all around. Yet Fuad and Souza both seemed comfortable with the uncomfortable silences. Me not so much.

After a lengthy beat I leaned in as close to Fuad as I could manage from the small couch. I didn't want to alarm the ladies, so I lowered my voice.

"Two questions Fuad," I said. "One—if you had this information, why not come to me earlier? Two—how do you know we won't just detain you right now and beat the information out of you?"

Souza closed his eyes and pinched the bridge of his nose. It looked like he was willing away a migraine. I'd jumped the gun. I'd fucked up his approach. Souza started to open his mouth when Fuad cut him off.

Fuad said, "Left-tenant, Jim. As always, I will answer your questions in order. First, I could not come to you with the index earlier because it was not complete. In fact, that night you found me in the *souk*, I was coordinating final efforts to obtain the information I needed. It wasn't until this morning that I had everything, including a complete listing of the *hawaladars* still operating within the United States. These people should be of particular interest to your federal law enforcement authorities, no? Second, you could detain me now, torture me, send me to Guantanamo Bay or one of your CIA's many dungeons. But you'd get nothing. The information in the index is vast. Memorizing all of the details would be out of the question. I cannot tell you what I don't have memorized. So, I saved the index to a computer disk. That disk is hidden in a location that necessitates my personal retrieval. Are these answers satisfactory?"

Souza jumped in. "Fuad, I appreciate you bringing this to us. I really do. But asylum is tricky. Not impossible, but tricky.

However, even if I take this up the chain of command and they decide to play ball, do you realize what's involved in starting a new life in the States? I don't want to insult your intelligence, but have you thought this through?"

"I'm very familiar with life in America. I lived there," Fuad said.

Didn't see that one coming either. Ol' Fuad was full of surprises.

"Are you fucking with us, Fuad?" I said. "You actually lived in the US? What the hell are you doing back here?"

"I came back for my family, of course. Specifically, my wife and daughter. My son is already in California. I was issued this while I lived with him in Los Angeles." Fuad pulled out a California driver's license and held it with thumb and forefinger. His finger blocked the last name and address blocks. I noticed Souza straining to try and memorize the details.

The license looked legit. Hologram, watermarked photo, the works. Fuad looked about the same age in the license photo. It had to have been issued fairly recently. This shit was getting wilder by the minute.

Fuad pocketed the license. "Gentlemen, I realize these things take time. That is why I invited you here as soon as I had the information."

Three static bursts popped through the handheld radio on my flak vest. It was Ox signaling from outside that we had trouble. Ox used our own brand of Marine-proof Morse Code. I gave Souza a nod—stay here with Fuad while I figure out what's shakin'.

I excused myself and walked to the front door and keyed the radio. "Talk to me, Ox."

"Suspicious car, Sir," Ox replied. "Circled the block twice. At least two occupants. Guy in the passenger seat eyeballed us pretty hard."

"Roger. Can you jam 'em?"

"Negative. Lost visual. If they circle back again, I'm gonna give 'em a love tap with the Deuce."

The 'Ma Deuce' was the nickname for the .50 cal. If Ox 'love tapped' anyone with that beast it would be a bloodbath.

"OK, let's try to avoid heavy guns on residential streets," I said. "Blast 'em only as a last resort. Let me grab Souza and we'll wrap it up. We'll be outside in a sec."

I walked back inside and waved Souza over to the door. I leaned in and whispered. "How do you want to play this? Looks like we've got some vultures circling outside. Should we take the whole family back to the Country Club right now?"

"Not a good idea," Souza replied. "We're not equipped to provide any kind of protective custody. If we bring them back, we have to detain them, and that might skyline Fuad and put a target on his family. Plus, there's just too many unknowns with his story right now. Let's leave him in the wild for a little while longer. I'll take this up the chain as soon as we get back and see if any of the big boys are interested in bringing him in."

"Yeah OK, roger that." I walked back into the living room.

"Sorry Fuad, we're going to have to cut this short," I said. "Trouble outside. You guys might want to stay indoors. We'll try and push another patrol through here later."

Ox came back over the handheld. "Car's back, Sir. I can see the front bumper peeking around the corner a couple blocks up."

"Don't engage yet, Ox." I turned to Souza. "We gotta bounce."

Souza was visibly agitated. He had reams of additional questions. We still didn't even have Fuad's full name/alias. Souza gathered up his notepad and asked Fuad for his contact info. No dice. The phones were down. No satphones. Fuad promised to contact us through the gate guard at the Country Club once a day. Souza wasn't happy with the arrangement.

Zahra and Adila emerged from the kitchen. I tried to look casual. "Ladies, thank you for the hospitality. The tea was excellent." I locked eyes with Adila. "Hopefully, we'll meet again soon." Adila smiled and busied herself with the tea tray.

I keyed the radio to let Ox know we were headed back out to the trucks. Fuad ushered us to the door and turned off the battery-powered lanterns. I thanked him again and waved goodbye to the shadows standing behind him. I couldn't be sure in the darkness, but I think Adila returned the gesture.

I followed Souza back to the trucks. The front half of the mystery car was still visible down the street. The rear passenger compartment was obscured by the corner of an apartment building. I radioed back to the CP and apprised the Ops Watch of the situation. Ops said Baker Company had a foot-mobile patrol in the vicinity. I rolled to Baker's freq and gave their patrol leader a rundown on the car. It took a bit of back and forth to confirm what street the car was on, but I finally vectored Baker to the car's position. The Baker patrol moved in behind the car from the east. If the car tried to leave, they'd have to come our direction.

After a tense couple of minutes, Baker popped back up on the net. No driver, no passenger, just a dead guy in the trunk. Hands and feet bound, throat slit. A single, clean slice. The killer wasn't some average Omar looking to settle scores with amateur-hour hack jobs. This was a professional gig.

The Baker boys checked for booby traps and removed the body. I went back and retrieved Fuad. He ID'd the corpse. It belonged to a guy in the Finance Ministry that helped facilitate the Oil-for-Food caper. My first reaction was that Fuad had arranged the body dump to lend credence to his tale about the skim. But Fuad looked genuinely unnerved at the sight of the dude's carcass. He had that same look of concern and mental calculation I saw that first night at the hospital.

"Do you guys have some place you can go, Fuad?" I asked.

Fuad sighed and shuddered. Like a dog shaking off a beating. When he looked back up his eyes beamed determination.

"We will be fine," he said.

———

Major McSorley and the Old Man were waiting for us back at the Country Club. I gave them the rundown. The Old Man pulled McSorley aside for a private discussion. Souza said he needed to transfer the video.

"Video?" I asked.

"Yeah, I recorded the meet with Fuad," Souza replied.

"With what?"

Souza pulled a device out of his flak vest. He held a beige plastic brick outfitted with a wire and what I assumed was a clip-on camera lens. The contraption looked like Tony Montana's cellphone in *Scarface*.

I laughed out loud. "The Smithsonian issue you that thing?"

"Marine Corps operates near the poverty line when it comes to tech budgets," Souza said. "And I thought we had it tight back on the beat. I should've brought some of the sheriff's gear with me."

It was the first time Souza had referenced his law enforcement day job in my presence. It seemed a minor admission, but it indicated an unspoken trust in our relationship that I wasn't sure existed an hour ago.

McSorley called us to the back of the CP. He asked Souza what he thought about Fuad's proposition. Would CIA be interested?

Souza admitted he didn't think we had enough for the Agency to bite just yet. He'd pull stills from the video and circulate Fuad's photo. He'd send up all the info we had to date. It would be a tough sell. We still didn't have a clue as to Fuad's real identity. We couldn't confirm whether his inferred *Mukhabarat* background was legit. We might never know how much of the alleged *hawala* network back in the States was already being looked at by the Feds. There were too many unknowns.

McSorely said the Old Man didn't want to bring in Fuad's family until CIA confirmed their interest. The Battalion didn't want to be saddled with the care and feeding of Iraqi civilians, especially since there were rumors that we might be leaving Baghdad soon. Souza said he'd try and leverage Fuad as much as possible in the interim. The guy obviously had some juice. We could dangle asylum as incentive. Get Fuad to hip us to problems of a more immediate, tactical nature while he waited for his family's golden ticket back to the Land of Freedom Fries.

I left Souza to pound away at his tiny laptop. The Battalion Intel Officer Capt Vandershot walked in as I was walking out. He seemed annoyed that he wasn't invited to Souza's debrief.

I cornered Vandershot. "Did you hear anything back from Treasury about those papers we recovered during the bank robbery?"

Vandershot side-eyed me. "Yeah, they got back to me yesterday. Why do you care?"

"I just want to know what we recovered," I said. "We come across all kinds of shit out on the street. Always good to know what might be worth taking."

I could tell Vandershot was deciding whether or not to share any of his precious intel. Dude was a varsity-level information hoarder. He finally relented.

"Treasury says the numbers look like the serials used for bearer bonds," he said.

I didn't know shit about bearer bonds other than what I'd seen in movies. *Beverly Hills Cop, Die Hard, Heat…* all the classics featured desperadoes willing to trade lead for bonds. But even in Hollywood the bad guys didn't rob banks with RPGs. This was next-level shit.

Ideas percolated. The bank heist congealed with the Oil-for-Food skim. The connections seemed logical but just out of reach. I'd run it by Souza tomorrow. Maybe there was another angle I couldn't see.

5

"The Country Club"
Baghdad, Iraq – Saturday, 18 April 2003

The sun was up by the time I came to. Eight hours of sleep left me foggy. My body wasn't used to such luxury. I checked my notebook. No patrols scheduled until the afternoon. I brewed up on the camp stove and headed to the CP. Souza was still at the field desk. It was clear he hadn't slept.

I handed him my canteen cup of instant Folgers. "Did the spooks get back to you about Fuad?" I asked.

Souza sipped the coffee and burned his lips. "Nah. I didn't get the report out until almost 3am. Then I spent the rest of the night on the hook, making cold calls. Tried to find someone who might be interested. Everything's confused right now. Some of the folks I wanted to talk to aren't even in Baghdad yet. Some of them were here and now they're gone. This transition to 'stability ops,' or whatever we're calling it, has everyone out of whack."

"You should hit the rack," I said. "You look like shit."

"That's the plan, I…" Souza trailed off mid-sentence as he looked past my shoulder.

The Ops sergeant with the busted knees poked his head up from behind a bank of radios. "Sorry to interrupt, Gentlemen. Lieutenant Wilde, the gate just called in, you have a message."

Souza and I locked eyes. Fuad? Already? We hustled out of the CP.

———

The Marine at the gate handed me a piece of folded paper. A note from Fuad. It outlined a new wrinkle. A new threat. Fuad wrote that he was taking Zahra and Adila out of Baghdad until he could be sure it was safe to return. He didn't say where they were going or how he planned on staying in touch.

I asked the gate guard to describe the person who dropped off the note. He said it was a young guy. A teenager maybe. Definitely not Fuad. He and the fam were probably long gone by now. I showed Souza the note and we strategized. We didn't have many moves. I told Souza to grab his kit. We'd take a couple of gun trucks and scope Fuad's pad. Look for signs of trouble. Canvass the neighbors. Souza didn't have a better idea, so he ran off to snag one of his Staff Sergeants that spoke Arabic.

McSorley didn't dig the idea of us going back to Fuad's. He pulled the patrol reports from the previous night to see if anything had popped off in Fuad's hood after Baker found the car with Mr. Slit Throat. Nada. The rest of the night had apparently passed without incident in that neck of the woods. I pleaded my case. Eventually, McSorely caved and gave me the greenlight to go check it out.

We rolled up on Fuad's apartment about twenty minutes later. It looked the same from the outside. No visible indicators of drama. Souza knocked on the door. No answer. I pried back the security screen with a vandal bar. Souza picked the lock on the interior door. No signs of trouble inside. The apartment looked exactly the same as it had when we left 12 hours before. We grid-searched the crib, room by room. It looked like some clothes were missing, but no signs of foul play. The joint looked purposefully sanitized. No phones, no electronic devices, no important-looking documents, no real clues. Souza's cop habits kicked in. He bagged a few teacups and glasses from the kitchen. There might be some prints. We didn't have any databases to run them against, but maybe they'd pop again in the future. It was worth a try.

Souza's Arabic speaker, Staff Sergeant Kinney, was already interviewing neighbors when we got back outside. The family that lived closest to Fuad acted like they didn't know who Kinney was talking about. Even with the language barrier it was clear the neighbors didn't fancy a chat. Especially not with us. And especially not about Fuad. Kinney interviewed a few additional locals. They admitted to knowing Fuad and Zahra, but they were stingy with details. Fuad's neighbors played it close to the vest.

A boy on a bicycle too big for his miniature frame stood watching us from across the street. Kinney walked over and gave the urchin some Charms and a bag of chocolate milkshake powder. The kid tucked the powder away in his pocket and started sucking on the hard candy. Kinney questioned the kid about last night. It was hard to understand the ragamuffin with the Charms stuck to his snaggleteeth. Eventually he got some sentences together. The kid said that a policeman on a motorcycle circled the block a couple of times. The cop spoke into a mobile phone and then took off. Souza and Kinney ran through the normal questions regarding the motorcycle guy's physical appearance. They jabbered away in Arabic until I heard Kinney stop asking questions.

Kinney switched to English for me and Souza. "The kid says the guy was wounded. In the face. Like he was burned or disfigured."

I soaked on that for a beat. The police motorcycle, a wounded face. A burn, an injury… a scar? A clearer picture started to gel in my mind. For the first time in months, I didn't feel ragged from lack of sleep. My mind focused, alignments aligned, details de-fuzzed. The scar. The heist man at the bank that greased his partner and jacked his compadre's backpack. Fuad's customer that night we found him selling Johnnie Walker out of his trunk, the shapeshifter that refused to make eye contact. The motorcycle cop I tried to saddle with the drunk cabbie. Three for three. All scars. The same scar. The same guy. Brain flash—the mental reminder I'd set for myself about the serial numbers Ox found in the bank. Potential bearer bonds. Scarface in on the skim. Scarface in on the heist. Scarface out on the streets in cop duds, perpetrating God knows what? Whatever the fuck Scarface was a up to, it seemed a sure bet it was connected to Fuad. I laid it out for Souza. He agreed, those are threads worth pulling.

———

Back at the Country Club, Souza and I got to work. He fired up the laptop and collated info. He pulled Be-On-the-Look-Out notices from the BOLO database. I scanned files. I eyeballed photos. We ran short on time. I had a patrol scheduled in an hour. Forty minutes in, I clocked Scarface's mug on a recent BOLO. That's him. Maybe. Mean-looking fucker staring back through the computer screen. His face looked like it had been cleaved in two and reassembled with a shitty spot-weld. I was 90% sure we'd found our man.

I sent a runner to grab Ox and Benny. I asked them if they recognized the guy. Ox gave me his 'they all look alike' shrug.

Benny piped up right away. "Yo, Sir, that's the fucking cop. The motorcycle guy. 100% that's him."

The more I stared at the bastard the more I agreed with Benny. 90% certainty edged up towards 99. The name on the BOLO read 'Izzat al-Zaidon.' Definitely a *nom de guerre*. The photo was cropped but it was clear ol' Izzat was wearing some sort of military tunic. A plain, olive drab number. None of the fancy epaulets or fruit salad favored by Arab poseurs the world over. The photo was a recent acquisition from a repository of Iraqi Government personnel files seized by the US Army a few days ago. The BOLO listed Izzat as *Mukhabarat*. Souza ran name checks on a dozen variations. Transliteration was a problem. Arabic names didn't jive neatly with western phonics. One potential match. A report from last week. A man with the same name was briefly detained up in Saddam City for trying to bring a pistol through a vehicle checkpoint. He got kicked loose after a senior Iraqi policeman vouched for him. The boss cop claimed Izzat was one of his boys. That would explain Izzat's motorcycle and policeman's garb. Easier to move about the city as a cop.

The patrol deadline loomed. I had to wrap it up with Souza. I told Ox and Benny to go get the platoon ready to hit the streets. I asked Souza to print out Izzat's photo. The printer produced copies at about the same rate as the Gutenberg Press. My patience redlined as the ancient machine burped and buzzed. I could have carved a woodblock of Izzat's photo in less time than the printer needed for two black and white copies. With the printouts finally in hand I ran out to the truck park.

———

The patrol was unsettling. The initial 'liberation' euphoria had soured. It was all bad vibes from the second we exited the Country Club. Hard brown faces casting the evil eye. Old men sitting in front of shuttered store fronts, sizing us up. We still didn't have an interpreter, but I tried to press a few locals anyway. I showed them Izzat's photo. I gauged reactions. No hints of recognition. Just hard stares and brusque wave-offs.

The sun blazed. This weather was the first taste of what lay in store once the real summer arrived. The midday streets were largely deserted. The city folk opted for rooftop siestas to beat the heat. Nothing shaking. Nothing brewing. It dawned on me that a quiet, uneventful patrol should be considered a good thing. I couldn't dig it. The platoon needed action. Grinding away in the heat like this would melt morale for good. Also—I wanted some leads on this Izzat fucker.

We rolled into the last leg of the patrol route. Babil District. Previously home to the Regime elite. Gaudy mansions nestled along the Tigris. *Miami Vice* gone rococo. Call it 'Lifestyles of the Rich and Tasteless.' The 'hood was abandoned. The previous occupants no longer welcome. Even those that managed to keep their faces off the 'Deck of Cards' knew that sticking around meant a death sentence, either at the hands of infidel invaders or uppity Shi'a looking for some payback. A couple of the homes had been looted, but surprisingly most of the mansions looked unbothered.

We were about to head back to the Country Club when Benny popped up on the radio. "Sir, we've got some cops waving at us back here. Trying to get our attention."

"Go see what they want, Benny," I said. "Stay alert. Lots of bad guys out here impersonating cops." The image of Izzat in his police uniform was burned into my eyelids.

Benny dismounted and approached Baghdad's finest with one hand on the butt of his Berretta. O'Reilly and Blanky pushed out on Benny's flank, ready to help him dump the cops at the first hint of chicanery. Benny jabbered back and forth with the tallest cop. Benny only knew two words in Arabic so the tall cop must have had some English. Benny gestured towards the river and then walked back to his truck.

"Sir, this cop told me there's something we need to see in one of these houses," Benny said. "He says its bad. I don't think he knows what to say in English."

I huddled with Benny and the Iraqi cops. The tall cop said his name was Ali. That was a good sign. No self-respecting Sunni would ever use 'Ali' as an alias. It would be like an Irishman naming his kid Oliver Cromwell. So that lowered the odds of Ali being *Mukhabarat* in mufti. Ali pointed to a house sprawled out on the bank of the Tigris. Ali said he wanted to show us something inside. The crib had a distinct '80s vibe. All white walls and glass brick. Definitely suitable digs for a proper villain. Benny posted security and followed me and Ali through an unlocked door.

The inside of the house was cluttered, lived-in. Kid's toys on the floor, dishes in the sink. Weirdly normal and domestic. Ali led us through a large TV room. Stacks of DVDs on the recessed bookshelves. The DVD collection boasted a high percentage of '*Skinemax*' style soft porn. Those UN import sanctions must've been tougher than I thought. I reckoned you had to take what you could get in a nominally 'Muslim' country. On the far end of the bookshelf was a metal door that looked like it belonged in a bank vault. Ali shouldered the door open and motioned for us to follow him inside.

Death funk. Strong enough to gag a maggot. I should've known we wouldn't make it one full patrol without stumbling across some sort of mutilation-torture caper. Ali flicked on an overhead fluorescent light. Apparently, the generators still had some juice. The room was small and windowless. An empty safe in the corner. A large desk with a computer, several notebooks, and a money-counter. A dead guy seated behind the desk.

He was bound to the chair, his face pulped. Dude didn't go easy. Both of his eyes had been burned out. All the fingers from his right hand were lopped off. The severed digits formed an ersatz Stonehenge on the floor.

Judging by the smell, the dead guy had been here a few days. Long enough for advanced decomp. Whatever had gone down, it was worth documenting. I sent Benny back to the trucks to grab a camera.

Ali pointed to the dead man. "This man. Saddam man. Very bad."

"*Mukhabarat?*" I asked.

"No. No *Mukhabarat*," Ali said. "Money man. His name Saeed Hasan."

"Money man? Did he work for the Finance Ministry?"

"Yes. This man work Finance Ministry."

Finance Ministry. The Oil-for-Food skim. Linkages re-linked. My mind raced. I forced myself to breathe deep and stay quiet. I scanned the room. There—under some papers next to the money-counter. A satphone. Add it up with the safe and the money-counter.

"Was this man a *hawaladar?*" I asked.

Ali side-eyed me. "You know *hawala?*"

"Yes," I lied. I didn't know anything beyond what Fuad told me. "Was this man involved with *hawala?*"

"Maybe *hawala*. I don't know." Ali frowned. He looked eager to explain but lacked the words.

"Ali, how did you find this room? How did you know this man was here?"

Ali's frown turned to worry. "Bad smell. Man told us bad smell. Show us."

It seemed unlikely that a random citizen called Ali off the street and led him to the scene. My guess is that Ali and his two cop buddies were casing houses door-to-door to see what of value might have been left behind by their erstwhile masters. That would explain the empty safe. Snatch the cash and then notify the Americans to make it seem like you weren't involved. Oh well, I didn't blame him. With the regime *kaput,* Ali would be shit-out-of-luck in the pension department. I was willing to chalk up anything Ali scored from the safe as reparations for future funds denied.

I pulled Izzat's photo out of my cargo pocket and showed it to Ali. "Do you know this man?"

Ali studied the printout. Instant recognition. Ali swallowed a couple of times. "Yes. He is bad man. Saddam man."

"*Mukhabarat?*" I asked.

"Yes."

"How do you know him?"

"My boss. He give my boss money."

"Do you know his name?"

"No. No name. Colonel. Rank is Colonel."

"Why did he give your boss money?"

"I don't know. Before America come Baghdad. He give boss money. But no policeman. This man *Mukhabarat.*"

Benny returned with the camera. We photographed everything. I made Benny roll the dead guy's fingerprints. Benny hit me with the 'why am I always on corpse duty?' stare. I ignored him and bagged up everything we could carry. I thought about dragging the body back to the Country Club but decided against it. The prints and the photos would have to suffice. The Country Club didn't have room for any more dead Iraqis.

I asked Ali to come back with us to the Country Club. I wanted Souza and Staff Sergeant Kinney to take a run at him in the mother tongue. Ali became visibly nervous. He probably thought the Country Club was just a layover *en route* to

Guantanamo. I assured him he wasn't being detained and said he could bring his two cop buddies. Ali's comrades didn't seem to dig that idea, but we talked them into it. The three Iraqi cops squeezed into the gun trucks and we headed back to the Club.

———

I walked into the HUMINT Exploitation Team's hooch. Souza was still asleep. Probably the first shut-eye he'd had in almost three days. Normally I'd have let him sleep it off, but I was too amped on the possibility of Ali leading us to Izzat. Kinney was awake, typing fast into one of those small rubber laptops. Souza had a poncho liner pulled over his head despite the heat. I kicked his boot. Souza bolted upright, confused eyes tried to focus. He recognized me after a beat and tried to lay back down. I lit a Miami and stuck it between his knuckles.

"Rise and shine," I said. "We got work to do."

We sat in the HET hooch and chain smoked while I brought Souza and Kinney up to speed. Kinney got Ali and his comrades set up in separate rooms and worked out an interrogation plan. Souza monkeyed around with Hasan's satphone. Eventually he pulled out another piece of vintage-looking spook kit and hooked it up to the phone. Within a few minutes he'd downloaded the numbers and call log. Souza speed-typed a report and sent the phone numbers up to the signals intelligence boys. Once the numbers were on task, we'd have a good shot at geolocating the phones. In the meantime, Souza ran the call numbers against an existing intelligence database. Lots of international calls. Jordan, Syria, Lebanon, France, South Africa. Lots of calls to Mexico. Two calls to numbers in the US. It felt congruent with Fuad's take on the *hawala* networks, but it still wasn't the concrete proof we needed to get CIA to bite.

Kinney returned from the interrogation booth. Ali provided some additional info on his boss. The boss' name was Thamir al-Tikriti. Thamir was related to Saddam. A second cousin maybe. Ali seemed certain that Thamir served in the *Mukhabarat* back in the early '80s. Sometime after DESERT STORM he'd transferred to the Special Republican Guard where he retired as a Brigadier General. Recently, he'd been brought out of retirement to serve as the Chief of Police in Baghdad. Ali said that up until Thamir fled a couple of weeks ago, he and Izzat met regularly at Police HQ. Ali didn't know the exact purpose of those meetings, but claimed Izzat regularly delivered large attaché cases that he assumed held money or other important financial documents. Ali wasn't sure where Izzat or Thamir were now.

Saeed Hasan remained a mystery. Ali and his buddies confirmed that Hasan worked for the Finance Ministry, but they couldn't provide any details. Ali didn't think the mansion was Hasan's house. Apparently, he wasn't high enough on the food chain to rate a sweet Babil crib.

I fired up my third Miami and closed my eyes, trying to assemble a possible narrative. Proper nouns danced through my brain-housing group.

"OK, so we have Izzat the spy potentially serving as some sort of bagman for Thamir the Police Chief," I said. "Thamir disappears, but Izzat stays behind in Baghdad to hit the bank. We know Izzat met with Fuad at least once, and I'm betting it wasn't just to buy black market whiskey. Fuad alluded to the fact he was gathering info that night we caught him at the *souk*. Then we get a kid witness saying a guy matching Izzat's description was circling Fuad's crib the same night Fuad leaves us a note saying he's going off the grid. Fuad also hips us to the Oil-for-Food skim-*hawala* caper. We find Hasan tortured to death in a room that fits the bill as a *hawaladar's* office. Hasan was probably killed a day or so before Fuad goes to ground, but we don't have anything to connect Hasan to Fuad, Izzat, or Thamir. Does that about cover it?"

"Pretty much," Souza replied. "We know Fuad and Izzat are connected and we know Izzat and Thamir are connected. Hasan is still a wild card. We can't be certain of how or even if he's connected to the skim. All that said, we don't have the dope on the call-log analysis yet. If we get lucky maybe the calls will link Hasan to the Finance Ministry, the Police, or maybe even the *Mukhabarat*. But don't hold your breath. Establishing linkages from satphones to those organizations is one thing, but sussing out any useful context is gonna be a long shot."

Staff Sergeant Kinney jumped in. "In the meantime, we've got Ali and his buddies in play. We set up a comm plan to keep in touch. Unfortunately, the cell network is still down hard and we don't have the budget or the inventory to start outfitting every Omar with a satphone. That said, the cops know to come back here to the Country Club according to the schedule I gave them. Normally I'd never want to 'group date' sources like that but under the circumstances, it was all I could do."

Souza and I nodded in agreement. Now came the hard part. The waiting.

We didn't wait long. Later that night, Ali reappeared at the Country Club gate, still in his policeman's uniform and looking harried. He told Kinney that Thamir's men were going door to door, killing folks and ransacking homes. Ali didn't know what they were looking for, but indicated they were heavily armed. Kinney had Ali study the city map. Ali said Thamir's crew were in a neighborhood near Fuad's apartment. I ran back to the CP to see if we had any patrols in the area. Rick was on Ops Watch. He told me there were no Marines in the vicinity, but there was a newly arrived Army National Guard unit a few blocks away. We got the Guard's boss on the hook and vectored their patrol towards the scene.

A couple minutes later we got reports the Guard patrol was in heavy contact. They'd cornered some gunmen in an apartment building about half a mile from Fuad's apartment. One of the Guard soldiers was hit. I winced. I'd laid a bet with one of the lieutenants in Charley Company that the Guard unit would take their first casualty inside a week. I'd just won $50 but wished I hadn't.

The Guard patrol leader, a Captain, popped onto our Battalion's radio net. He screamed for a medevac. Rick told him he was close to our Battalion Aid Station here at the Country Club. They could get their wounded to us by ground faster than if we launched a medevac chopper. The Captain lost his shit. He didn't know where he was. Rick tried to talk him on to our position. No dice. The Captain came back on the net yelling that they were pinned down and taking fire from both ends of the street. They couldn't evac their wounded soldier. I could hear the guy sobbing in between transmissions.

The Guard needed backup ASAP. The duty roster listed my buddy Taco's platoon as the designated Quick Reaction Force. Major McSorley gave Taco the greenlight. Taco and his boys peeled out of the Country Club to rescue the Guard. They rolled hard. Gun trucks maxed, out for blood. Rick told the Guard Captain that help was on the way. He tried to hash out some coordination measures so the Guard patrol wouldn't blast Taco's boys by mistake.

Rick coordinated with the Battalion Air Officer to rally some gunships. There was a section of Cobras available, but it would take them 10-15 minutes to get on scene. Taco's platoon made it in five.

Back at the Country Club, we listened to Taco coordinate with the Guard Captain. Heavy guns barked in the background of each transmission. After a couple of minutes, Taco came back on the net. He confirmed they'd cleared the bad guys out of the apartment building. His boys had to grease a slew of 'em but managed to take three alive. Taco dispatched one of his trucks to guide the Guard back to the Country Club with their wounded soldier. The initial report wasn't good. The joe took a round to the head. It blew his helmet off.

I raced down to the Battalion Aid Station to let the surgeon, Dr. Ranier, know he had a gunshot patient inbound. Dr. Ranier gathered a couple of Corpsmen and began to prep their field-expedient operating room.

By the time I got back to the CP, I saw one of Taco's trucks leading a column of Guard vehicles into the Country Club. I waved them down and directed the vehicles to the BAS. Two soldiers hopped out of the lead truck and pulled their wounded buddy from the backseat. The initial report was accurate. Headshot. I could tell the guy was already dead, but the Surgeon and his Corpsmen scrambled to get him on the operating table.

The Guard Captain came running up from the last truck in the column. He tried to make his way into the OR. I ran over to stop him, but a couple of his soldiers beat me to it.

About five minutes later, Dr. Ranier walked out of the OR and spoke a few inaudible words to the Captain. The Captain stormed off and threw his helmet against the truck. He covered his face with his arms and dropped into a crouch. He was sobbing and rocking back and forth on his heels. Dr. Ranier walked over and tried to comfort the Captain. The Captain stood up and pushed him away. Turns out the dead joe was the

Captain's cousin. Most everyone in the Guard unit was related to one another.

———

Taco's boys rolled back triumphant. A high-back Humvee parked near the interrogation hut. A hog-tied Iraqi was unceremoniously launched out of the truck. He landed face-first, his bound arms and legs unavailable to break the fall. Hog-Tie started moaning. He sounded like those underwater recordings of whales talking to each other.

I bent down to wipe Hog-Tie's hands with the gunshot residue detection kit. The wipe came back purple. Bingo. Hog-Tie had fired a weapon recently. The kit doesn't lie. Taco's boys got the right guy. Even if Hog-Tie wasn't the dude that shot our joe, he was definitely in the game.

Hog-Tie tried to look back at me through his busted face. The Marines had tuned him up something fierce. One of his front teeth popped through an after-market harelip. Hog-Tie's shirt was drenched too. He smelled like microwaved pus.

I had to jump out of the way as two more bound Iraqis came sailing out of the back of the truck. One of them had a prosthetic leg that broke away at the knee on impact. His fake leg dangled from where it was flexi-cuffed to his wrists.

Taco sauntered up with a grin. He was cleaning bits of flesh out of his Texas A&M class ring. I noticed the divots in Hog-Tie's face. I could almost make out the A&M seal on his cheek.

"Make sure we save this fucker's peg leg," Taco said. "I want to get that shit wall-mounted. Make a hell of trophy."

"Nice work." I pointed to Hog-Tie. "I just swabbed this fucker's hands. Positive for gunshot residue. Looks like you boys bagged the right guy."

Taco launched a huge stream of tobacco juice onto Hog-Tie's back. "Fuckin-A right we got the right guys. I saw this bastard light up one of the Guard trucks with my very own eyes. Woulda dumped him but he dropped a mag during a reload and I thought maybe we should bring back a couple live ones for the 'gators."

Taco's boys carried Hog-Tie and his companions into the interrogation hut. Souza walked out of the hut to collect the capture tags. Taco filled out the processing forms.

A Corpsman walked over to begin the detainee medical screenings. He took a look at Hog-Tie's face.

"Sir… how do you want me to write this up on the intake form?" the Corpsman asked.

Taco chuckled. "Just say he was resisting."

———

I was out hard. Deep, black, dreamless sleep. A boot nudge my shoulder. Benny was standing over me. It seemed like every time I was pulled out of the ether, it was Benny doing the pulling. Apparently, he never slept. Benny told me that Souza and Kinney had finished interrogating the detainees Taco's platoon brought in. I shook off the cobwebs and sleep-walked to the CP.

Souza was in his usual spot behind the laptop. He looked as tired as I felt. We both needed some real sleep soon or we'd start making serious mistakes.

Kinney walked in with coffees and a fresh pack of Miamis. He laid out a summary of the interrogation findings. Hog-Tie and both of his comrades claimed they were cops. Hog-Tie admitted working for Thamir al-Tikriti, but said he didn't know the former Police Chief's current whereabouts. Hog-Tie also claimed they were going house to house to look for children who'd been kidnapped by unidentified 'gangsters.' Apparently, these 'gangsters' started pulling kidnap-for-ransom capers about two days after US forces rolled into the city.

Kinney brought Ali in after the interrogation. Ali didn't recognize any of the three detainees. He gave Kinney a few questions to test the detainees' knowledge on basic facts all Baghdad policemen should know. All three failed.

Ali helped Kinney sort the detainees' personal effects. Hog-Tie had a small, burgundy, triangle-shaped patch sewn into the inner pocket of his jacket. Ali said the patch was something members of the Special Republican Guard sometimes wore for identification purposes in case they were accidentally detained while operating undercover. Obviously, the patch could be worn by imposters, but given Thamir's previous affiliations and his willingness to shoot it out, it was possible these men actually were Special Republican Guard.

Conclusions were tough to draw. Was the door-to-door shakedown a last-ditch attempt by Thamir to find the index and eliminate Fuad? Possibly. Fuad's neighborhood housed quite a few former mid-level regime types. Maybe his neighbors had been in on the skim and were known to stash hard currency in their homes. Again, possible, but we didn't have anything definitive to work from. Fuad, Thamir, and Izzat were still in the wind. The one likely *hawala* connection we'd found was already dead. Beyond lending credence to the notion that there was money or skim-related information still out on the streets, the interrogations hadn't told us much more than we already knew.

I looked at the file photos of the three detainees on Souza's field desk. The photos didn't help me conjure any additional lines of questioning. No workable leads magically appeared. Hog-Tie's split lip made me laugh though. It was a hell of souvenir. If that fucker survived imprisonment, he'd never forget the night he met Taco's boys.

6

"The Country Club"
Baghdad, Iraq – Sunday, 19 April 2003

My head pounded from too many cigarettes and not enough water. I had no idea what time it was, but the sun was already high and merciless. A wave of relief hit as I remembered we weren't on the hook to patrol until after sunset. I crawled into the shade of the truck and tried to fall back asleep. Someone kicked my boot. Benny again. He said our company commander, Major Miller, was back from the Babylon conference and he needed to talk to me.

I found Miller in the CP. He looked even leaner than before he left for Babylon. Six foot and no more than 150 pounds. A bantamweight with eye bags. We posted up in a small office. I could tell by his face that the 'Secret Planning Mission' at Division HQ hadn't revealed any welcome 'secrets,' or much in the way of a 'plan.'

"No shit, Jim, there was talk of us going all the way to Damascus," Miller said. "Can you imagine? As if through sorcery we could magically get to Syria with enough ammo and fuel to fight Bashir's boys." Major Miller wasn't a man who rattled easy, so whatever the neocons in DC were cooking up must have been exceptionally harebrained, even by contemporary standards.

"Sir, I hope to Christ you talked them out of that nonsense," I said. "We're not going to Syria, are we?" I didn't think we were, but I sensed my boss needed a chance to vent a little here in the 'circle of trust.'

"No, we're not," Miller said. "Sanity prevailed. The Division Commander embarrassed some of the Pentagon folks on the video teleconference yesterday. Started asking them all sorts of basic planning questions that they couldn't answer. I think he successfully stuffed the Genie back in the bottle."

We rapped for a few minutes. Miller brought me up to speed on the latest higher headquarters scuttlebutt. I gave him a very brief synopsis of what we'd been up to in his absence. I noticed Miller's eyes wouldn't focus while he talked. The dark eye bags and gaunt cheekbones gave him the appearance of the Grim Reaper's stunt double. His words started to drag. Little black dots were stuck to his gums and teeth. I quickly realized what I was looking at. The workaholic bastard had been dipping instant coffee grounds to stay awake. Not a good sign. His odds of stroking out now seemed to outweigh his chances of getting zapped in combat.

McSorley walked in with a laptop. He and Miller exchanged a quick glance. McSorley opened the laptop and turned it so that the screen faced my direction. McSorley pressed enter and took a seat next to Miller.

"You need to see this, Jim," McSorley said. He and Miller exchanged another sideways glance.

A shaky video feed filled the screen. At first it looked like random combat footage. It could have been any street in Iraq. But then the picture steadied and I realized I was looking at Ox. I felt a surge of anger flush my face. Fucking CNN. It was Eddy's video from the raid on Fuad's suspected stash house.

McSorley let the video roll. Eddy zoomed out. Ox aimed at a man seated in the middle of the street. My voice rang loud in the background, "Hit him again Ox!" Ox fired. The seated man flattened in a pink puff of smoke and tissue. A chorus of cheers erupted somewhere off camera.

"Lotta press outlets running with this one, Jim. They're saying that we're out here shooting unarmed civilians," McSorley said as he switched off the video.

"That fucker was armed, Sir," I said, the anger rising in my throat. "I get it—it's hard to tell on the video. But that asshole had a fucking AK. Ox dropped him with the first shot, but the guy started to get back up. He was definitely going for the rifle. It was right there on the ground behind him."

"Yeah, I got it, Jim. No one here is saying that it was a bad shoot. We're just giving you a heads up."

"A heads up for what, Sir?" I felt like there was something McSorley and Miller weren't telling me.

"Jim," Miller said. "We just wanted to make sure you were aware the video was out there. At this time, we haven't heard anything regarding an investigation, and the Old Man will obviously do his best to keep it that way. But sometimes these things can snowball, especially since this video is out in the public domain now. The press are getting more critical of our presence here. Some of the lefty media types back home are butt-hurt and looking for ammo. We just didn't want you to get blindsided."

"An investigation? What the fuck, Sir? That was a righteous kill. Ox is a fucking war god. I was gonna add this one to his award citation. Now I gotta worry about some fucking lawyer or goddamn NCIS trying to jam us on this bullshit?" I wanted to have a little talk with Miguel and Eddy. The CNN boys deserved a beating for releasing an edited video that made us look like thrill killers.

"Calm down," Miller said. "We don't have any indication that anyone is taking legal or investigative action. Again, we just wanted you to know that the video was out there." Miller could sense I was on the verge of losing my shit. "No need to tell Corporal Oxford or anyone else about it. At least for now."

There was a knock at the office door. McSorley barked, "Enter!"

Souza stuck his head in. "Sorry to interrupt, Gentlemen, but Fuad left us another message."

Miller looked at me with a 'who the fuck is Fuad?' expression. I'd purposefully left Fuad out of the conversation when I'd given Miller the 'while you were gone' recap. I wanted to pursue the Fuad angle, but I needed to come up with an approach that Miller would buy. I hadn't come up with one yet.

McSorely waived Souza into the office and had him re-close the door. Reluctantly, I brought Miller up to speed on everything that had transpired with Fuad. I could tell Miller was annoyed I hadn't told him all of this during our earlier conversation.

I wrapped my spiel. McSorely added a few superfluous details. Miller held up his hands to indicate he was tracking the main gist of the drama.

"Another young fella dropped this off at the checkpoint a couple of minutes ago," Souza said as he held up Fuad's latest note. "Different courier than the one Fuad used last time, from what we can tell, but Fuad gave us his location. He has the family stashed on a farm near the Diyala River. He wants to meet down there. Says he has new information."

McSorley said, "That's out of our Area of Operations. Getting you guys down there would be a hassle. And unless I'm missing something, it seems unnecessary."

Souza replied, "Agreed, Sir. Normally I'd say let him wait it out down there. But, I finally heard back from our CIA bros.

They want Fuad. They think our Fuad is actually a senior *Mukhabarat* officer named Noori Shammar. They're sending a guy over here in a couple of hours. They've asked if we can escort him down there for a meet."

Miller and McSorley looked at each other. I felt like they were telepathically agreeing to push back on CIA's request. I needed to cajole.

"Please, Sir," I said. "The music's playing. Let us dance." I gave Souza an exaggerated wink.

The two majors stayed silent. I could tell they were both mulling over the pros and cons of trying to sell the Diyala trip to the Old Man. Almost as if operating off a single brain they both said 'OK' at the same time.

Miller said, "You've convinced me it's worth a shot. But tell CIA to send their guy over quick. We need to have all the details nailed down before we take this to the Old Man. It's not going to be easy to get him onboard."

———

Souza and I poured over the maps and overhead imagery of the location Fuad provided for the farm. The imagery showed a single farmhouse and what looked like a storage shed set back about 75 meters from the river. The problem was there was only one road leading to the farm and it ran right through a village that sat about a half mile east of the farmhouse. We'd pushed through that village on the way up to Baghdad a couple of weeks ago. The dense date palm groves, irrigated fields, and elephant grass, made it look like a set piece in a Vietnam movie. It had some unpronounceable Arabic name, so we ended up calling it 'Nam. Unlike most of the locals we encountered on the march up from Kuwait, the villagers in 'Nam were overtly hostile.

We even encountered a couple of ambushes outside the village proper. Ox smoked a few locals and one of the other platoons dropped some additional villagers during our brief stay. It seemed unlikely that we'd be welcomed back with open arms. To further complicate matters, the villagers had posted lookouts along the single access road that connected to the highway. If we rolled in hot, the lookouts would no doubt alert the village. The prospect of getting ambushed again in 'Nam seemed likely.

I brought Ox and Benny into the CP to help with the planning. Ox came up with an idea. He said he had a scheme that could get us into 'Nam without alerting the bad guys. Charley Company had 'appropriated' a large civilian dump truck earlier in the week. We were banking on the fact that the lookouts wouldn't alert on a civilian vehicle. Ox pointed out that the high walls of the truck bed could conceal a squad of combat-loaded Marines. We could drive the truck all the way inside the village with no one the wiser. Pull a Trojan Horse. Pop out and swarm the fuckers before they had time to run. Souza and Mr. CIA could follow us in another civilian vehicle. Once we had 'Nam pacified, they could pass through unmolested and conduct the meet with Fuad. Compared to most 'plans' we'd come up with over the past couple of weeks, the dump truck charade wasn't bad. But we'd need a driver that could pass for Arab.

"Benny, you think you can drive that dump truck?" I asked. I could tell by Benny's face he wasn't sure if he should answer truthfully.

"Uh, yes, Sir," Benny said. "I can drive it. I drove my dad's big rig when i was sixteen. Dump truck's a piece of cake."

"OK, you're going to be our driver. We need someone who can pass for Iraqi."

"Sir… I'm Mexican."

"Yeah, like I said. We need someone who can pass for Iraqi."

"Wait, just because I'm brown that makes me the stunt Iraqi?"

"Well… yeah. Don't worry about it, we'll get you outfitted in some *hadji* gear, maybe some aviator shades. You'll look the part. And it's not like you have to talk or anything. We just don't want the lookouts to sound the alarm before we get inside the village."

"That's fucked up, Sir." I could tell Benny was a little salty that I considered him the most Iraqi-looking Marine in the platoon. But it was true. Most of the boys, myself included, looked like emaciated hillbillies. We'd never pass the sniff test. Benny was our best bet.

"I need someone I can trust if the ruse doesn't work," I said. "If we get compromised on the way in, the rest of us will be sitting ducks. I need my best vehicle commander at the wheel if shit hits the fan."

Benny stared at me for a beat, trying to detect whether I was just blowing smoke up his ass or if maybe I had a point about him being the best man for the job. After an awkward ten or fifteen seconds he finally relented.

"OK, Sir," Benny said. "You need me to drive? I'll drive. Not like you're giving me a choice. Let's go roll these fuckers."

I ran the dump-truck plan by Major Miller. Surprisingly, he gave us the greenlight straightaway. Of course, we still had to get the Old Man's stamp of approval, but Miller's lack of pushback was a welcome, albeit minor victory. I chalked it up to the fact he was probably delirious from his terminal lack of sleep.

———

CIA sent a dude named Brent. He and his posse arrived at the Country Club 30 minutes late in an armored Chevy Suburban.

Brent had a couple of bearded hard cases with him, a driver and a door gunner. Brent rode shotgun. Souza met Brent in the parking lot and led him to the CP.

The Old Man sat at the far end of long table, bifocals perched on the end of his nose. Brent, Miller, McSorely, and Souza sat in the other chairs. Kinney, Ox, and Benny stood against the wall. I was on the hook to brief the movement into 'Nam. Lieutenants always draw the toughest crowds.

The Old Man stayed silent throughout my brief. I noticed Brent didn't take any notes. Souza kept eyeballing McSorley and Miller. I wrapped the brief and asked if there were any questions. The Old Man let out a long sigh and pinched the bridge of his nose. I was mentally prepared to get flamed with a barrage of unanswerable questions. After an uncomfortable silence, the Old Man stood.

"Do it." The Old Man walked out without another word.

I stayed silent. Stunned. The 'plan' was still pretty sketchy. I certainly didn't have it dialed in. Add in the fact that the Old Man was notorious for asking a million questions and it was a goddamn miracle he gave us the go order. First Major Miller, now the Old Man. I was on a roll. I didn't know whether to feel happy or scared. Miller and McSorley exchanged another telepathic look and then Miller shrugged. It was on. 'Nam here we come. Fuad, you better be worth it.

———

Benny looked fucking hilarious. Captain Vandershot loaned him some man jammies that he wore over his camouflage pants and combat boots. Souza loaned him a checkered keffiyeh that he wrapped scarf-like around his head. Benny insisted on wearing his own wrap-around Oakleys. Brent laughed and called Benny's look 'Beirut bomber chic.' I started having second thoughts on whether the 'Nam lookouts would buy-off on our bullshit.

After a couple quick rehearsals, we were ready to roll. I packed a squad of our best shooters into the bed of the dump truck. I crawled into a spot nearest the tailgate. We pulled a canvas tarp over the bed of the truck. We needed something to conceal the fact we had a squad of trigger-pullers along for the ride. The raid was timed for 5pm so we'd still have some daylight. I hoped the heat would keep the lookouts off their game. Now I was worried we'd have our own heat casualties. It was minimum 130 degrees underneath that fucking tarp.

The trip to 'Nam was mercifully short. Benny maxed out the dump truck as we barreled south. I could track our progress by peering through a small crack between the tailgate and the wall of the dump bed. The village popped into view. Benny keyed the handheld three times to prompt us to get ready to pounce.

Benny cruised past the lookouts. We rolled into the middle of the village. The few villagers out on the road didn't pay us much attention. Ox dropped the tailgate. We poured out.

I hit the ground and spotted two locals sprinting for the river. The taller of the two popped into a hut and came out the back door carrying a large duffle bag. They were unarmed. Even out here in the sticks, shooting unarmed civilians in the back wouldn't fly. I sent four Marines to cut them off at the river.

Two minutes later the squad finished clearing the dwellings. We rounded up the two dozen or so villagers that were either too old or too salty to run. The Marines assembled the villagers next to our truck. Most of the villagers were elderly women. A couple waifish kids thrown in for good measure. The only two 'military age males' I'd seen were the two that raced off towards the river.

Souza and Brent drove up in a beater Datsun pickup. It was obviously a local 'acquisition.' One of Brent's shooters hopped into the bed of the Datsun and they took off towards Fuad's farmhouse. We'd planned on staying no more than half an hour, so whatever Fuad had to say he'd have to say it fast.

Ox walked back from the river with two military aged males in tow. He was carrying the duffle bag I'd seen the taller of the two runners grab from the hut. The Marines zip-tied both men and sat them next to one of the huts. Staff Sergeant Kinney separated them for field interrogation.

The dude Ox caught with the duffle started squirming. Ox bitch-slapped him and settled his ass down quick. Ox had that effect.

Ox said, "This dude threw the duffle into the river. He tried to get the water buffalo to trample it into the mud. As if that was going to keep me finding it. What a fucking idiot."

Both captives stared at the ground to avoid eye-contact with the Marines. Ox opened the soaked duffle bag and dumped out the contents. A couple of folding-stock AKs, a rusted Takarov pistol, and an ancient Enfield rifle that looked like it was left over from the British occupation. Not exactly an arsenal.

Kinney conducted his field interrogations. The tall guy claimed the weapons were for self-defense. The village was weary of carpetbaggers coming down from the city to loot what little they had. Hence the 24/7 lookouts posted on the access road. His story sounded legit. Attacking Marines with that old-ass Enfield and a couple AKs was a suicide trip. These folks didn't look like the martyring type.

The Marines didn't find anything else incriminating in the huts. I assembled the village elders and had Kinney translate for me. I told them that we'd be back. I was letting them keep their weapons so they could defend themselves. But my largesse came with a caveat. If anyone from the village ever took another shot at a Marine we'd come back hot, kill everyone, and raze the village. The tall guy appeared to think that was fair. He tried to smile but the left side of his face was swollen shut from Ox's slap.

————

Half an hour passed. Souza and Brent hadn't returned. I decided to go check on them. I put Benny in charge of 'Nam and walked off down the road towards Fuad's farmhouse. Brent's shooter met me at the door. Whatever Brent was pitching to Fuad was something beyond my 'need to know.' I didn't care. I just wanted to see Adila. I heard woman's voices behind the house. I walked around to the back and saw Adila and Zahra hanging laundry. My footsteps must've startled Adila. She turned around excitedly.

Adila recognized me right away. "Jim!"

"Hi, Adila." It was tough to take my eyes off of her, but I made myself do so to properly greet Zahra. "Hello, Zahra."

Zahra nodded in response. Her expression was hard to read. Definitely suspicious but still not overtly hostile or protective. Something beyond her daughter's welfare weighed heavy on those sad eyes.

Adila stepped closer. "I didn't know you were coming."

Once again I had to prevent myself from stepping in and inhaling the citrus scent that, even outdoors, followed her everywhere. "We had some business in the village," I said. "I thought I'd walk down here and visit."

We chatted for a bit. Small talk. I didn't really know what to say. All the things I would have liked to ask Adila were off limits with Zahra in the mix. I did elicit some laughs and smiles though. Without realizing I had moved, I found myself standing close to Adila, definitely within the touch barrier. She laughed at something I said and leaned in towards me. I reached out to grab her hand but caught myself.

Zahra coughed. Adila and I looked up, but Zahra avoided our eyes. She busied herself with a bedsheet. I heard voices spill from the house. It sounded like Souza's laughter. Brent's shooter came around the corner and said they were wrapping up with Fuad.

Reluctantly, I bid farewell to the ladies. Adila offered a sad smile. I could feel her eyes on me as I headed back to the Datsun. It was the same quasi-telepathic sensation I'd felt that first night Souza and I left their apartment. Adila's presence challenged my emotions in ways I was wholly unprepared to process at the time.

Fuad and Brent were shaking hands near the farmhouse door. Fuad noticed me and waved. I gave him a casual thumbs up and hopped in the bed of the truck. Souza walked over and told me they were taking Fuad back to the Country Club. He had some actionable intel. Anticipating my next question, Souza said Fuad's cousin was coming down from Baghdad to stand guard over Zahra and Adila. I didn't like the idea of leaving the ladies at the farmhouse without our protection, but it wasn't my call. It was CIA's show now.

Fuad gathered his wife and daughter for a quick huddle. He hugged them both, grabbed a satchel bag he'd stashed by the door, and got into the truck. Souza, Brent, and the bearded shooter climbed in after Fuad and we drove back to 'Nam. A minute later I hopped out of the little pickup and rallied the platoon for the trip back to the Country Club.

———

The drive back was more pleasant. We were no longer burdened with the tarp, so the Marines posted up against the walls of the dump truck. The fresh air felt great. The Marines smoked Miamis and bullshitted while keeping eyes peeled for potential targets.

The sun was setting as we pulled back through the Country Club gate. My platoon was scheduled to go back out on patrol in a couple of hours, but I knew whatever Brent and Souza were cooking up with Fuad would take priority. I talked to Major Miller and he got another platoon to cover us for the night patrol. I hustled into the CP where the Old Man and Major McSorley were waiting for the debrief. I gave them the 'executive summary' and said I'd have more after following-up with Souza, Brent, and Fuad.

I found Souza brewing up outside the CP. His eyes were blurred, unfocused. He worked the camp stove with zombie hands. The coffee wouldn't have any effect at this point.

"Brent is in the conference room with Fuad right now," Souza said. He offered me a waxy paper cup of joe. I accepted the offering even though the air felt hotter than the coffee.

"What happened with Fuad out on the farm?" I asked.

"It was interesting. I don't think I was supposed to be in the room while Brent made his pitch, but Fuad insisted I stay. Made it a little awkward."

"I can imagine. I bet Brent and his Agency bros hate the fact that they're down here slumming it with the Marines."

"Without Marines their movement is pretty damn limited. They'll take what they can get at this point," Souza said. He spat some coffee into the dust and continued. "Anyway, Brent straight-up offered Fuad $10K for his intel. I couldn't believe it. That's more than my Team's annual source budget. But ol' Brent was ready to make it rain within fifteen minutes of meeting the guy. Brent's trigger man, the bearded dude in the back of the Datsun… that fucker had the $10K in his assault pack. He threw that shit out on the table there in the farmhouse. Stacks of cold hard cashish. Row upon row of crispy new US Benjamins."

"What did Fuad say?" I asked.

"He didn't care about the money. Or more likely realized it was worthless if he couldn't get out of Iraq. Brent knows that. I think he brought the cash just to show Fuad he's got the goods. Fuad kept circling back to asylum for the whole family. Brent told him asylum was a possibility but that he'd have to give them something actionable first. Something that would help validate the rest of his story about the Oil-for-Food caper and the US-based *hawaladars*."

———

Fuad's 'actionable intelligence' ended up being another humdinger. He told Brent that Thamir al-Tikriti was still in Baghdad. Fuad had it on good authority that the former Police Chief was holed up in an old factory out near the Olympic Stadium. According to Fuad, Thamir was *the* key intermediary in the Oil-for-Food skim out of Iraq. Thamir used dozens of *hawaladars* to move the money through a series of small transfers. It was Thamir's records that Fuad stole to compile the first draft of the index. Along with most of Saddam's extended family, Thamir fled north when US troops reached the outskirts of Baghdad. A few days ago, Thamir was tipped to the fact that Fuad was looking to trade the index for asylum. Thamir returned to Baghdad, presumably to kill Fuad and disappear the index for good.

I had a million questions cartwheeling through my brain. I started with the obvious one. "How does Fuad know all this?"

Souza swallowed the last of his coffee dregs. "He was cagey about the source. Brent actually did a pretty masterful job of trying to elicit some additional details, but Fuad deflected. Eventually Brent told Fuad that if we were going to roll on Thamir, he'd have to come with us. If we're walking into an ambush, Fuad's going to be along for the ride. He's gotta have skin in the game. Plus, capturing Thamir alive is one of Brent's conditions for the asylum deal, so having Fuad in the mix might help those odds. He might be useful as bait."

"Thamir must be a player if Brent's willing to play ball," I said. "I half expected you guys to shuffle Fuad off to some black site and torture him for the info in the index."

"What do you mean 'you guys?'" Souza gave me the fish eye.

"You guys. You and Brent. Spooks."

Souza's face beamed pure indignation. "I'm a Marine, asshole. Don't lump me in with CIA. Don't get me wrong. Brent's got some moves. He knows his shit. But I'm not one of them."

"All this pushback coming from a reservist? Kinda 'pot and the kettle' don't you think? I mean come on, you might be a full-time cop back in the world, and a full-time spook here in the sandbox, but you're still just a part-time Marine." I put on a big shit-eater while Souza's jaw dropped as he tried to form a retort. "But I guess I'll allow it since you haven't gotten anyone killed yet." Souza's slack jaw turned sheepish. In spite of himself he cracked a smile. I could tell by the change in expression that Souza realized we'd crossed the 'comfortable enough to talk shit' boundary. He was part of the crew now. A made man in the infantry mafia.

Brent came out of the conference room. He waved me and Souza into an adjacent office. The three of us crowded around a computer desk. Brent ran us through his latest conversation with Fuad. The abandoned factory where Thamir was supposedly squatting used to belong to the Transportation Ministry. Brent had Souza pull it up on imagery. It was a massive complex with two standalone buildings, wide open perimeter parking, and a couple of massive loading docks. Fuad's source claimed that Thamir would only be there through tonight. If we were going to move on him, we'd have to do it fast.

Brent said, "It's your Battalion Commander's call on whether we hit the factory. My bosses would like to get hands on Thamir, but we don't have the ass right now to roll across Baghdad and take this guy by force. That's if he's even there." Brent stopped and looked directly at me. "Do you think you can sell it to your Boss?"

I smiled. "Why not? I seem to be on a roll lately. I still can't believe the Old Man let us roll on 'Nam in a stolen dump truck."

———

Thamir turned out to be a harder sell than 'Nam. I did my usual song and dance for the Old Man. I dialed up the obsequiousness. Brent caught my drift and played up the possibility of Thamir leading us to other regime heavies. It was ugly, but we eventually got the Old Man's approval. However, the greenlight came with extra duty.

The Old Man had received a call earlier in the day from an Army battalion commander operating across the river. The Army battalion had a lead on the location of a prominent, but very dead Shi'a cleric named al-Fahi. This al-Fahi character was a fairly renowned rabble rouser who, as rumor had it, was executed by Saddam's crew a couple of days before we entered Baghdad. The Army's higher headquarters wanted to confirm the identity of the body for use in pending war crimes charges against a couple of senior regime officials they'd rolled up. The burial site was in our area of operations. The Army asked for the Old Man's help in obtaining a biological sample. The Old Man tasked me and Souza to nab the guy's fingerprints and DNA. The Boss was worried about the optics associated with what amounted to the grave robbery of a respected religious figure. He ordered us to do it on the downlow before we headed out to grab Thamir.

I looked at Souza. He wore a 'why me?' expression that he probably hadn't conjured since the last time his Sheriff saddled him with jailer duty. Apparently grave-robbing wasn't on his Iraq bucket list.

In a desperation move to get us off the hook I turned to Brent. "Does CIA wanna help us on this one?" I asked. "Sounds like your kind of gig. You guys love sneaking around in the dark and digging up bodies, right?"

Brent had already turned to leave. "Not a chance. But hurry up, would you, we need to get out to that factory pronto. I don't want to risk losing a shot at Thamir."

I let out a sigh and resigned myself to yet another long night. Digging up al-Fahi and tracking down Thamir all before midnight was a tall order. I'd been dealt the proverbial ten pounds of shit in a five-pound bag.

———

Souza shagged the Datsun. He looked considerably cooler in his civilian garb than I did in mine. I didn't pack civvy duds in my war kit so I had to scrounge some from my buddy Rick in the Ops Shop. Rick was a big dude. I looked like a kid who'd raided his older brother's closet.

Our luck improved. Slightly. The Army's source claimed al-Fahi wasn't actually buried. His corpse was allegedly stashed in a refrigerated trailer behind the central morgue. The drive from the Country Club to the morgue would be at least 20 minutes barring any drama en route. Despite the fact that we wouldn't have to actually dig, Souza's disappointment in the mission quickly transformed into a palpable nervousness. It was a reasonable reaction. The gig felt unplanned, reactive, half-cocked.

The Old Man insisted we keep the absolute lowest of profiles. The clandestine exhumation game required a heavy dose of discretion. We rolled solo. No gun trucks to back our play. I felt naked. Souza was jittery. I wasn't sure if it was nervousness, sleep-deprivation, or both.

In an effort to lighten the load I scoured the Datsun's dashboard for a distraction. There was a cassette next to the tape deck. The cover art featured a chick in a sequined mask. I assumed it was a belly dancer compilation. I popped the tape in the console and goosed the volume. We got hit with a burst of trebly Iraqi jingle jams. The opening track meshed counterfeit Casio drum machine beats with '80s retread synth riffs. It sounded like the soundtrack to one of those Golan-Globus movies Ox dug so much. Maybe a scene where Arab terrorists are celebrating before getting wiped out by ninjas.

I tried to dance in my seat, but the rhythm was hard to follow. I felt woefully unsynchronized with the beat. No doubt I looked like a pasty, underfed Bollywood reject. Souza sized me up with something approaching pity.

I kept dancing and pointed in his direction. "You too cool to dance? I know you dig this track."

Souza groaned. He held down the fast forward button long enough to bypass the current song. He pressed play and a slightly slower jingle jam crackled through the Datsun's bargain basement speakers.

"I think you've proven this shit is undanceable," Souza said. "But it's not your fault. All of it sounds the same. I bet you this chick's biggest fans couldn't tell you where one song ends and the next begins."

Souza had a point. I wished I'd snagged "Little Richard's Greatest Hits" from Ox's truck. But I couldn't let the jingle jams defeat me. I continued my whack-ass seat dance until

Souza started laughing. We probably should've been paying more attention for possible threats, but dancing seemed more important in the moment.

———

We found the morgue after a couple of detours. It was blacked out and deserted. It seemed like the kind of place the locals would steer clear of even during daylight hours. Souza parked the Datsun in the morgue's loading dock, facing out towards the service road in case we had to make a quick getaway. We hopped out of the truck and I shouldered a prybar I'd brought along for the gig. Souza grabbed the bag with the fingerprint kit and the tissue sample vials.

Souza gave me a 'let's get this shit over with' nod and we started out across the parking lot. I spotted the reefer trailer. It looked like a converted mobile home that the morgue boys jury-rigged with window air conditioning units.

A heavy stench engulfed the trailer. The biological decay of the morgue's forgotten residents was coupled with a sharp chemical tang. The dueling odors created a uniquely sinister pong. The whole scene gave me an acute case of the heebie jeebies. The trailer was pure nightmare fuel.

Souza and I advanced slowly. Being lightly armed without backup, I was on full mental alert. Somehow the morgue stench jumped sensory boundaries and started to impede my hearing. The death miasma felt palpable. It attenuated all ambient sounds. I strained in the darkness, trying to discern anything that might indicate a threat. But try as I might, all the external sounds were drowned out by the faint static wash of the blood pulsing through my skull. I breathed hard through my nose and forced myself steady.

Souza found the door to the trailer and yanked down on the handle. The metal hinges groaned as the door swung outward. Instinctively, I spun around to scan the perimeter of the parking lot. The trailer noises compromised our position but I didn't detect any movement. If bad guys were waiting for us out in the darkness, they were doing a masterful job of staying hidden.

I handed Souza my red lens penlight and he grid-searched the inside of the trailer. He fixed the beam on one coffin-shaped box that looked large enough to accommodate a body. It was the only such box in the trailer. If al-Fahi was in here, this had to be his crate.

Souza and I locked eyes. I wedged the prybar under the lid and froze. My brain retreated to a vivid flashback of a Vietnam movie I'd seen as a kid. Something about the Viet Cong boobytrapping dead bodies. I snatched the penlight from Souza and studied the box for wires and detonation cord. It was clean. I shook off the paranoia and regripped the prybar. Souza lent a hand. It took a couple of hefty tugs, but we managed to yank off the lid.

The box was filled with thick plastic bags. They looked like those vacuum-sealed biohazard bags you see at hospitals. The bags were filled with goo.

Souza whispered, "Are you thinking what I'm thinking?"

"If you're thinking liquified human, then yeah, we're on the same page," I said.

"Fuck me. Why would they seal him up in plastic like this?"

"I don't know. But we don't even know it's him. It could be our boy al-Fahi. But the Army's source could be wrong. Maybe the source just fed the joes what he thought they wanted to hear. Maybe he was angling for some reward money. This could be any old Omar. Bagged up to prevent easy identification. I'm just glad it's your job to get the sample."

"My job? Who the fuck said it's my job?" Souza's voice kicked up a notch.

"You have the collection vials. That makes it your job. Plus, you're a cop in real life. Cops do forensics, not grunts. But don't worry, I'll supervise," I said.

"Fuck you and your supervision. This shit is heinous."

"That goo ain't gonna analyze itself, hoss. You best get to sampling. Quick like, lest we get made out here desecrating the grave of a beloved cleric."

Souza grumbled some more under his breath. He reluctantly broke out the tissue sample kit and a little tub of VapoRub. He smeared a line of the ointment under his nostrils. Souza didn't offer to share. He pulled a Leatherman tool and punctured the top bag. I gagged. Liquified human is a very distinct aroma. It overpowered the already heavy fog of decay that blanketed the trailer. Souza chuckled under his breath as I started dry-heaving. He filled a couple of plastic vials and started putting his kit away.

"What about the other bags?" I asked.

Souza looked up at me like I had a dick growing out of the center of my forehead. "What the fuck you talking about? I have the sample. No thanks to you. Now, let's get the hell outta here."

"How do you know all three bags are the same person?" I asked. "Shouldn't you take samples from all three to be sure? What if al-Fahi is only in the bottom bag? By the way, can I borrow some of that VapoRub?"

"Fuck no you can't borrow my Vapo. You're going to sit there and suffer while I open these other bags."

Souza started working faster. Within a couple minutes he had goo samples from all three bags. He looked green around the gills.

"You about to chuck there, Steve?" I smiled at the prospect of not being the only one to lose my lunch, which was nothing more than a pitiful mix of stomach acid and coffee.

"No. I'm good. It's just…" Souza broke off mid-sentence. He slow-blinked a couple of times.

"What's wrong man?"

"Nothing. I'm OK. I was just thinking about these bags of goo. This used to be a person. Now all that's left is slime. His family probably doesn't even know his remains are out here. Even if they did, they can't even give this poor bastard a proper send-off. No way his loved ones should have to see this. And I can't even imagine our higher-ups explaining in court how we got this shit. It's fucking ghoulish."

"He's gone, Steve," I said. "I don't think it really matters what's left."

"No. It matters. Believe me. It matters."

Souza packed up his gear and motioned for us to head out. We hustled back to the Datsun and b-lined it for the Country Club. Even with the windows down, I couldn't evict the death stench. That shit was hardwired deep in my psyche.

We got back to the CP in record time. I dropped off the DNA samples with Major McSorley and ran back out to the staging area. Benny had already run the platoon through the pre-combat checks for the Thamir snatch op. The boys were ready to roll.

Brent and his CIA crew were waiting by the gate. He raised his arm and pointed to his watch. It was the unofficial hand and arm signal for, 'we need to get this show on the road.' I nodded in confirmation.

Souza popped out of the CP with Fuad in tow. The gang was assembled. Time to boogie. I gave the signal to saddle up and we lit out to find Thamir.

———

The derelict factory Fuad identified as Thamir's hiding place was actually a compound of four separate buildings. What looked like two large buildings in the imagery were four smaller structures connected by an overhead. We didn't have the manpower to hit all of them at once. The 'plan' was to set a perimeter and work the buildings two at a time. Not ideal, but time was a luxury we couldn't afford. It was almost midnight by the time the boys got into position. There was still no electricity in this part of the city. The factory compound was blacked out. No lantern light or any other signs of habitation. We were in for another long night in the ink.

Brent and his CIA guns were set-up across the street at the Olympic Stadium. The stadium was huge by Iraqi construction standards. Apparently, Saddam's son, Uday, needed the extra space to properly torture the underperforming athletes he oversaw as head of Iraq's Olympic Committee. The stadium's upper decks reached six or seven stories, well above the tallest building in the factory compound. Battalion loaned us a couple of Scout Snipers. The snipers perched on top of the stadium. Their job was to start plunking squirters, or anyone else who looked shady.

I split the platoon into two assault teams. Souza and Fuad embedded with Benny's team. Fuad was reluctant to go in unarmed, but I didn't give him a choice. If we found Thamir inside, we'd need Fuad to identify him. And I still didn't trust him enough to give him a heater. If this was some sort of trap, Fuad would eat the first burst before he got a chance to take any of us with him. Fuad might not sellout for $10k in CIA cash, but if he tried to fuck us, I was ready to pay him 32 cents worth of lead.

I gave the 'go' signal over the handheld and we started clearing buildings east to west. The first building my team entered was a large open warehouse. There was an amateurishly drawn Transportation Ministry logo on one wall. Thousands of vehicle license plates littered the factory floor. It looked like someone had deliberately cut open the storage pallets and scattered the plates by hand. The discarded plates and the lack of ambient light made it difficult to move across the building without raising a racket. We clanked our way through every nook and cranny but didn't find any signs of life. I was leading my team into our second target building when Benny hit me up on the handheld.

"Sir, we found him," Benny said.

"You guys nabbed Thamir?" I asked.

"I said we 'found' him Sir. He's dead. Single tap to the head."

"Roger, I'm headed over after we clear this second building."

We secured the second building. My team started site exploitation and I hustled over to Benny's position. Benny led me into an office that overlooked the factory floor. Fuad was standing in the corner. Souza was taking photographs and bagging evidence.

Behind a desk on the far wall was Thamir's body. I pulled out my red lens to survey the damage. Single entry wound in the forehead. Eight-ball hemorrhages in both eyes. Brains and skull fragments plastered all over the wall behind the desk. The rest of Thamir's body looked unbothered. No signs of torture.

I turned to Fuad. "You sure this is him?"

"It's him," Fuad said. "That man is General Thamir al-Tikiriti."

"Fuck. He's going to be hard to interrogate."

Souza popped off a few more photographs of the scene. The flash of the digital camera threw Thamir's corpse into macabre relief with every shutter click. Thamir's blacked out eyeballs gave his face a particularly horrific appearance in the flash. I suspected the visual would feature regularly in my dreams for the rest of my life.

I radioed back to Brent to see if his CIA overlords wanted Thamir's body. He said yes. I had Doc Strickland break out a poncho liner. Benny and I loaded Thamir's girthy cadaver into the makeshift stretcher and heaved. The fucker weighed a ton. Had to be 260lbs easy. Souza said he and Fuad were going to continue going through the few documents left in the desk to make sure they didn't miss anything. I told them we'd meet back on the perimeter. My knees popped and groaned as Benny and I lifted Thamir and shuffle-stepped out the door.

Benny and I got to the top of a short staircase when I felt a vibration, followed immediately by an eerie suction noise. Then the world went black. Dark black.

I came to on my back. A crushing weight squeezed my chest. My head pulsed like a tuning fork struck with an aluminum bat. When my eyes finally regained focus, I was staring into two black eyeballs atop a bristly mustache. Thamir's face. We were piled up brow to brow.

I yelled for Benny. In my peripheral vision I saw a pair of boots running towards me. Thamir's body disappeared. The air above me was a dirty red. It took a few seconds before my brain registered it was a red lens flashlight shining through a cloud of dust. The dust sparkled. Metallic. The air felt superheated. I blacked out again.

———

I had a vague sensation that I was being carried by a giant. It felt as if my head was stationary but the earth was bouncing up and down with each of the giant's steps. The giant gingerly placed me in the back of a truck. I knew we were driving, but I didn't know where or how. I couldn't hear anything other than a static hum. The hum warbled in time with the rapid tuning-fork vibrations inside my skull.

The next thing I remember was waking up in the Battalion Aid Station. I had the feeling that I'd been conscious, but my short-term memory was shot. Call it a bad case of the 'Time Warp Blues.'

A Corpsman I didn't recognize helped me sit up. I was naked, wrapped in an olive-drab blanket. It was dark outside. The Corpsman was talking to me, but I couldn't really decipher what he was saying. I had an overwhelming urge to lay back down and sleep. The Corpsman wouldn't let me. I'm not sure how long I sat there. Minutes felt like hours.

At some point Dr. Ranier walked in and started asking me questions. My hearing was starting to return. If I focused on Doc Ranier's mouth as he spoke, I could partially decipher what he was saying.

Dr. Ranier said, "Jim, do you know where you are?"

I seized up in a coughing fit. I hacked up a wad of phlegm and wiped my mouth. "I'm back at the Country Club," I said. "This is the Battalion Aid Station, right?"

"Yes. Good. That's correct. You're safe with us here in the BAS," Dr. Ranier said.

"What the fuck happened, Doc?"

"There was an explosion. You lost consciousness. But you're OK. No shrapnel, no broken bones, no internal bleeding. You got your bell rung pretty hard, so you're probably going to be in pain for—"

I cut him off. "Explosion? At the factory? Who got hit, Doc?"

Dr. Ranier's eyes narrowed, his face tensed. Panic dripped down the back of my throat.

Major Miller stepped into view on the other side of my cot. "Jim, Chief Warrant Officer Souza was killed in the blast. Fuad was killed, too."

"What the fuck are you talking about?" I swung my feet off the cot. Rubber legs. I tried to stand anyway.

Dr. Ranier forced me back down on the cot. "Jim, I know this is upsetting," he said. "But please, I need you to try and remain calm."

"Who else? What about my guys? Any of my boys get hit?" It felt like every muscle in my body contracted at once. A head-to-toe cramp.

Miller said, "No Jim. All your Marines are fine. Corporal Benitez got a little banged up. The explosion knocked him down some stairs, but he's already been released from the BAS. He's with the platoon now."

"When can I get out of here, Sir?"

Miller sighed and rubbed his fatigue-ravaged face. "When Doc says you're ready."

7

"The Country Club"
Baghdad, Iraq – Tuesday, 21 April 2003

Dr. Ranier didn't release me for almost 24 hours. I walked straight to the CP and tracked down Major Miller. He pulled me into the conference room and filled me in on the details of the previous night. An explosive device was placed behind the desk where Thamir's body was found. The explosion was command detonated with a battery-powered cordless phone. Souza and Fuad were still in the office when the bomb went off. They were killed instantly. The room and the desk absorbed a lot of the blast. Benny got launched down the stairs outside the office. The other Marines had already vacated the building and were unhurt. Right after the blast, Ox ran into the building and carried me out. Ox got me into Brent's Chevy Suburban and the CIA crew raced me back to the BAS while the platoon scoured the streets for the bomber.

I couldn't focus. The idea of a dead Souza haunted me. I ran down a list of questions. He was married, right? Kids? Had his family been notified yet? Had his bros back in the LA County Sherriff's Office been notified? Did I need to call anyone? I realized Miller had stopped talking. Brain flash—Fuad's dead too. What about Zahra and Adila? Did they know? Wait… were they still down on the farm in 'Nam? Was Fuad's cousin still guarding them? We needed to take action.

"Sir, we gotta go back to 'Nam," I said. Miller recoiled slightly. I realized I was talking way louder than what my ears registered.

"Jim, we have lots on our plate," Miller said. "The only thing you need to focus on right now is getting healthy and getting back to the platoon."

"I'm good to go, Sir. I'm ready to rocknroll. But we need to go back to 'Nam. Right now. Fuad's wife and daughter are still down there. Whoever popped Fuad and Steve will go after them, too. We gotta protect them."

"Jim, we don't know Fuad was targeted," Miller said.

"Of course he was, Sir. You told me yourself that the IED was command detonated. You think the bomber just got lucky and happened to kill the one guy who had the Oil-for-Food information and the details on the *hawala* network? Come on, Sir, I know you don't believe that."

"Even if Fuad was targeted, we're not a witness protection program. We can't go snatch up the family members of every Iraqi who gives us dirt on the bad guys."

"Sir, I don't give a shit about Fuad. He was in the game. He lost. It happens. Boo-fuckin-hoo. But Zahra and Adila don't deserve to get left hanging like that. I'm not saying we have to give them asylum, but we should at least take them out of the mix for a little while. Otherwise, they're dead."

Miller wasn't buying my humanitarian jive. I decided to change tack. "What does Brent think? Does CIA want to talk to the wife and daughter?"

"I don't know," Miller said. "I didn't get a chance to ask. After Brent dropped you off, he and his guys went back to the Agency compound across the river."

"Let's get him on the hook, Sir. I can race down to 'Nam with the boys, we'll secure Zahra and Adila and then we can pass them off to CIA."

Miller reluctantly agreed. I spent the next hour trying to get Brent on the line. No joy. I purposefully didn't tell Miller that I couldn't get ahold of Brent. Zahra and Adila were running out of time. I resolved to go get them. There would be plenty of time to work the CIA angle on the back end.

———

I rallied the platoon and told them we were headed back to 'Nam. No dump truck this time. We'd roll in hot.

Staff Sergeant Kinney walked towards the HET hooch. I motioned him to meet me on the far end of the truck lot. We needed to get out of earshot of the other Marines for this conversation.

"I'm sorry about Souza," I said. "I know you guys were tight. The op was my responsibility. I jumped all over Fuad's lead on Thamir. That's on me. I should've played that one more carefully."

Kinney gave a short nod, but didn't say anything. I could tell he at least partially agreed with the notion that I was responsible for Souza's death. He wasn't wrong.

"So yeah, Souza's death is on me. But I don't plan to let it go unanswered. The first step is securing Zahra and Adila to see if they can provide additional leads. Obviously, your Arabic skills will be a huge advantage as we move forward on this. So, what I need to know right now is this… are you in? Will you help us track down those responsible for killing Souza even if we have to go off script?"

Kinney didn't even blink. "I'm in, Sir. Whatever it takes. Whatever the stakes. I'm all the fucking way in."

"Good man," I said. "Grab your gear and meet us at the trucks. We're heading back to 'Nam. We're going to go get some answers."

———

We raced south. I saw the lookouts posted to the access road. Two kids this time. The older one had a walkie-talkie. Ox waved. The kids waved back.

No one shot at us as we rolled into the village. Apparently, the elders took my warning seriously. The guy who tried to bury the weapons in the river was standing on the side of the road. His face was still visibly swollen from Ox's slap. Ox smiled and waved to the guy.

I dismounted about 50 meters out from the farmhouse. The trucks set up in a perimeter. I left Ox in charge and took Benny and Kinney with me to the farmhouse. We approached cautiously. It was too easy to miss potential danger in the date palms and elephant grass. I positioned myself away from the doorframe like Souza would've done and banged on the screen. No answer. I sent Benny around back and to see if he could peek inside the house. He circled around. Nothing stirred. No noise from inside the house. I tested the door. It was locked. The idea that it might be boobytrapped sprinted through my mind, but I kicked the door in anyway.

The door flew open. "Zahra? Adila? Is anyone home?" I shouted louder than I had intended.

No answer. Sunlight flooded through the back of the house. The front half was all shadows. I motioned to Benny and we started clearing room by room.

Benny called out from the bedroom. "Sir. You need to see this."

I ran to the bedroom. I tried to mentally steel myself for a mutilated Adila. Instead, I got a dead Zahra. Single tap. Forehead. No signs of torture. The scene looked similar to Thamir's murder. Her arms were thrown over her head. Rigor had set in. Zahra's handsome jaw was thrust straight up in the air. The backs of her cheekbones were purple where the blood had pooled. It takes a hard motherfucker to look a woman in the face like that and pull the trigger. My blood boiled. My concussed skull throbbed.

No sign of Adila. We tore the house apart. No clothes. No bags. No personal items. Nothing. Probably a good sign. I couldn't imagine kidnappers bothering to pack for her. No sign of Fuad's cousin either. I harbored serious doubts this cousin actually existed. If he did, he was supposed to protect the women. He failed.

We wrapped Zahra in a bedspread and drove her body back to 'Nam. Kinney pulled aside a couple of village elders and explained the situation. They agreed to bury Zahra. Kinney didn't have time to separate the elders, so he addressed them as a group. Had anyone seen anything suspicious since the last time we were here? Did anyone visit with Fuad's family? Has anyone seen Adila or Fuad's cousin? Head shakes and blank stares. The villagers claimed not to have seen anything. I found that unlikely. There was only the one road in and out. If Zahra's killer drove to the farmhouse, they would have travelled right through the village. Kinney agreed the villagers were holding back, but couldn't figure out what they were trying to hide. I debated hooking the guy that Ox had slapped. He seemed like a prized member of the community. Maybe if we threatened to take him away it might jog the village's collective memory. But if they called my bluff we'd be saddled with yet another detainee with nothing to show for it. I decided against detention. I also promised myself that if I found out later that the 'Nam villagers were complicit in Zahra's death, I'd drive back down here with as much ammo and quick lime as I could carry and erase these fucks forever.

————

On the drive back to the Country Club I wracked my brain for another lead. My noggin still felt scrambled. Concentration didn't come easy. I replayed the explosion at the factory. What was I missing? Brent and his guys might have seen something from their position at the stadium. But they'd gone off the radar. It might be days or weeks before I could track them down. Then I remembered—the scout snipers were posted at the stadium too. Miller didn't mention debriefing the snipers.

I tracked down the snipers, Sergeants Davis and Cole. They were sleeping in the sniper platoon's hooch, resting up for a night mission. I woke them up and made them rehash the op. Both men claimed that just after they heard the explosion, they tracked movement on the north side of the factory compound. They heard engine noise. Davis claimed he caught a brief glimpse of a motorcycle driving away from the factory along a revetment that cut under the perimeter fence. The bike was only visible for a couple seconds and he wasn't able to get off a shot. Davis said it looked like one of those old Russian bikes that the Iraqi motorcycle cops rode. I froze at 'motorcycle cop.'

Major Miller was waiting for me as I exited the snipers' hooch. I gave him the rundown on what transpired in 'Nam. Zahra dead. Adila in the wind. Miller shrugged. He was done with the Fuad family drama. The Battalion had other priorities. He sensed that I was invested. I didn't give him a chance to change topics. I told him about the police motorcycle that Davis saw fleeing the factory. I colored in the rest. Izzat had a police bike. Izzat was a known associate of both Fuad and Thamir. Izzat was *Mukhabarat.* Izzat was in on the skim. Then I dropped my remix of the conspiracy theory. Izzat was Fuad's source. Izzat used Thamir to lure Fuad to the factory. Izzat smoked Thamir to prevent any chance of a double-cross. Izzat detonated the bomb that killed Fuad and Souza. Izzat killed Fuad to protect the money transferred abroad through the *hawala* network. Izzat killed Zahra in case Fuad had passed info from the index to his wife. Izzat may have kidnapped Adila. My narrative lost steam. It was clear by Miller's expression he wasn't buying my 'Izzat as the single architect of evil' story.

Miller stared at me with pitiful eyes. "Jim, you're going home."

"What?" It was the only word I could muster. Going home didn't make sense.

"That's what I came over here to tell you," Miller said. "Division sent us our redeployment orders. We're leaving Iraq in six to ten weeks. It looks like it'll be a quick turn. We'll train for a few months back home and then be back out here early next year. The Old Man needs an officer in charge of the advance party. He picked you."

"Sir, what the fuck are you talking about? I can't leave the platoon. I brought the boys up here. I sure as fuck intend to be the one that takes them home."

"I knew you'd feel that way. And if it was up to me, I would have let you stay with the platoon until we got back to California. But the Old Man was insistent. He wants to send you home so you can start putting the training syllabus together. You're the senior platoon commander in the Battalion. You've had your time."

"Sir. Please. I'm fucking begging you. Don't make me do this. I dropped papers before we left. I'll be a fucking civilian by Christmas. This is my last dance. Let me ride this out. Find someone else."

"That's not the way it works, Lieutenant. You know that. You're on a helo to Kuwait tomorrow. Then back home by the end of the week. Go pack your gear."

Part Two

The World

8

Jessica's House
Carlsbad, California – Saturday, 24 May 2003

June Gloom. Or 'May Gray' if you want to get technical. The cold ocean haze did nothing to slake my hangover. Muted, gray sunlight flooded through the windows. I didn't recognize the bedroom. The door to the master bath was open. I needed to get the Devil out.

I finished up in the bathroom. My shirt and jeans were on the floor. No shoes, socks, belt, watch, or wallet. My Ray-Bans were on the nightstand. I put them on. The gray light dulled a notch. I shivered. Time to face the music.

A TV was on downstairs. I padded down the stairwell and walked slowly into the kitchen. A girl sat at a breakfast nook watching the news. She gave me a mischievous smile. She was sixteen tops. What the fuck did I do?

"Hey, handsome." An older woman's voice behind me. Raspy. I turned around. Bottle blonde, brown eyes, green kimono. Generous estimation—early-40s.

My voice was thick with booze fumes and smoke damage. "Uh, good morning."

"Well, actually, it's afternoon," she said. "But hey, it's Saturday, so who's counting. Come with me."

The lady grabbed my hand and led me to a patio table in the backyard. There was a pot of coffee and a couple mugs laid out. She poured two cups and folded herself next to me on the bench seat. I grabbed the mug. My hands were shaking.

"That's Rachel in the kitchen," she said. "My daughter. She wasn't supposed to be here. She was staying at her girlfriend's this weekend but, apparently, they had a falling out. She came back this morning."

Thank God. I shuddered in relief. I've made plenty of bad judgement calls, but stat rape was never my scene. I tried to shake the cobwebs. Less than 24 hours back in the World and I'd already dodged one felony. It would be a miracle if my luck held through the weekend. I wish I could say last night's blackout was a one-time thing, but the binge drinking had been out of control long before Iraq. Apparently, six dry months in the desert hadn't been enough to shake old habits. Now I had to figure the score with this woman beside me.

She lit a cigarette and blew gray smoke into the gray sky. She offered me one. I wasn't sure I could handle it in my current state. I declined. She smiled. I took off my Ray Bans. Huge mistake. I pulled them back down over my eyes.

"I'm Jessica, by the way," she said. Her grin was a carbon copy of her daughter's. Deviousness ran deep in this family. "I'm guessing you don't remember much about last night?"

A few disjointed recollections. The week I was supposed to spend in Kuwait turned into a month. Just before I died of boredom, I wrangled a flight out. I landed in California yesterday morning. I remember turning my weapon in at the armory and signing out on block leave. I remember my old college roommate Navy Mike picking me up in 29 Palms. I remember driving to the coast. Carlsbad, I think? Some outdoor bar with f ire pits.

I mentally replayed the scene in the bedroom upstairs, grasping for clues. A very specific detail emerged—no condoms. Raw-dogging a Carlsbad Cougar my first night back was pretty aggressive, even by my standards. But I was so fucking relieved I hadn't slept with her daughter that it seemed a forgivable transgression.

The pneumatic drill in my head subsided for a beat. Long enough for me to string together some words. "I don't really remember anything about last night," I said. I took a long pull of the coffee. "I'm Jim, by the way."

"I know." Her voice a carcinogen purr. It was a promising sign. Women who smoked in the 21st century tended to not make a big deal over their other bad decisions.

"Sorry I'm such a mess. Are we in Carlsbad?" I asked.

"Ha! At least you remember that much."

Rachel poked her head out the back door. "I'm going to the movies with Troy. Be back later."

Jessica didn't even look back at her daughter. "OK hon, have fun. Call me later if you need a ride."

Rachel pulled the door shut a little harder than necessary. The reverberation bounced around in my skull. I was hurtin' for certain. The coffee helped, but only a little.

Jessica stubbed out her smoke. "Your buddy Mike said he'd come pick you up around 5:00. That's in three hours."

"Again, sorry about last night," I said. "I've been gone a long time. I'm off my game."

"Don't worry about it. You weren't *that* bad. Just let it never be said that I don't support the troops." The naughty smile and the raspy voice were a lethal combination. I was starting to see what must have caught my eye last night. I was still game, even without the booze.

"I wasn't *that* bad?" I groaned.

"Heh. Let's just say I'm certain you could do better. In fact, I'm willing to bet on it." Jessica stood and undid the belt on her kimono. She let the robe slide to the patio floor and slowly walked back inside the house. Her bare ass had a tractor beam effect. It pulled me out of the hangover and right back into her bedroom.

———

Jessica seemed satisfied with Round 2. Still not my best performance, but I was working on a nine-month handicap and a case of near-fatal dehydration. Even better, the sex halved my hangover headache.

In the gray light of day, it was clear that Jessica was a lot older than me. I didn't care. The bed felt great. The softness of her body felt downright exotic after months of sleeping in combat gear.

The shifting gray in the window indicated it was getting later. Navy Mike would be here soon. Jessica dozed on my shoulder, her drool pooling in my armpit. I gently shook her awake.

"Can I use your computer real quick?" I asked. "I have to check my email."

In my excitement to party last night, I'd forgotten to let my Mom and Sister know I'd finally made it back. Truthfully, I wasn't even sure they'd have noticed. Mom and Sis were the only permanent female fixtures in my life, but what little connection remained was predicated solely on the fact we were blood. I didn't communicate with them any better than I had my ex-wife or girlfriends.

Jessica slid out of the covers. Her laptop sat buried under a bundle of clothes on the dresser. Still naked, she bent over to boot up the computer. The view was spectacular. I'd always admired how certain older women didn't harbor the body image hang-ups so common to girls my age. I got aroused at how comfortable Jessica seemed in her own skin. She immediately noticed my arousal as I slid out of bed at half-mast.

"Looks like he might still have some fight left in him," she said. Jessica raised an eyebrow and gave my dick a little pat as she walked past me. She slid back into bed and stretched.

I opened the web browser and realized I still didn't know where my wallet was. "Have you seen my wallet?"

"All your stuff is there on the dresser, under my sweater."

I picked up the sweater and caught a whiff of fire pit smoke. This must have been what she wore last night. I savored the image of her pulling off the sweater when we returned from the bar. Not that I could actually remember it.

I found my wallet. I felt woozy. The headache started to re-congeal in the back of my brain. Maybe getting out of bed wasn't such a good idea. Maybe I should forget the email and just crawl back under the covers with Jessica.

It had been months since I logged on to my email account. I couldn't remember the password. Anticipating this situation, I'd written down a bunch of user IDs, PINs, and passwords before we deployed. I still had that list hidden somewhere in my wallet. I opened my wallet and saw a piece of card stock I didn't recognize. It was Jessica's business card. Some realty company I'd seen in advertisements along the coast. Her personal cell number was scrawled across the back of the card. I smiled and kept digging until I found the password list. It was stuffed deep in an inner pocket next to the condom I'd neglected.

I logged on. My inbox was swamped. Hundreds of emails. I forgot all about emailing Mom and started deleting in bulk. One message caught my eye. The sender's address looked like a random jumble of letters and numbers. The subject field was blank save for a single period. The date showed it was sent five days ago. Curiosity got the better of me. I opened it.

The message was brief.

Greetings, Lieutenant Jim. My name is Hamid. My father Fuad told me to contact you. Please call me as soon as you can.

No signature block. Just a phone number with a Los Angeles area code. My alcohol-fried braincells snapped into gear. Memories, flashbacks, a big tangle of emotions. I remember Fuad talking about his son Hamid who lived in Los Angeles. He mentioned his son that night at the apartment when he showed me and Souza his California driver's license. I couldn't deal with this right now. Iraq would have to wait. Hamid would have to wait.

After logging off, I turned around and leaned against the dresser. Jessica was only half covered by the sheets. The S-curve of her hip taunted me. I looked at my watch. Mike wouldn't be here for 45 minutes. Plenty of time. She clocked me with predatory brown eyes. I crawled under the sheet and buried my face between her thighs.

———

Navy Mike dropped me off at a hotel in Point Loma. Mike was a ship driver. His ship was in port this week down at 32d Street. He had duty tonight and had to get a move on. I thanked him for picking me up and playing wingman in Carlsbad.

I had ten days of block leave before I had to be back in 29 Palms. Not enough time to fly back to Virginia to see Mom and Sis. Plenty of time to get in trouble on my own. I had no plans until Monday. I had to be up in LA for Souza's funeral. The fact that Steve's send-off was scheduled for Memorial Day seemed a little too on-the-nose. No doubt the funeral turnout would be massive, even by LA standards. Marines, LA Sheriffs, other assorted cops and veterans' groups. I needed to steel myself for the spectacle.

In the meantime, I had to make some decisions. Hamid's email bothered me. How the fuck did he get my email address? Was the person on the other end of the email actually Hamid? Was Hamid actually Fuad's son? Was Fuad still trying to play me from beyond the grave? My initial thought was to just delete the email and move on. Put Iraq in a box. Try to get my life in order. I only had a few months before I'd be out of the Corps and without a paycheck. But even with Jessica's scent on my lips I still couldn't shake the thought of Adila. I'd thought about her every day during my purgatory in Kuwait. Was she still alive? Does this 'Hamid' character know what happened to her? Establishing contact with someone I believed to be the son of a senior Iraqi intelligence officer didn't seem like a smart play. The 'what now?' decisions loomed large.

Before I made any decisions, I had to take care of some housekeeping. I needed a car. I needed a cell phone. I'd sold my truck before leaving for Iraq. Cabbing around Southern California was out of the question. Fortunately, my return to the World coincided with the long weekend. The used-car crime cartels were big on holiday-weekend sales events. I checked the paper. Lots of full-page color adds with red, white, and blue Memorial Day bunting. The San Diego dealerships were in a full-bore, lot-clearing arms race. I found one within walking distance that looked promising. The ad said they were open until midnight. Plenty of time to hoof it, buy a car, and score some dinner.

The used car lot ended up being about an hour away on foot. The long walk helped me sweat out the last dregs of the hangover. I found a '96 Chevy Impala that fit the bill. The reprobate working the sales lot kept trying to get me to finance through the dealership. Greaseball wanted to bilk me at some ungodly, usurious rate. Fuck that. I was flush. Six months in the desert with no bills. Plus, it was the end of the month. The sales geek was staring down a deadline. I sensed he needed to unload the Chevy to make his quota. I lowballed the fucker. I paid cash. I drove the 'Pala off the lot 30 minutes later.

Haggling with the car salesman left me with a healthy appetite. I drove the new whip north to a Mexican joint on the outskirts of Old Town. It was one of those older establishments with a full bar adjacent to the main dining area. I found a stool on the far side of the horseshoe and ordered big. After gorging myself, I hobbled to the head to get rid of the 60 ounces of Tecate swishing around my bladder.

There was a payphone next to the bathroom door. I decided to check in with duty officer in 29 Palms. A Staff Sergeant whose name I didn't recognize answered. When I identified myself, he told me to stay on the line. I could hear him rustling through some papers on his desk. He found a message from Regiment. I was to report back to 29 Palms immediately.

What the fuck did 'immediately' mean? Tonight? I'd already had too much to drink to risk a four-hour trek back to the high desert. I was on leave for fuck's sake. What the hell could be so important that they needed me back in the middle of a holiday weekend? I told the Staff Sergeant to tell Regiment I'd be there tomorrow.

I drove back to the hotel. The thought of calling Jessica crossed my mind but I shelved it. I walked over to a liquor store and bought a six pack and a prepaid cellphone. I tried unsuccessfully to regain the beer buzz I'd kicked off at dinner. Eventually I gave up and fell into a dreamless sleep.

9

Marine Corps Air-Ground Combat Center
29 Palms, California – Sunday, 25 May 2003

The drive back to 29 Palms was brutal. The Memorial Day Weekend traffic crawled. I stopped for a late breakfast in Temecula. I called the Regimental Duty to let them know I was on my way. I made it to the Yucca Incline about mid-day. The superheated desert teed up Iraq vibes. Not the scene I was looking for having only been back in the World for 30 hours.

The gate guard hassled me over the Chevy's dealer tags. My tolerance for fuckery was already in the red. I pulled the Sergeant of the Guard out of his airconditioned shack and bullied my way on base without the proper registration docs. The base was usually deserted on Sundays, but it felt extra empty today. No one stayed in the high desert over a long weekend by choice.

Despite the lack of people, it took me a while to find covered parking. I finally found a stall a couple blocks from the Regimental HQ. It was worth the walk. The 'Pala would turn into a skillet if I left it exposed to the sun. I damn near melted walking the 40 meters between the parking stall and the headquarters building.

A weary looking Staff Sergeant manned the duty desk. I told him who I was and he pointed me to a waiting room. I plopped on the couch and thumbed through some old _Marine Corps Gazettes_ that were left on the government-issued coffee table.

I dozed off and lost track of time. The Staff Sergeant walked in and said someone was waiting for me down the hall. He led me to a small conference room off the quarterdeck.

A woman in her early-30s and an older dude sat at the far end of the table. Notepads spread before them. They both wore polo shirts and khaki pants. I could see a white t-shirt under the open collar of the older guy's polo. The skivvy shirt was a tell; this dude was some sort of federal agent. Pancake holsters tend to rub you raw if you don't wear an undershirt. Fed-issued Berettas and Glocks were notorious for gouging flanks. Especially if you boasted a little 'tactical girth' in the love handle region, which this cat had in spades.

"Lieutenant Wilde," the man said. "I'm Special Agent Lawson and this is Special Agent Cruz. We're with NCIS." Lawson and Cruz both held out their badge and creds. Neither offered to shake hands.

Lawson gestured for me to take a seat at the far end of the table. I studied both faces as I sat down. The girl was attractive. Not just because I was fresh back from Iraq. She was the real deal. She had that no-nonsense look that street-wise Latinas cultivate in early adolescence. She vibed 'I grew up with asshole brothers and I work in a male-dominated field so fuck with me at your peril.' I was smitten. Her partner was a different story. I could tell from jump this guy was a dick. Officious, jaded, the kind that rides his badge because it's the only leverage he has left in life. Dollars to donuts Lawson was on the backside of several failed marriages and would be on the job for life to pay for kids he hated.

"What can I do you for?" I said. I kept my tone icy. I played the 'I'm a combat vet so the world owes me' approach.

Lawson jumped right in. "We're here to discuss the events of 12 and 15 April of this year. In Baghdad. In your own words, can you walk us through what happened on those dates?"

This was an ambush. NCIS trying to jam me up on some bullshit. My blood pressure spiked. I struggled to stay frosty. I kept my eyes on Lawson.

"I didn't exactly keep a diary," I said. "I'm afraid you're going to have to refresh my memory. What was I 'supposedly' up to those days?"

Lawson consulted his notebook. Pure theater. He had his version memorized. "The 12th of April was a Saturday. Your platoon was dispatched to a bank in central Baghdad. There was an attempted robbery. Lots of civilians killed."

"Attempted? Nothing attempted about it. Those clowns blasted the vault room with an RPG."

"Walk us through what happened that day." Lawson readied his pen to take notes. Apparently, this dickhead thought I'd just start talking.

No dice. I wasn't playing this game. "I'm not walking you through anything without a lawyer."

Lawson's head popped up from his notebook. A look of surprise was quickly clouded by anger. Cruz turned her head, trying to hide a smile. She was amused. I'm guessing she'd just won a bet.

Lawson struggled to keep his cool. "Lieutenant, I don't think you understand. We're not charging you with anything. You're not in custody. This is an interview, not an interrogation. We're just trying to figure out what happened at the bank on April 12th and what happened during the raid on April 15th."

Ah yes. The 'raid.' That would be suspected Iranian stash house Fuad led us to. The one where CNN filmed Ox dropping the wounded guy. Miguel the reporter and Eddy, his Limey cameraman. The leaked footage. McSorley and Miller warned me. I wasn't sure what NCIS had on the bank caper, but if they were lumping it in with the raid video, it couldn't be good.

Fuck this Lawson prick. I came back icy. Straight out of the freezer. "I don't think *you* understand," I said. "I'm not talking to you without a lawyer."

Lawson fumed. I held my stare until he broke eye contact. He was probably used to strong-arming junior Marines and Sailors into telling him what he wanted to hear. I didn't play that game. Amongst all his rambling advice on dealing with shitheads, the last thing Uncle Mitch told me before he died was, 'Never talk to cops without a lawyer.' At the time it struck me as a little odd coming from a cop, but it was probably the best nugget he ever threw my way.

After an unhealthy silence, Cruz finally spoke up. "OK, please coordinate with your lawyer," she said. "We'll be in touch. Do you have a phone number we can use to get back with you?"

"Of course." I grabbed two of Cruz' business cards from her notebook. I stuck one in my shirt pocket. I wrote my prepaid cell number on the back of the other card and handed it to her. This time her smile was more patronizing, less amused.

Lawson was still irate. Cruz flashed him a look that said, 'keep your cool.' Lawson started packing up his notebook and pens. I stood up and beat him to the door. Without looking back, I gave an over-the-shoulder wave. I floated a breezy "Ciao." I strolled half-speed to the quarterdeck. Cruz might not have been impressed with my little business card stunt, but I sure as hell felt her eyes on me as I walked out of that room. The sensation of feeling Cruz' gaze conjured a mental image of Adila. The thought of Adila made my stomach ache.

I sat sweating buckets in the car. Even in the covered parking with the A/C blasting it was nuclear fission hot. But it wasn't just the Mojave. It was the 'interview' that had me all lathered. I played the hardman with Lawson because my pride wouldn't let me look weak in front of Cruz. But tough guy kabuki aside, this was serious shit. The video of Ox plugging that guy could turn things sour. I knew Marines that had been jammed up for less. My thoughts jumped back to the bank. What the fuck was NCIS doing sniffing around that mess? Back in the World less than 48 hours and I already had too much shit on my plate. First Hamid, now NCIS. I needed to lay low for a few days.

———

I pointed the Impala west. I made LA by sundown and checked into a hotel on the gritty side of Venice. The hotel was walking distance to a favorite haunt down by the pier. The bar's generous collection of booze beckoned. I walked in. The place hadn't changed a lick in the half decade since my last visit. Stale taps, greasy chow, and a favorable girl/guy ratio. Encouraging signs at the end of a shit day. I found a spot at the bar and placed my order. The bartender looked like she'd worked the joint since Jim Morrison was a regular.

It was time to make some calls. I needed a lawyer. My buddy Easy was at the top of the list. He left the Corps 18 months ago after his first hitch. Now he lived up here in Venice. I wasn't exactly sure what kind of law he practiced, but at the very least he'd know who to trust. Easy picked up on the second ring. I told him I was back in the World and needed some legal advice. The stars aligned. Easy was two blocks away. He said he'd meet me in five.

Easy walked in two minutes later. His hair was longer and his midsection was a touch thicker than I remembered, but he still maintained the alpha ape swagger he wore during his stint in uniform. "Jimmy! Long time no see, brother."

"Easy, my man. Thanks for coming, Homie."

"For sure. Look at you! All skinny and shit. How long you been back?"

"Less than 48 hours… but it's been an eventful couple of days."

"No doubt. Fuck the small talk, Brother. Order another round and give me the skinny."

I ordered shots with a couple beers. I gave Easy the rundown on the 'interview' with NCIS. He listened carefully. I could see the legal strategies congealing behind his eyes. At the end of my spiel Easy ordered another round of drinks. He stretched on the barstool and handed me a business card.

Easy said, "All good Brother. I'll rep you pro bono. My firm can carry the work. I've rustled up a ton of clients recently and they owe me. My info is on the card. Office is closed tomorrow because of the holiday. Drop by Tuesday morning and I'll have you fill out the paperwork. I'll get ya through the interviews and we'll put these NCIS fucks back in the box."

"Thanks, Brother," I said. "That was almost too, dare I say it, 'easy.'" Having Easy in my corner made things seem much more manageable. The fact we were four rounds deep probably helped as well.

"You know how I do, Brother." Easy raised his shot glass. We toasted. The dude definitely lived up to his moniker.

We sank another round. I ordered a burger to help absorb the booze. With the legal business handled for now, we shifted to sea stories. We caught up on the exploits of mutual friends, talked shit about our ex-wives, and got our swerve on. Inevitably the conversation shifted to Iraq. I realized I hadn't really talked about it since leaving Baghdad.

Easy said, "Tell me, Brother. What the fuck is the plan over there? What are we supposed to be doing?"

I was buzzed. I knew whatever I said would be an oversimplification. "I'm not sure there really is a plan. We seemed to be winging it. The original plan was get to Baghdad. We got there and then shit got confused real quick. Folks were happy we booted Saddam, but the goodwill only lasted about a week. After that, it just felt like we were fighting everyone and no one all at the same time. I realize that statement probably doesn't make sense."

"Nah, I get it, Brother," Easy said. "Makes perfect sense. I knew those clown shoes in DC didn't know what the fuck they were doing. I listened to their bullshit on TV all day, every day. The dudes pushing the invasion were fucking dorks. Goddamn chicken hawks who never served a day in uniform. Anyway, fuck it, dude, I'm just glad you're back home safe and sound."

"Don't get me wrong, I feel like we did *some* good," I said. "We greased a lot of bad guys. So, if nothing else, at least those assholes won't be around to victimize others. But it seems like such a wasted opportunity. I mean we really coulda handled some business over there if we'd been given the greenlight."

Easy belched and ordered another round. "I feel ya. And I'm sure you and the boys took care of business. Never had any doubts about that. All that other political shit… that's not on you, Brother."

I didn't want to go down the self-pity rabbit hole. Iraq was fucked. Who cares? That was the gig. I'm a professional. I could handle the disappointment. But there was a lot that still bothered me about the place. Souza's death and Adila's disappearance were at the top of that list. Still, I didn't want to hassle Easy with all this Debbie Downer bullshit. I changed topics. I asked Easy if he had a girl. He played coy. That meant he was banging some lawyer chick he worked with. Probably one that was married. You'd think he know better than to dip his pen in the company ink. But once a Marine, always a Marine.

Easy looked at his watch. It was getting late. He was playing in a Memorial Day charity softball tournament in the morning.

The games started early. He begged off to bed. We made plans
for me to visit his law office Tuesday morning. Easy paid our tab.
I left a big cash tip for the relic behind the bar. She collected the
bills with a wink and a smile that cracked her battle paint.

Against my better judgement I bought a pack of darts on
the walk back to the hotel. My mood was instantly lifted by the
ocean breeze and smoke combo. It was one of those righteous
harmonies you couldn't simulate in the desert. One surprise
though, the Camel Wides didn't taste as good as Miamis.

Talking about Iraq with Easy also got me rethinking
the Hamid angle. With all the drama of the past two days,
getting involved with another Iraqi seemed like an unnecessary
complication. But curiosity is a bitch. The whiskey-fueled devil
on my shoulder kept telling me to call him. I got back to my
hotel room and sat on the bed staring at my cellphone. The room
swirled a bit as the booze kicked in. I dialed Hamid's number.
No answer. No voicemail. No dice. I washed down a couple of
sleeping pills and dropped into the ether.

10

Los Angeles National Cemetery
Los Angeles, California – Monday, 26 May 2003

Souza's funeral procession stretched half a mile. The crowd featured a full-on sheriff's motorcade augmented by what seemed like hundreds of LAPD and California Highway Patrol cars and motorcycles. I stood sweating in my dress blues as the hearse pulled into the Los Angeles National Cemetery. The hearse was a big Cadillac job. It struck me as obscenely oversized knowing that what was left of Souza probably wouldn't fill a cookie jar.

I flashbacked to Souza's comment at the morgue a few hours before he was killed. About the horror of a family being left with nothing but the liquified remains of a loved one. The smells from that night came flooding back. It took a couple of hard, sour swallows to get my stomach back in check.

The funeral service crawled. I struggled to maintain my bearing. Souza's wife looked unbelievably young and vulnerable. His son stood perfectly still in his toddler-sized suit, squinting into the sun. The little boy didn't flinch during the rifle salute. Maybe he was numb. Or maybe he'd simply inherited his dad's grit. Maybe both.

After the eulogy, I started to make my way to the front of the crowd. I felt compelled to tell Souza's wife that I was with him when he died. I made it to the front row. Mrs. Souza was sobbing against her mother's shoulder. We made eye contact. She looked devastated. Hopeless. I chickened out. I broke contact and hustled back to my car.

Two men in lightweight summer suits approached. A skinny Asian guy on the left and a fat white guy on the right. They looked like the number 10 walking at me.

"Jim Wilde?" the fat guy asked. The dude's whole body jiggled when he spoke. He looked like a 250-pound sack of smashed assholes.

"Yeah. Who are you?"

"I'm Special Agent Brian MacFarlane and this is Special Agent Bradford Li, FBI."

Fuck me. Back in the world less than 72 hours and I was already on my second set of Federal Agents. "What can I do for ya?" I asked.

"We'd like to ask you some questions about Jawad Shammar," MacFarlane said. "You might know him as Hamid."

Hamid? That was fast. My first impulse was to shine these suits until I could get Easy involved. But something told me that if the Feds were asking about Hamid, they might have a line on Adila. My curiosity was piqued. I decided to risk it.

"Can we talk about this somewhere else?" I asked. "I'm dying out here in my blues."

I followed the Feds to a non-descript strip mall. I changed out of my blues in the parking lot and the Feds ushered me into a small office. It looked like a low-rent legal firm. Li entered a code on a keypad next to the door and an auto-lock disengaged. I guessed it was some sort of Fed off-site, but they didn't bother to explain.

MacFarlane said, "Jawad Shammar. Or Hamid. You know who I'm talking about, correct?"

"I've never met the guy," I said.

"But he contacted you a few days ago, yes?"

"He emailed me sometime last week. I didn't see the message until Saturday. That was my first full day back in the States."

"What did the email say?"

I didn't like MacFarlane's tone. It was the typical 'treat everyone as a suspect' Fed bullshit. I decided to take him off his game.

"Is this about Adila?" I asked. I threw on a scowl of mock suspicion.

"Who's Adila?" MacFarlane asked.

I noted the change in tone. MacFarlane legitimately didn't know about Adila. Li looked confused as well. These guys were searching. They weren't trying to jam me. Not yet anyway. I decided to break Uncle Mitch's rule and give them the full backstory even though Easy wasn't present. I spilled the whole she-bang. I recounted how Fuad appeared out of thin air that first night at the church. The Oil-for-Food rumors. Fuad's request for asylum. His relocation to the farm down at 'Nam. My theory that Fuad was lured back to Baghdad and killed so that he couldn't expose the money trail. Zahra's murder. Adila's disappearance. Izzat at the center of it all. I didn't have the facts to prove Izzat's role, but I skewed the tale to make him seem like a supervillain. The only thing I didn't mention was the bank heist. I wanted to see how that was going to play with NCIS before I started connecting the dots for the Feds. MacFarlane and Li listened in silence. They scribbled notes. It was obvious they were playing catch-up.

I'd showed my cards. Most of them anyway. Now it was time to see if they'd reciprocate. "So how do you guys tie-in on Hamid, or Jawad, or whoever he is?"

MacFarlane looked at Li and then back at me. "Jawad Shammar is dead. He was killed four days ago here in Los Angeles."

Three of the four family members killed in less than a month. An unlucky coincidence? Hardly. This shit had to be about the money. Like Uncle Mitch used to say, 'it's not *all* about the money, it's *only* about the money.'

All the drama pointed in one direction—Iraq was now bleeding into California. Call it a hemorrhage. If someone was willing to grease Hamid here on US soil, then Fuad's index might actually exist. It might still be out there somewhere. Maybe with Adila.

"So, what now?" I asked. "Do you want the phone number Hamid left for me on the email?"

MacFarland looked at Li again before answering. "We already have it," he said.

"Ok, so you're up on his email and phone. And maybe my email as well. What do you need me for?"

"Tell us about Fuad."

I recounted everything I'd already told them. Fuad's California Driver's license, the fact that Adila had lived in the UK, the family's near-perfect command of spoken English. I held nothing back. Was this the Feds playing 'Repeat and Control?' Maybe. They didn't press me on any details. I wrapped up my summary and sat back in the uncomfortable government surplus chair. I studied the G-Men's eyes for clues. I didn't see any.

MacFarlane checked his notes. It felt like he was stalling, waiting for me to start talking again. I stayed silent. After a tense interlude he spoke up.

"If you're contacted by anyone from an email or phone number you don't recognize, you let us know right away," MacFarlane said. "If any strangers contact you in person, you let us know right away. If you come across anything related to Fuad's family, Iraq, the Oil-for-Food deal, or anything like that, you contact us right away. Understood?"

The Fed-tone returned to MacFarland's voice. He was trying to re-establish control at the end of our little discussion. It still felt kosher though. I didn't get a squeeze vibe. Whatever the angle, their real target wasn't Jim Wilde.

I shrugged. "Easy day. If I hear anything, you guys will be the first to know."

———

Holiday traffic put me in a chokehold on the way back to Venice. I checked my phone. Two missed calls. One was from Easy. He wanted me to come in earlier tomorrow than we originally planned. The second message was from Special Agent Cruz. No details, just a 'call me when you get this.' I checked the timestamp. She called almost two hours ago. That was long enough to call her back without seeming anxious. I dialed her number. Cruz answered right away. Even in business mode her voice was sexy. She and Lawson wanted to talk to me again tomorrow. New information had come to light. I told her I couldn't drive back to 29 Palms. She said there was an office at LA Air Force Base we could use. She gave me the address. I agreed to be there at 4pm. She hung up without saying goodbye.

I got back to Venice and checked my email in what passed for the hotel's business suite. Nothing. I ruminated on the meeting with the Feds. The FBI wasn't giving me the full picture on Hamid. The Feds don't investigate homicides. This had to be about the Oil-for-Food deal and the *hawala* network here in the States. I knew enough about the FBI to know that they had plenty of finance nerds capable of following dark money all over the world. It was a safe bet they were already savvy to the Oil-for-Food business.

After mentally replaying the meeting with MacFarlane and Li a couple of times, I decided to keep myself on the hook. If I played along with the Feds I might just stumble across a lead on Adila. I assumed that if she was still alive, she was probably stuck in Iraq. But who knows? She'd made it out once before. Maybe she'd make it out a second time.

Even though I'd convinced myself to play the FBI's game, I didn't like the idea of playing solo. Easy would cover me on the legal front, but I needed someone in the game, someone with a badge, someone who could potentially back my play if things got hot. I went through the checklist and kept coming back to Cruz. Even though we'd only just met, she was the only one who fit the bill. She was only tangentially involved at this point, but I convinced myself that if I could entice her into the fold, Cruz could help me. But would she? It was worth a shot.

I called Cruz back and asked if she could meet me alone before the 4pm interview with Lawson. She hedged. Going behind her partner's back was bad form. I played to her ego. Her partner was a geek. She was a boss. Her partner sucked. She had moves. I knew the Feds would talk to her but only if she liaised alone. They wouldn't give Lawson the time of day. They'd shut his goofy ass out of anything serious.

Cruz saw through the flattery. She'd had plenty of practice parsing through men's bullshit. But she was curious, and curious was enough. She agreed to hear me out before the official meeting. I gave her the name of a diner near the airport. It was a date. I celebrated the small victory by heading back to the bar by the Venice Pier and getting smashed.

11

Century City
Los Angeles, California – Tuesday, 27 May 2003

Easy's office was in Century City. One of those glass and chrome deals made popular in 80s crime flicks. His office faced west. Seventeenth floor. No June Gloom up here. Soft orange glow all the way to the coast.

I nursed my fourth consecutive hangover. The new morning routine. Not much different from the old routine. At this rate, I'd have to redeploy to Iraq just to dry out. Betty Ford had nothing on Baghdad.

Easy greeted me at the elevator and hustled me into his office. I told him about the meet with Lawson and Cruz. Easy cleared his schedule. His eyes twinkled. For a dude named Easy he sure as hell relished conflict. I gave him my take on the Lawson/Cruz dynamic. Lawson's a dick. He doesn't care about facts. He'll burn me just for the collar. Cruz seems legit. She knows the score. Lawson might be the senior agent, but Cruz wears the pants. Easy asked me straight up if Cruz was hot. I admitted she was. He laughed and shook his head. Apparently, my criteria for picking allies wasn't as objective as I thought.

Easy and I went back over the bank heist and the raid. He asked me a million questions. We nailed down the chronology. We hardwired the details. We identified 'known unknowns.'

Easy peppered me with potential follow-up questions. We discussed oblique lines of inquiry and elicitation stunts. He showed me a couple of hand signals he would use during the interview. The most important one was Easy's right hand on his notebook. That was the signal for 'shut the fuck up.' I felt good. I was ready.

We weren't meeting Lawson and Cruz until 4pm. Easy had a full plate so I got out of his hair. I needed some time alone to rethink how best to play the one-on-one with Cruz. Back in Venice I fought the temptation of a liquid lunch. A beach walk helped clear my brain. Focus. Think. Anticipate. I felt better, more engaged than I'd been since my last day in Iraq.

I rolled to the diner 15 minutes early. It was a move born of old habits seasoned with a new paranoia. I suspected that NCIS, the Feds, or both, had me under surveillance.

The diner crowd was sparse in the pre-dinner rush hours. There were only a few customers. All old-timers. None of them vibed Federal Law Enforcement. I grabbed a corner booth facing the entrance.

Ten seconds later, Cruz walked through the door. Pantsuit tailored to the bone. Dangerous curves on full display. It didn't seem possible her jacket could conceal a gun. The timing of her arrival led me to assume she'd already clocked me in the parking lot. She might have even followed me all the way from the hotel.

Cruz took a seat in the booth. She forced me to scoot down so that she was facing the door. We had three feet of Formica tabletop between us. Awkward. We both ordered coffee. Cruz waited for the waitress to get out of earshot. She put her hands on the table and fixed me with cat eyes.

She said, "Start talking."

"Did you follow me here?" I asked.

"I wouldn't tell you if I did. You've got me out on a limb here, so let's cut the chit-chat. What did you want to tell me?"

"Are you recording me?"

"Seriously? Either you start talking or I start walking. Chop-chop."

The 'chop-chop' sounded like a mom getting her five-year-old ready for kindergarten. Not the start I was shooting for. I leaned back in the booth and tried to relax.

"I got hit up by the FBI yesterday," I said. "Long story short, the son of an Iraqi I met in Baghdad was killed here in LA a few days ago. I wasn't even back in the States yet, so I'm alibied, and I don't get the feeling the Feds are trying to jam me on this one, but they're holding back. They've got something brewing and I want in."

Cruz stared. Her eyes narrowed. She was intrigued. She tried to hide it.

I laid out the whole story. Meeting Fuad that night at the church. The meeting at his apartment. The Oil-for-Food skim. The *hawala* network. The index. I ran down my theory about Izzat using Thamir to lure Fuad back to Baghdad. I almost got choked up recounting the night Souza and Fuad got blown up. I gave Cruz all the grisly details on Zahra's murder. I speculated on Adila's disappearance. I added more conjecture on the bleed over between events in Iraq and here in LA. I wrapped up with Hamid getting clipped. The tale sounded ridiculous when I said it out loud. I could tell Cruz intuited that I'd deliberately omitted info regarding the bank caper during my rundown of the drama.

The waitress came back and refilled our coffee. Cruz waited again until the waitress left. She frowned and pinched the bridge of her nose. The gesture was clear. I was a headache she didn't want or need.

"What exactly is it that you want me to do, Jim?" she asked.

She used my first name. I took it as a good sign. "Liaise with the Feds and see if they have a bead on Adila," I said. "You can use your investigation into the Baghdad bank robbery to shoehorn yourself into their case. Wrap the bank heist into the missing Oil-for-Food funds and tie all of it back to Fuad's family. Three out of the four are already dead but maybe there's a chance at saving Adila. She deserves our protection. And I'm assuming you guys have better access in Baghdad right now than the FBI. You can use that access as part of your interagency cooperation pitch. Convince the Feds to bring you into the fold on what they've got going on here in LA in exchange for tying up the loose ends in Iraq."

Cruz chuckled. "Wow, this Adila woman has you all worked up. She must've really left an impression." Cruz shook her chin back and forth. "You Marines and your 'Sergeant-Save-a-Ho' complexes. So predictable. Tell me this, Mr. Knight in Shining Armor, even if I somehow managed to get NCIS in the tent and we did get a fix on Adila, what are you going to do about it? If she's not already dead, she's probably still back in Iraq. You going back there on a solo mission to rescue her? Nice try, James Bond."

Behind the sarcasm, I felt that I'd touched a nerve. Cruz was jealous that I cared about Adila. Not 'jealous' jealous, but her reaction came off a little too harsh, a little too personal. My ability to read women had never been great, but I suspected it had been a while since Cruz thought a guy cared about her the way she thought I cared about Adila. And that's just it, I did care about Adila, but not to the degree Cruz assumed. I filed Adila in the 'missed opportunity' category. I'd welcome the opportunity to help her since we'd fucked things up in Baghdad, but a month's honest reflection told me there was no real future between us.

Even if I still sometimes tried to convince myself otherwise. We were worlds apart. The reality was insurmountable.

What I really wanted Cruz' help with, and what I had to be careful about revealing, was revenge for Souza. Souza's death left me with a debt I was only too anxious to settle. I hadn't wasted much time reflecting on Iraq. I'd avoided the big 'what does it all mean?' self-reflection hocus pocus. But I knew I'd regret it the rest of my life if I didn't do everything I could to avenge Steve. I'd been brooding on a revenge kick the whole time I was stranded in Kuwait. But seeing Steve's wife and kid at the funeral was the clincher. I might be too weak to offer the remaining Souza family any emotional support, but if I'd learned nothing else from my time Iraq, it was this—sometimes violence *is* the answer.

I stalled. I didn't want Cruz to read my thoughts. I made a show of draining the rest of my coffee. My mind raced. My leg started gently bouncing up and down underneath the booth.

While I shuffled in my seat, I raced through all the possibilities for revenge I'd conjured earlier and I tried to temper my expectations. If there were Iraqi spooks creeping around LA trying to get a fix on the Oil-for-Food cash, then there was a good chance they'd be tied in to Izzat. The way Izzat traveled in the same orbit as the Oil-for-Food skim, the bearer bonds, and all the associated killings convinced me he had to be involved. Unfortunately, when I was being honest about it, the chances of Izzat making it out of Iraq alive seemed dim. I chewed on that for a bit. Cruz watched me with deteriorating patience.

Ultimately, I decided Izzat wasn't the only viable target. I'd settle for putting down a few of his associates. That would be enough to help even the score for Souza, at least in terms of sating my personal vendetta. More dead Iraqis weren't going to do shit for Steve's family, but I knew deep down that I'd never be able to put Iraq in the rearview mirror if I didn't at least make a play. Was I being selfish? Probably. But acts of violence are almost always selfish.

I looked at my watch. The next meeting at LA Air Force Base was in less than 30 minutes. It was hard to hold my focus on Cruz' eyes. She had a way of looking at me that was simultaneously disarming and endearing. I reckoned she had to be an absolute puppet master in the interrogation booth. Her mere presence made men want to confess their deepest secrets.

"So, Angela, is that a yes? You'll help me?"

Cruz' face hardened. The 'Angela' was too much. She can call me 'Jim,' but Marine Lieutenants don't get to call her by her first name. Not on the job anyway.

She closed her eyes and sighed again. "I'll think about it."

———

Easy and I made it to the conference room on time. Lawson and Cruz were already there. Easy introduced himself. Lawson seemed more cheerful than I expected. His happy-go-lucky demeanor seemed rehearsed. It put me on edge.

Lawson said, "Jim, we have some good news."

I stared back. Silent. I'm not biting, asshole. Tell me what it is you're going to tell me. Lawson did the thing where he looked back over his notes. He wasn't reading anything. It was a nervous habit.

Lawson cleared his throat and continued. "We finally got a hold of the full, unedited video from CNN. The video of the raid on April 15th. I'm happy to report the full video clearly demonstrates that the wounded man you ordered Corporal Oxford to fire on was, in fact, armed and reaching for his rifle. It's been ruled a good shoot. We closed the inquiry."

Again, Lawson paused, expecting me to respond. He was trying to build rapport. Trying to play the good guy. Repair the damage from the first interview. He wanted me to drop my guard so he could hook me on the bank caper. Fat chance asshole.

Easy said, "I'd like a memorandum from your Field Office that outlines what you just said." Easy switched to a mock conspiratorial tone. "Just in case *someone* decides they want to harass my client regarding that episode in the future," he said.

Lawson stuttered. "Well… well, we don't really provide memoranda in such cases. As a matter of standard practice."

Easy smiled. He enjoyed steamrolling guys like Lawson. It was probably the main reason he stayed in the law game. "I'll be requesting one, anyway," Easy said. "Formally. Through your counsel's office." Easy didn't care about a memo. He just wanted Lawson off-balance. Easy wanted Lawson to know he wasn't his only touch point at NCIS. It worked.

"OK…uh, that leaves us with the other matter to discuss. The bank robbery on 12 April." Lawson looked back down at his notes. Awkward silence.

Cruz chimed in for the save. "Lieutenant Wilde, as we discussed during our first meeting, you aren't being charged with anything. You can decide not to talk to us, but that may *complicate* our investigation. The sooner we can establish some facts about the bank incident, the sooner we can decide how to proceed."

I smiled. Casual. Mr. Unflappable again. "How can I help?"

Lawson started to say something, but Cruz cut him off. She was running the interview now. "You can help by walking us through the events of that day."

I looked at Easy. He gave me a nod. I recounted the scene at the bank exactly how we practiced it in Easy's office. Lawson got lost in his notes. He tried to interrupt me several times to ask for clarification on specific points. Cruz silenced Lawson with death ray stares. She didn't need to take notes. She intuited what parts of the story needed to be challenged later on. My earlier assumption about her prowess as an interrogator was confirmed. She knew Lawson's interruptions might give me an opportunity to massage the chronology, to deflect, to run the narrative in circles.

I obliged Cruz and got back on track. I talked for 20 minutes. I laid out the whole fiasco. How we got called to the bank while the robbery was already in progress. How my boys dropped most of the heist crew. How Ox found paper scraps with bearer bond serial numbers. How another platoon arrived and relieved us. How we boogied out of there *before* the French TV crew arrived and started filming wild dogs munching on bodies.

I finished my story and leaned back in the chair. Cruz was about to start asking the standard 'repeat and control' questions when Lawson interrupted again.

"Lieutenant did you take anything else from the crime scene?" MacFarlane asked. "Anything besides the papers that Corporal Oxford found in the vault room?"

Cruz flashed Lawson another Medusa gaze. Her feline eyes narrowed into gun ports. This wasn't part of the plan. Lawson jumped the gun. He was showing their cards too early.

Easy pounced. "Agent Lawson, are there any allegations pertaining to my client that I should be aware of?"

Lawson stuttered again. "I'm… I'm just asking Lieutenant Wilde if he took anything from the bank. Or if any of his Marines took anything. Maybe there were additional items recovered from the bank that didn't get processed for intelligence exploitation? If you can identify any such items, it will help us reconcile your recollection of the events with other witness statements."

Easy placed his right hand on his notebook. I tallied the signal. I stayed silent. Easy took over.

"Agent Lawson, my client has already provided you a full accounting of the events that transpired at the bank on April 12th," Easy said. "If you have questions regarding what was processed *after* the robbery, we can schedule another interview. Otherwise, it's time for us to call it a day."

Now it was Cruz' turn to look down at her notes. Lawson derailed the interview. She knew it was time to cut bait. "OK, Gentlemen, thank you for your time," she said. "We'll be in touch."

Lawson looked at Cruz with a hurt-puppy expression. No doubt the version he'd replay for their boss would feature Cruz letting us off the hook right before he got me to cop to looting the bank. Easy and I stood up to leave. Cruz followed. When Lawson wasn't looking, she pointed towards the door and held up all five fingers—*meet in the parking lot in five minutes.*

———

It was hot in the parking lot. My Ray-Bans fogged over as soon as I stepped outside. I thanked Easy for reppin' me. We promised to keep in touch throughout the week. Easy had to go back to the office in Century City. I told him I could handle Cruz alone. Easy didn't like that idea, but he had other paying clients to deal with. He got in his car and rolled out to battle traffic.

Cruz exited the building alone and speed-walked to my car. I fixated on the swing of her pant-suited hips. The Ray-Bans hid the fact I was scoping her. At least I hope they did.

Cruz said, "I contacted our FBI liaison. They want to meet tomorrow. The Federal Building on Wilshire. Meet me there at 5pm."

"OK, I'll be there," I said. "And by the way, just so *you* know, we didn't take anything else from the bank. There wasn't anything else to take. Some loose dinars laying around. Small denominations. Nothing anyone would bother trying to smuggle home."

"That's something you could have told us in there," Cruz said.

"When it comes to the official stuff, I say what Easy allows. Which I'm sure you can appreciate. Despite your boy Lawson's best efforts, I'm not getting dragged into some bullshit bank robbery investigation. That's what this is about right? That's the angle you guys are working? Someone dimed me out? You hearing rumors that ol' Jim Wilde and his boys were out there looting Iraqi cash?"

"You know I can't talk about that. I'll see you tomorrow, Jim."

"It's a date… Angela."

12

Federal Building
Los Angeles, California – Wednesday – 28 May 2003

The Federal Building on Wilshire looked out of place in the West LA lineup. The post-deco façade made it look more like a prison. Call it mid-century American brutalism. I reckoned the architecture would be the least brutal aspect of the afternoon. Dealing with the FBI was always excruciating.

Cruz met me in the lobby. She handed me a visitor's pass and we took a seat in the waiting area. Typical FBI bullshit. Always on *their* time. I was tempted to chat her up. Flirt with her. Nix that. It's time to behave. I need Cruz on my side. I couldn't risk jeopardizing my only link to the bigger game that was starting to unfold.

Ten minutes later, Special Agents MacFarlane and Li walked into the waiting area. No handshakes. Just curt nods. They led us into a conference room on the ground floor. I noticed right away it was wired for sound and video. No attempts were made to hide the overhead mics and bubble cameras. We sat down. Everyone pulled out their notepads.

MacFarlane took the lead. "Mr. Wilde, when we spoke on Monday, you failed to mention that NCIS had interviewed you regarding the bank heist in Baghdad. Why did you choose not to disclose that?"

I played it oblivious. "I assumed you already knew," I said. I gestured to Cruz and Li. "Don't your agencies coordinate these things?"

"We do coordinate," MacFarlane said. "But what I'm trying to figure out is why you left the bank heist out of the story you told us yesterday?"

I deflected. "How does the bank connect to Fuad's family?"

Silence all around. Accusatory looks from MacFarlane and Li. Frustration from Cruz. They haven't slapped the bracelets on me yet. That means they need me.

I broke the silence. "I'm here to help," I said. "Tell me how all this connects. Or don't tell me. Whatever. Just tell me what you need me to do."

MacFarlane continued to try and bore holes in my head with his stare. His fleshy face failed to intimidate. Li looked back and forth between MacFarlane and his notes. Finally, MacFarlane spoke up. He spoke for 15 minutes straight. I wouldn't have believed the tale if MacFarlane hadn't been such a square. There was no way he could've come up with this stuff on his own. MacFarlane's backstory covered a lot of ground. He spat the highlights in tight bursts. Jawad was *Mukhabarat* like his dad. Jawad came to California on a bogus student visa eight years ago. Jawad's Kuwaiti passport listed him as 'Hamid al-Duri,' an identity he stole from a Kuwaiti about his age that was killed during the Iraqi invasion in '90. The Feds picked up on the fake identity before he entered the country, but let him in anyway in hopes he would lead them to any other foreign intelligence assets in the US. Initially, the Fed's gamble looked promising. Jawad was a graduate engineering student at USC and the FBI knew Iraqi Intelligence had people in USC dating back to the late-70s, just after Saddam took the reins. The FBI put Jawad under surveillance off and on for years. Unfortunately, the op didn't yield any actionable results. Jawad never interacted with any of the known *Mukhabarat* already in the US. In fact, he rarely interacted with anyone. Until January of this year.

MacFarlane paused to take a sip of water. My head was spinning. It was hard to keep MacFarlane's story straight as he rattled off details.

MacFarlane continued the Jawad saga. Back in January, Jawad met with a couple of bad actors in Ensenada, Mexico. Bad guy #1 was Anton Colombani, a shot-caller in a Corsican organized crime family with deep connections in the Levantine underworld. Bad guy #2 was a Mexican national and known *Mukhabarat* asset named Rudolfo Santana. Santana used his position in the shipping industry to help Saddam evade post-DESERT STORM import sanctions. Uncle Sam didn't have coverage on the meeting, so whatever was discussed remained a mystery. However, the Feds had information indicating that Colombani had entered the US under a false identity ten days ago. The Feds liked Colombani for the hit on Jawad. My story about Fuad's index bolstered that theory. If Fuad managed to get a copy of the index to Jawad, gangsters like Colombani wouldn't hesitate to kidnap, torture, and kill their way to the *hawala* codes. There was enough money at stake to bring out the heavy hitters. To add to an already spicy recipe, the Feds had sources that claimed Colombani was still in the US. Most likely in the greater LA area.

MacFarlane's story was a lot to take in. Iraq spillover was one thing, but now we had Corsican gangsters and Mexican smugglers in the mix. I couldn't feature how I fit in. But after watching Souza get blown up and Adila disappear, I was hot to trot. I tried not to look too eager.

Special Agent Li finally spoke up. "Some new information indicates that there were, in fact, bearer bonds stored at the bank in Baghdad," he said. "We've spent the past few hours running this down with Special Agent Cruz's colleagues at NCIS and the analysts at Treasury. I can't get into the details, but we believe the bonds were stolen the night you responded to the robbery. We also have reason to believe that they may be headed back here to California."

Now I was starting to lose the thread. I turned to Cruz. "So does that mean you guys are done jamming me up about the bank?" I asked. "Or do you still think I took the bonds?"

Cruz exchanged glances with MacFarlane and Li. "The investigation is still open," she said. "I'll leave it at that."

I gave Cruz my best whipped dog look. I got icy eyes in response. Cruz didn't tolerate theatrics.

It was MacFarlane's turn to run a new approach. "Lieutenant Wilde, I don't think you stole any bearer bonds," he said. "The bonds are difficult to convert. There are maybe three or four fences on the west coast that could handle them and, let's just say you don't strike me as someone who moves in those circles. Now, that said, the bad guys might not share that assessment. They might think you have the bonds, or at least access to someone who has them. In their part of the world, there's rarely a distinction between military officers and criminals. So it's not out of the question that they would think you, a Marine Officer, might try and sell the bonds. That's our play. That's what we want to leverage."

This was getting interesting. "But I saw Izzat flee with the bonds," I said. "Well, technically I saw Izzat clip the other robber and take the backpack that, from what you've told me, I assume contained the bonds. That aside, why would this Corsican asshole, his Mexican buddy, or any other bad guy think I have the paper?"

"They don't," MacFarlane replied. "We have no reason to believe that any of the bad actors we're tracking think that you're currently in possession of the bonds. But we have ways of floating the idea that a certain Marine Lieutenant fresh back from Iraq happens to be in possession of the bonds, and that's a notion that could quickly gain traction amongst our targets. Might even shake a few out of hiding."

I smiled. "The old 'tethered goat' operation huh? Put the word on the streets that I've got the paper and let the bad men come at me? I know that game. But what about the *hawala* index? That would be the real score for you guys, right? You'd have a map of the Arab World's underground finance ops right here in the US."

Li said, "Here's the deal. We don't know for sure why Jawad was killed. Maybe his father sent him a copy of the index. Maybe he came into possession of the bonds stolen in Bagdad. Maybe none of the above. Although we don't know exactly *why* he was killed, we have a pretty good idea *who* pulled the trigger. For reasons I can't get into just now, Colombani is our prime suspect. It appears that he personally did the job, which is a big deal in his family. His unwillingness to delegate the hit to a subordinate demonstrates the importance of what's at stake. That said, the first step is to play the bond angle and draw Colombani or his associates out in the open. Step two is to use Colombani to generate leads on the index and the bonds. Colombani's crew uses the same *hawaladars* in Jordan, Syria, and Lebanon that the Iraqis likely would've used to move the Oil-for-Food skim internationally. There aren't many *hawaladars* that can cover such high value transactions, even when the money is broken up over multiple, smaller transfers. Therefore, given the previous links between the Corsicans and the Iraqis, there's a high probability of cross-pollination between Colombani's network and the *hawaladars* used by the *Mukhabarat*. We want to use you to try and draw one or more of the players out of the woodwork.

Normally we'd use one of our own undercovers in your role, but there's a good chance some of the players on the Iraq side might now know what you look like. Like you said, Fuad approached you and knew your name before you'd even introduced yourself. That fact alone speaks to the notion that you likely were targeted for development as some sort of player in whatever scheme Fuad had cooking. That doesn't leave us with many options. Using one of our undercovers would be extremely risky given that we don't know exactly what the bad guys know at this point. Using you is risky as well, but we're willing to take that chance if you are."

Li's transparency regarding the state of their investigation shocked me. I wasn't used to the FBI being so forthcoming. Using me as bait seemed like a long shot, but I was game. Still, I didn't want to seem too anxious. I waited a beat. I studied faces. Cruz's look said, 'this is exactly what you wanted, don't fuck it up.' She was right.

I leaned back in my chair. "Sign me up, coach. I'm in."

———

The Feds kept me for another hour. I had to sign a bunch of paperwork. We went over the game plan. They showed me file photos of Colombani and Santana. Colombani looked older than I expected. His swarthy face was framed by a drape of white hair that was so yellowed at the tips that I could smell the nicotine through the photograph. Santana looked younger, but his babyface held that blank gangster stare. Shark-eyes bored into a flat face. If he didn't have such a good base tan, he could've passed for a Russian. Both men vibed hardcase. Even though they were only peripherally involved, greasing either one still felt like it would be a good step towards evening the score for Souza.

Colombani and Santana immediately joined Izzat at the top of my 'to do' list.

It was dark by the time I pulled back out on Wilshire. I drove back to the hotel in Venice and for the first night since returning to the World, I decided not to drink. I tried to hit the rack early. Without the booze it was damn near impossible to fall asleep. I tossed and turned on the shitty hotel bed. Mental snapshots of Adila, Souza, Fuad, and Izzat flicked though my brain like an old-time stop-motion animation film. The enormity of what I'd just volunteered for started to sink in. Colombani, or whoever did Jawad, was playing for keeps. The more I thought about it, the less convinced I was that MacFarlane and Li were up to the task of covering my six. I doubted either Fed had ever been in a gunfight. Same for Cruz. She definitely had more street *wasta* than the Feds, but I couldn't bank on the fact that she'd be there guns blazing if things got real. She was still a relatively junior agent and, as NCIS, an outsider to what was now the FBI's show.

During my time in Iraq, I'd become accustomed to having real trigger pullers like Ox and Benny covering my every move. That level of insurance wouldn't be available on the streets of LA. I needed something additional. Preferably someone outside the law who had the moves to help out in a jam. I also needed a gun. One that couldn't be traced to me in case I had to get down in a hurry. I had someone in mind who could help me out on both fronts. But first I needed another phone as I assumed the Feds were now monitoring my prepaid. I threw on a shirt and walked towards the pier until I found a convenience store. I bought another burner and dialed my lawyer.

Easy answered on the second ring. "Hello?"

"Hey Brother, what's shakin'?"

"Jimmy?"

"Yeah man, it's me. I'm calling you from a new phone."

"I noticed. That's not a good sign. What kinda trouble you getting yourself into, hoss?"

"The kind that requires lawyer-client confidentiality. You free to meet?"

"I'm on my way to a work thing. Dinner with some of the new attorneys. But if you can meet me here, I can excuse myself for a few minutes."

"Where's here?'"

"Yamashiro's. It's in the hills. You know it?"

"I'll find it. See ya there."

———

Yamashiro's looked like it had probably peaked a decade or so before, but the place still pulled a slick crowd. The hostess pointed me towards a long table. Easy sat with half a dozen suits. I walked wide and tried to catch his eye. The lo-fi electronic beats and the panoptic seating arrangement made me feel like I was walking in circles. Easy was backlit in an aqua haze that gave his shadow a Jack-O-Lantern outline. I couldn't tell if he noticed me. I looked conspicuous with my deployment haircut and bargain threads. I was itching to get out of there as quick as possible.

On the second pass, I thought I saw Easy's silhouette acknowledge my presence. I pointed to the bar. He nodded. I found two stools by the server's station. Easy sauntered up a minute later. I gave him the rundown on the Feds plan to use me as bait to lure Colombani. Less than three hours after leaving the Fed Building and I'd already violated MacFarlane's non-disclosure instructions. Fuck it. I needed Easy in my pocket for this one. Fuck it always wins.

Easy took a long pull from his Manhattan. Silence. He stared at his glass.

I kept going before Easy could respond. "I also need a gun," I said. "Something that won't come back to me. If there's a chance of me brushing elbows with the bad guys, I'm not rolling slick. I don't trust the Feds to cover me as enthusiastically or as competently as a Marine infantry platoon."

Easy finished the rest of his drink and signaled the bartender for another round. "As your lawyer, I advise you to forget about all of this. Go back to the Feds, tell 'em 'thanks but no thanks.' Let the NCIS investigation into the bank caper play out. Enjoy the rest of your leave. Call your new 'friend' in Carlsbad. Get laid. Leave Iraq where you found it. Don't bring that shit back into the World."

The bartender dropped a fresh round on us. Easy took a heavy pull, swallowed, and turned to face me eye-to-eye. "That's what I recommend as your lawyer," he said. "But if my legal advice doesn't cut it, I might have some other recommendations."

Call it a win. I cheered Easy's glass. We both broke into grins. Easy chuckled.

"My man Jimmy Wilde," Easy said. He slapped my back. "Divorced, war hero, and rogue stooge for the FBI all before his 26th birthday. Off to risk life and limb to avenge fallen comrades and impress some random NCIS chick. You're such a fucking Marine it hurts."

"Cheers to that," I said.

I felt a little sheepish. Easy had me dialed. My life was defined by pointless grievances and doing stupid shit for women who weren't impressed… or didn't even care in the first place. But even if I put Cruz aside, getting payback for Souza still meant something. It seemed silly when I dwelled on it. For most of the time I knew the guy I wasn't even sure I really liked him. But the

Corps has a way of building bonds that aren't always intuitive. Like combative siblings we'll talk shit to each other all day, every day. But if someone outside the clique tries to step up, then God help them. We'll close ranks and get down before the echo of the first insult fades. My time in the Corps was coming to an end. I was goddamned determined to make anyone even remotely associated with Souza's death pay before I took off the uniform for the last time.

Easy said, "I need to wrap-up with the folks from the office. But let me make some calls. I've got a guy you need to meet." He made a pistol with his hand and mimed a double tap to my chest.

I waited until Easy was back amongst the law dogs and slipped out the back door. I lit a cigarette and felt better. Easy was in my corner. The drive back to Venice flushed all the crazy shit out of my head. I stretched out on the overtaxed hotel bed for a second time that night and fell asleep in seconds.

13

Off Highway 62
Joshua Tree, California – Saturday, 14 June 2003

Two weeks passed in a blur. I was in regular contact with the Feds but there was no movement on the case. No mysterious emails, no phone calls, no contacts. No word on the NCIS investigation either. I figured if NCIS actually had anything they would've arrested me or set up another interview by now. I debated calling Cruz to wrangle an update, but I didn't want to come off as anxious.

I spent my days bumming around Venice, trying not to get drunk before nightfall. After a couple of near-blackout nights, I started to taper off on the booze. It occurred to me that I'd been the FBI's tethered goat for quite a spell now. If Colombani or any of his ilk were looking to make a move, I needed stay closer to sober.

I checked in with the duty officer back at 29 Palms. The Battalion's return was pushed back at least a month, maybe more. I felt guilty. The boys were still back in the shit, sweltering through an insanely hot Iraqi summer while I was out here sucking up ocean breezes in perfect California.

MacFarlane's boss made some backchannel moves with Headquarters Marine Corps and I was put on Permissive Temporary Additional Duty orders. The new orders threw me into administrative limbo, but at least I wasn't burning my personal leave.

The conditions of my orders stated I had to stay within two hours of the FBI's LA Field Office. That meant flying back east to see Mom and Sis was out. I still hadn't talked to them on the phone. Mom sent a few terse emails inquiring about when I might be back. Her notes were always clinical, dispassionate. It didn't bother me. I knew she didn't mean to come off so cold. It was a coping mechanism she'd developed after my stepdad's death. I tried to assuage her with vague plans about a prolonged visit over the holidays, but I think we both knew we were just going through the motions. We always defaulted to saying the things that we thought normal families would say. My sister was even less of a factor. She never bothered to weigh in after a perfunctory email response that contained a lot of words but didn't equate to more than 'I'm glad you didn't die in Iraq.' I didn't blame Sis. She was busy with college and I hadn't really existed in her orbit for years. The Marine Corps was a much more engaging family than Mom or Sis had ever been, but that family was still back in Iraq. For better or worse, I was untethered.

To help pass the time while I waited on the Feds' call, I reconnected with Jessica, my Carlsbad fling. She seemed genuinely surprised that I called her back. We hooked up a few times over those two weeks. We scheduled visits when her daughter was out of the house. By our second 'date' we'd fallen into a comfortable routine. Sex, dinner, long mornings in bed, more sex. She liked to keep our public outings brief. I got the feeling she was going out of her way to compartmentalize our relationship. She shied away from anything that would make us seem like a couple. She actually flinched when I kissed her goodbye on the front porch one morning. She had me firmly fixed in the fling category. It felt a little cheap, but like most guys in my situation, I really didn't care. We were both using each other in that sense. I kept her distracted from normal mid-life existential bullshit. In turn, Jessica kept my mind off of Cruz and, to a lesser extent, Adila, who despite my best efforts, kept creeping into my thoughts.

Easy called one Saturday morning as I pulled out of Jessica's driveway. Even through the garbled cellphone reception he sounded mischievous.

"Jimmy, you ready for a little road trip?"

"Sure thing," I said. "Where are we headed?"

"The guy I mentioned that night at Yamashiro's. He's back. We need to go see him ASAP."

"I'm ready to roll. I'm leaving Carlsbad right now. I'll pick you up in two hours."

———

I picked up Easy at his office in Century City. We sped east in the Impala. Easy gave me the details. Easy's guy was a dude named Randall. Randall lived out in the desert near Joshua Tree. Randall was a gun guy. He could get me heeled with an off-the-books heater, but I'd have to play it cool. Randall was cagey. Randall knew Easy. Randall didn't know me. Per Randall's instructions, Easy had to make the introduction in person. I was cool with that. Cold calling a guy to wrangle illegal firearms seemed like a sketchy proposition. Easy's presence would help normalize the transaction. Or at least make it as normal as asking someone to spot you a ghost gun could ever be.

Randall was a retired Marine Chief Warrant Officer 4. Infantry guy. A legit Gunner. A not-so-reformed wild man and loner who lived in the high desert by choice. I was always a little suspicious of people who chose to live in the Mojave. It's

America's halfway house. If you're an outlaw, cult member, or even just a garden variety fringe-dweller, it's best to do a few years in the hi-desert before jumping back into 'real' society. I figured Randall's exile in Joshua Tree was probably some sort of self-imposed parole. Or maybe he just needed the space to bury all the bodies, secrets, and regrets that I assumed littered his past. Or maybe I was way off the mark. Maybe I was trying to squeeze Randall into convenient categories to try and make sense of the situation. Ultimately, I decided that 'sense' didn't so much apply to my current predicament.

Easy dove deeper on Randall's backstory as we barreled east. "Randall retired about five years ago," he said. "I got him out of a battery beef when I was still with the Staff Judge Advocate's office. That's how we met. Dude is a legend. One of the few guys that actually racked some confirmed kills during DESERT STORM. Bagged a couple Iraqi joes out in Khafji. Back in the 80s he was loaned out for some wet work down south. Inter-Agency stuff. Big time voodoo. I saw a photo of him once. He was wearing those old 'Nam-era tiger-striped cammies. No rank, no insignia. He was jungled up with a squad of Contras. They had a couple of dead Sandinistas laid out at their feet like big game trophies. Dude's the real deal."

Color me intrigued. "He sounds like my kinda guy. And this Randall character can score me a *pistola*?"

"He can indeed. Get this, the dude smiths his own weapons. He's got a workshop at his place out near J-Tree. All the machinery, the tools, the works. It's the full Magilla. He manufactures all his guns and ammo from scratch. No federal registry, no ballistics databases, nothing. Everything is bespoke and completely off the radar. Of course, he's not licensed to do any of it. Hence the low-profile. The fact that he's kept his little operation going these past few years without getting busted is a testament to his discretion. You might say he's earned his paranoia. All that aside, once he meets you and we have a beer or two, he'll come around. He trusts me and I trust you, so it'll all work out."

I couldn't suppress a chuckle. "Easy, my man. For a lawyer, you sure enough associate with a lot of outlaws."

"Outlaws pay better."

"I'm not paying you shit."

"Well technically you're not an outlaw… yet."

———

Randall's crib was set about a quarter mile back from a two-lane road off Highway 62. We pulled up to an old ranch gate tricked out with video surveillance cameras. Easy pressed the intercom. Randall answered by activating the remote lock. The lock buzzed and the gate swung wide.

We parked in a large pre-fab storage shed. Randall appeared in the doorway. He had the outlaw vibe down cold. Gray-streaked ponytail, Fu Manchu, snakeskin boots. The boots looked expensive, but I noticed they had rubber soles. That was a good sign. Leather soles were for dancing. Rubber soles were for fighting.

Randall said, "See you boys found the place alright."

"I see you've expanded the spread, Randall," Easy replied.

"Yeah, I've added a few things here and there. Who's this young fella, Easy?"

I stuck out my hand. "Jim Wilde. Pleasure to meet ya, Randall."

Randall's hand felt like rhinoceros hide. "Welcome, Jim Wilde. As you can imagine I don't get many visitors out this way. But I figure if Easy says you're ok, you gotta be mostly on the up and up."

"I try to be… until it's time not to be," I said.

"I take it this must be one of those times then. Otherwise, you boys wouldn't be out here in the middle of the desert."

"You're damn sure right about that, Randall," Easy said. "I'll let Jimmy lay it out for ya."

I gave Randall the rundown on the FBI bait op. Randall was unfazed. He chained smoked Lucky Strikes and didn't ask questions.

I finished the tale. I didn't editorialize. I admitted that revenge for Souza was a driving factor. I didn't try and hide the fact that Cruz and Adila also influenced my decision to participate. Randall let out a huge cloud of Lucky smoke. His leather face cracked into something resembling a grin.

"I swear it's like looking into a mirror 25 years ago," Randall said. "Throwing yourself to the wolves to impress some sexy broad with a badge. I need to see this Special Agent Cruz with my own eyes." Randall choked through another chuckle. "Good to know they still make Marines like they used to."

"What I really want is payback for Souza," I said.

Randall's grin remained, but his eyes hardened. "Then you've come to the right place."

Randall took us into the house. A spacious ranch affair. We posted up at his hand-carved bar. We talked shit for a spell. Randall asked about Iraq. He seemed genuinely disappointed to have missed out on this latest round of action. He also seemed happy for our company, although I suspected he'd never admit it. Eventually he turned back to the question of armament. He took us out to his workshop.

Randall's set-up was top shelf. Anyone with this gear had to be a real-deal craftsman. The workshop smelled of lubricants, oils, and competence.

I was curious. "What made you decide to start making guns?" I asked.

Randall stuffed out a Lucky on his bootheel and field stripped the butt. "A long time ago I met a cowboy," he said. "Old-school character. I'm talking drive the herd to market on horseback kind of old-school. Anyway, he was an exceedingly capable man. He could cowboy, he could shoot, he could build. Any task you threw his way, he was up for it. One day I asked him how he got so goddamn good at everything. And he told me, 'Son, a man should be able to do anything his ancestors did. That's the gift of history. All that knowledge and know-how is right there waiting for you to use it.' I thought about that statement damn near every day for years. Eventually, it just faded into the background like so many of life's lessons. But then I finally punched out of the Corps and I was sitting out here on the ranch drinking every goddamn day. That ol' Cowboy's words came back a ringin' in my ears. My great grandpa was a gunsmith and I'd been around weapons my entire life. I knew the knowledge was out there. I just needed to take advantage. So I did. I taught myself. Felt compelled to do so. Like if I didn't, I was somehow shirking my ancestral duty."

I nodded. Any man who thought *not* building weapons was skating out on his bloodline was a man I could trust.

Randall pulled a pistol off the peg board. "This here is an exact copy of a .45 caliber Colt 1911. I machined the casts myself off the factory specs. No mods. The weight, the balance, the pull, everything is exactly the same. Except of course there's no serial number or ballistic record. I named her *La Malinche* after that Indian gal that translated for Cortez and his Conquistadors. This here *pistola* is the best translator ever invented. Ain't a man alive that don't understand the language of lead."

I'd only fired a .45 a couple of times. I was much more comfortable with the 9mm, but I didn't want to give Randall the impression I was being picky.

"That'll get the job done," I said. "How much?"

"Let's not make this a cash deal," Randall said. "I'll let you take this one for a promise."

"Ok. What did you have in mind?" I asked.

"It's difficult for me to buy a lot of the materials I need for my operation," Randall said. "For example, if I start buying large quantities of gunpowder I wind up on a federal watchlist. *No bueno*. So, in exchange for the .45, I'll need you to make some purchases for me in the future. A little here, a little there. Help old Randall stay off the Fed's radar."

That sounded like a more-than-fair proposition. "Sold," I said. "You just let me know what you need and I'll deliver. I really appreciate this, Randall."

"Always glad to help Marines, even greenhorn lieutenants. In fact, I'm actually a little jealous. I have my own reasons for keeping a low profile these days, but I'll say this—you find yourself in a pickle, maybe give ol' Randall a call."

"I guarantee you, Randall, if I run into any trouble *La Malinche* can't sort, you'll be at the top of my 'call in case of emergency' list."

Easy piped up. "Just for the record, I don't think I can afford to represent both of you pro bono. So, let's maybe keep the felony gunplay to a manageable trickle. Deal?"

Randall chuckled again. His laugh echoed like bullets casings on a hardwood floor. "I don't want to speak for the young *desperado* here," he said. "But speaking for myself, I don't like to make promises I can't keep."

————

We didn't get back to Easy's office until almost 3am. I thanked him for the intro with Randall. Easy was definitely taking an expansive approach to client services. For the umpteeth time in the past month I felt lucky to have him on my side.

I steered the Impala south towards the hotel. I'd just exited the 405 when burner phone #1 rang. It was MacFarlane. He seemed surprised I answered at this hour. He said we needed to meet. I told him I could be at the Federal Building on Wilshire in 20 minutes. I U-turned and hit the 405 North. There was no traffic that early in the morning. I made it to Wilshire in what had to be an LA County speed record.

Maybe some of Randall's paranoia had already rubbed off on me, but I parked a few blocks away from the Federal Building. *La Malinche* was stashed in the Impala's A/C vent. I didn't want the Feds to stumble across her if they decided to monkey with my car while I was inside. Technically, I was on their team for the time being. But that formality didn't engender a lot of trust and confidence in the Bureau's long-range motivations. Or the probability they'd try and slap a locator on my ride the first chance they got… if they hadn't already.

MacFarlane and Li were waiting for me in the lobby. Much to my disappointment, Cruz wasn't with them. This time they took me up to a small office on one of the upper floors. The building was damn-near deserted at this hour. We had the room to ourselves. Li handed me a foam cup half-filled with weak-ass Fed coffee.

MacFarlane said, "Colombani took the bait. He called one of our confidential informants a couple of hours ago. Your name came up. Our CI agreed to broker a meet with you. It's showtime. You ready for this?"

Drinking all night with Randall and Easy left me worse for wear but I lied. "Born ready," I said. "What's the plan?"

"Our CI is a known fence," Li said. "He's moved bonds before. He owes us. The general idea is that you were put in touch with him through a third party because you want to unload the bonds. Our CI is willing to 'betray' you to Colombani for a flat fee. That way Colombani thinks our CI is just looking for the easy score. He gets paid without the hassle of reselling or cashing the bonds. And he curries favor with Colombani. Of course, knowing Colombani, it's a safe bet that if this was for real, he'd just kill you *and* our CI and save himself the fee. Obviously, we won't let that happen. We'll take him down as soon as we have a positive ID."

Li seemed pretty cavalier about the whole op. It was a very 'un-FBI' approach. The suits were usually cautious to a fault. I decided the G-men must be getting desperate. I wasn't sure if that was good or bad.

"I follow so far," I said. "What exactly do you need me to do?"

"The general protocol for these types of meets includes some sort of 'proof' that you're actually in place with the bonds," Li said. "So, you'll have to actually be on scene with our CI so that Colombani, or one of his crew, can confirm that you're present. Otherwise, Colombani won't come anywhere near the meet site."

"You actually think Colombani will show in person or will he just task this out to his minions?"

"We can't be certain either way, but there's a good chance he'll cover this one personally. There's very little honor amongst thieves and he's probably not working with his regular crew here in LA. Therefore, we don't think he'll risk using a third party who might double cross him and skip out with the bonds. That said, Colombani most likely will use a spotter to confirm your presence, so we need you to be there in the flesh."

"I can do that," I said. "Just tell me when and where to be."

"We'll set the meet for tonight. We'll ping you with the time and location later."

"Do I get a gun?"

Li exchanged a sideways glance with MacFarlane. "No," he said. "We'll have plenty of armed agents on scene. We'll make sure you're safe."

I didn't feel safe. "What about Cruz? Is she in on this?"

"We're coordinating with her office," Li replied.

Somehow that was the exact kind of non-answer I expected.

14

The Huston Hotel
Santa Monica, California – Sunday, 15 June 2003

The alarm buzzed at 3pm. It took me a minute to realize where I was. I'd crashed hard when I finally got back from the meeting with the Feds. I racked almost eight straight hours. It felt like the longest I'd slept in ages. That should've been a good thing, but my circadian rhythm was still fucked. The booze, the shifty schedules, the slow-burn stress of not knowing what lay in store, all of it conspired to make me feel groggy and on-edge at the same time. Not a good headspace for a showdown with murderous Corsicans. Usually, I'd seek some bourbon therapy but the Feds had been adamant that I needed to stay stone sober.

I laid in bed for an hour. I guzzled the hotel's tepid courtesy coffee. MacFarlane called. He said a Fed undercover would pick me up at the hotel at 9pm. There were some counter-surveillance considerations that precluded me rolling to the meet in my Impala. Keeping *La Malinche* on my person was a no-go as I was damn certain the Feds would pat me down before putting me in the room with their CI. For my own piece of mind, I had planned to keep the pistol stashed in the 'Pala in case things went totally FUBAR. Having a gun a hundred meters away in the glove compartment probably wouldn't do me much good in any scenario that involved professional triggers, but knowing the pistol was there would be mentally reassuring. Now, even that minor assurance was out of the question.

A few minutes before pickup time MacFarlane called again. He confirmed my contact was approaching the hotel in a gray Dodge Magnum station wagon. The Dodge struck me as an interesting choice for an undercover whip. Maybe the organized crime scene wasn't all Range Rovers and tracksuits after all.

The Dodge pulled into the parking lot right on cue. I hid *La Malinche* in the bathroom. I scoped myself in the mirror. My reflection looked less nervous than I felt. I grabbed my coat and hit the door.

The undercover introduced himself as Greg. He was a white dude, mid-30s, average height. He wore a shiny golf shirt and expensive jeans. Greg looked like an Orange County dad that spent weekends chauffeuring his daughter across the Southwest for travel league soccer games. He certainly didn't project a hardcore criminal vibe. But what did I know? Maybe that made him more believable. I realized I was making these judgements about his car and his appearance as a way to distract myself from what was about to happen. I'd done the same thing in Iraq. I'd find myself making unnecessary map and radio checks to keep my mind occupied until the shooting started. Coping mechanisms come in all flavors.

Greg briefed me as he drove. The meet was set for a hotel called The Huston up in Santa Monica. It was an old, art deco-era job that had been updated with all the 21st century gadgets. Access in and out was tightly controlled. The parking garage and surrounding streets were covered by CCTV. All in all, the joint was as secure a public location as possible for this sort of gig.

The Feds had rented out several rooms next to the suite where the CI was stashed. Greg handed me a keycard that would get me into the lobby, the elevator, and the CI's suite. He also handed me a backpack that held a hard-case binder. Greg said I needed something that made it look like I was carrying the bonds. At least it wasn't the old attaché case with handcuffs get-up.

Greg dropped me off in the parking garage. I was instructed to walk through the lobby and take the main elevator up to the 11th floor. Another armed undercover would get in the elevator with me for the trip topside. Greg ran me through some additional security precautions. I nodded along, anxious to get it over with.

I clocked faces as I walked through the lobby. No one stood out. No one vibed assassin. The reception area was wide open. No weighty, hardwood desks to take cover behind if a gun fight broke out. If Colombani wanted to clip me here, my chances of surviving the attempt seemed slim.

A woman in a hotel uniform pressed the 'up' button as I approached the elevator bank. I reckoned she was my armed escort. I surreptitiously checked her out in the reflective chrome of the elevator's interior. I tried to spot the tell-tale bulge of a service weapon along the contours of her vintage bellhop jacket. I didn't see any bump. It occurred to me maybe she wasn't a Fed. Maybe I'd jumped in the elevator with one of Colombani's crew. A case of nerves hit me like puppy love. Butterflies in the belly and sweat on the palms. I side-eyed the woman. I white-knuckled a fist inside my coat pocket. I was prepared to pulp her face if she made a move. I hated the idea of hitting a lady, but I resolved to cave her head in if she got buggy in the elevator. We stopped on the 11th floor. The woman's reflection went spooky in the chrome doors. I peeped the funhouse mirror image for any sign of a weapon I might've missed at first glance. Still nothing. I stepped back against the handrail and made an 'after you' gesture.

The woman gave me the briefest of smiles and walked out ahead of me. She pushed open an 'Employees Only' door on the far side of the elevator bank. I watched her pull a cell phone out of her pocket as she disappeared behind the door.

It took a few steps before I could stabilize my breathing. I calmed myself and found room 1111. The room number seemed an inauspicious omen. I pulled out my keycard and let myself in. A fat man in an open-collar dress shirt waved me inside.

The suite was spacious. The décor reflected a distinctly 21st century interpretation of the Roaring '20s. Period-authentic construction materials were substituted with subtly disguised injection-molded plastics and other polymers that didn't exist 80 years ago. The contrast of the faux fixtures in a legitimately old building gave the room a movie set affect. I hoped it wouldn't host the scene where my character got gunned down.

The fat man motioned for me to take a seat at a small breakfast table near the balcony. I kept my eyes on fatty. I wasn't sure what someone who could fence bearer bonds was supposed to look like, but this guy wouldn't have fit my first 100 guesses. He was swarthy, unshaven, and sported a wet-earth smell that reminded me of an Arab spice market.

Fatty said, "Jim, please… be seated."

I didn't reply, but I set the backpack on the breakfast table and sat down as instructed.

Fatty took a seat across from me. He watched the door. He stayed silent.

Finally, I gave in. "What's your name?" I asked.

"Probably best if you don't know. But for the purposes of our meeting tonight you can call me Geoff. Our guests know me as Geoff. Geoff with a 'G.'"

"So, what happens now Geoff with a 'G?'"

Geoff, or 'Fat Geoff' as I'd already rebranded him in my head, pulled a cellphone from the pleats of his prodigious pants. I wasn't sure he'd be able to operate the tiny buttons on the phone with his thick sausage fingers.

"I call Colombani, let it ring once and hang up," Geoff said. "That's the signal that you're here. But I'd guess his people already made you in the lobby. Did anyone catch your eye?"

I debated whether to mention the woman in the elevator. I didn't trust Fat Geoff. I gave a noncommittal shrug.

Fat Geoff started to say something when the fire alarm started blaring. The plastic disc above the door strobed in synch with the 'waahhhh-waaahhh' of the siren. Fat Geoff jumped up and knocked on the door that connected the suite to the adjacent room. MacFarlane opened the door and gave us the hand signal to stay put. About a minute later he returned and yelled over the alarm noise that we had to evacuate.

MacFarlane pulled us into his room. Undercover Greg and Special Agent Li were in the room with a couple of other Feds gone full gear queer in Kevlar vests, assault rifles, sap gloves, and ballistic glasses. All the tactical Feds needed now were subdued Yankees caps and about 20 less pounds of trunk fat and they could've passed for Delta Force.

MacFarland split us into two groups and ordered us to evacuate along separate routes. The Feds nodded their acknowledgement in unison. Apparently, they'd planned for such contingencies. I wasn't sure any plan would be worth a damn if we were about to shoot it out in a crowded hotel hallway.

I followed Greg into the hall. Flames licked the frame of the 'Employees Only' door I'd seen the elevator woman enter. A greasy smoke poured into the hallway. The scent of burning polyester tickled my nose. The overhead sprinkler system activated just as we left the hallway.

We raced to a stairwell on the far side of the hotel. There were dozens of people streaming down the stairs from the upper floors. I stayed close to Greg as we pushed our way past the slower guests. We hit the parking garage and Greg hustled me into the Dodge. A hotel employee manually raised the automatic arm at the garage's ticket booth as we rounded the corner of the parking lot. Greg punched it. I looked back and saw the bellhop woman from the elevator hustle out of the parking garage and get into a tinted Lincoln Navigator. The Lincoln ran a red light and tucked in a few car lengths behind us.

I tapped Greg's rearview mirror. "Hey Greg, I think we're being followed. Black Lincoln Navigator a few car lengths back."

Greg scanned the mirror. His eyes narrowed as he studied the Lincoln. Greg picked up a handheld radio from under his seat.

"Control, X-Ray 1," Greg said. "We picked up a tail. Black Lincoln Navigator with dealer tags. Request local PD initiate traffic stop."

A staticky voice came back over Greg's handheld. I couldn't make out the reply.

"What now?" I asked.

Greg's eyes danced between mirrors. "I'll run the Lincoln in circles until the locals can vector a black & white. PD will stop 'em and run the tags and licenses. Once we shake free, I'll take you to the debrief."

We drove around Santa Monica for a spell. The Sunday night traffic was thin which made the tail easy to track. Greg got a radio call that a local patrol car was en route. We stopped at a red light and the Lincoln pulled into the number two lane behind a delivery truck. The light turned green and Greg waited a beat before driving through the intersection. Once we cleared the block I craned my neck around to try and spot the Lincoln. It was gone.

Greg's eyes darted back and forth between side and rearview mirrors. No joy. The SUV had vanished. Greg called it in. The staticky voice on the other end of the radio said there were no other patrol cars available to intercept the Lincoln. Greg let out a barely audible 'fuck' and pulled onto the 405 South. We drove south on the freeway for a couple of miles and Greg exited again. We cut squares through Venice and then east through Culver City.

———

Greg dropped me off in a gas station parking lot. He pointed to a sedan parked at the pumps. He told me another agent was waiting in the car and would take me to the debrief site.

I walked over to the sedan and the driver motioned for me to get in. The driver was an older guy in typical Fed attire sans tie. He drove me back to the same West LA strip mall office where MacFarlane and Li interviewed me after Souza's funeral.

Li opened the office door as I approached. It was noisy inside the office. MacFarlane was talking to Fat Geoff in the corner. The tactical Feds sat around a conference table talking with their hands like fighter pilots. Li offered me a seat at a small desk in the corner.

I felt a hand briefly pat my shoulder. Cruz was standing behind me. "Hey, Jim," she said.

"Hey, Angela. I didn't know you were participating in tonight's festivities."

"Of course. I'm still on the case."

"Good to know."

MacFarlane shouted for everyone to shut up. The tactical Feds were dismissed and Li took Fat Geoff into another room. Once Li returned and the room was cleared, we got busy with the debrief.

I gave MacFarlane and Li the blow-by-blow. I described the petite, olive-complexioned woman in the hotel uniform. Italian? Latina? Arab? Something like that. I noted how the woman stayed silent during our elevator ride. How she avoided eye contact. How she disappeared behind the 'Employees Only' door on the same floor as Fat Geoff's room. How she carried a cell phone that didn't look like the two-ways that hotel employees carry. How I thought she might've started the fire in the room behind that door. How the same woman hustled out of the parking garage during the evacuation. How she climbed into the black Lincoln that followed us around Santa Monica for the better part of 15 minutes. How the Lincoln disappeared before the police could conduct a traffic stop.

The Feds listened and took notes. When I wrapped up, they exchanged a couple of quick glances. Li confirmed that the woman in the hotel uniform wasn't one of theirs. He didn't offer an explanation as to what happened to the undercover agent that was supposed to ride with me in the elevator, but he did call an underling to grab the hotel's surveillance footage. MacFarlane asked some perfunctory follow-up questions regarding the description of the woman and the Lincoln. Cruz stayed silent.

"What happens now?" I asked.

"We wait," MacFarlane replied.

"Wait for what? It seems pretty clear the whole fire drill was set up to try and get me outside on my own. So, I'm guessing Colombani, or whoever we're up against, correctly sniffed out that hotel-meet as a trap."

"All of that is supposition, Jim," Li said. "But in the meantime, we'll take extra precautions."

"Supposition? I think it's pretty damn obvious the chick in the Lincoln ID'd me."

"Agreed, but we've got you covered," Li said. "You'll be safe."

"What about Fat Geoff? Now the bad guys know he's involved with you, right? Or do you think that fucker had planned to sell me out from the get-go?"

MacFarlane cut me off. "Geoff is our concern. We'll handle it. In the meantime, like Special Agent Li just said, we'll take precautions to keep you safe and wait it out."

'Precautions' and 'wait it out' didn't sound like much of a plan. I was OK playing the tethered goat as long as we had some offensive options up our sleeve. Now it sounded like I'd have to go into hiding.

I regretted signing on for this caper. It would be hard to get payback for Souza if the Feds sat on me 24/7. I thought through my options. I could only come up with two approaches. One—convince the Feds to keep me in the game. Two—figure out a way to shake free of the law's persistent stare. The first approach seemed more feasible. But the second sounded more appealing. If the Feds were convinced I wasn't in danger, I stood to gain considerable freedom of movement. I needed to convince them to cut me loose so I could go back on the hunt. That would have to happen soon. Once my Battalion returned from Iraq I'd get sucked back into the daily grind of Marine Corps garrison life. My window of opportunity for tracking down the people associated with Souza's murder was closing fast.

———

The Feds wanted me to leave my car at the hotel and maintain the reservation under my name in the hopes that it might lure Colombani's crew out of the shadows. I protested, said I needed to retrieve my gear from the hotel room. I'd been in the same clothes all day. Now I smelled like a mix of body odor and burnt acrylic bedspreads. Cruz said she'd take me to the hotel and then to the FBI safehouse. The Feds weren't keen on that idea. They didn't like the concept of non-FBI knowing the locations of their safe houses. I reminded them that Cruz would still need to interview me regarding the Bagdad bank heist investigation. If she had access to the safe house, then that would save the time and effort of carting me around town for follow-on interviews. It would make the FBI's job easier. I tried to make it sound practical, but it was the prospect of alone time with Cruz that drove my argument.

MacFarlane's phone blew up. His boss wanted him and Li back at the Field Office. MacFarlane and Li exchanged one of their insider glances. MacFarlane relented. Cruz would have access to the safe house.

We left the strip mall at 1am, tired but wired. My mind flashed through all sorts of scenarios. I tried to play it cool since I was with Cruz, but I caught myself constantly checking for tails on the drive to Venice.

"Now that we're alone, what do you think of this 'wait and see' plan?" I asked. "What's the likelihood of the bad guys trying to do me at the hotel in Venice?"

Cruz didn't answer right away. I could tell she was thinking through her reply carefully.

"I think it's our only legitimate play right now," she said. "I know you Marines always default towards taking action, but sometimes doing nothing is the smart play. Sometimes criminals need to be given an opportunity to make the first move. To make the *wrong* move."

Intuitively Cruz's recommendation made sense. But I wasn't sold. Waiting around for the bad guys to take the initiative seemed like a good way to run out of options.

I said, "These folks don't seem like run-of-the-mill dumb fuck criminals to me. That shit at the hotel was pretty slick. It worked. They got me separated from the herd and exposed the Fed's trap. And what's your take on Fat Geoff? Whether he sold me out or was legitimately trying to help the Feds, he's dead either way, right? I gotta think Colombani's crew is hell bent on disappearing him now that he's served his purpose."

"Geoff is the FBI's CI, not mine. He's not a problem I would waste too much energy on. Geoff is replaceable. Crooks like him know the score. If he gets himself killed, there'll be some other asshole ready to step up and make a deal."

"Damn, Angie, you're a cold customer."

"Don't ever call me Angie."

I'd touched a nerve. "My bad, Angela. But you didn't answer my question. Do you think Geoff was playing the Feds the whole time? You think he tipped Colombani that the meet was a trap? The fire drill thing seemed pretty complicated to pull off on the fly."

"It's certainly possible Geoff's on the make. But again, he's not my concern. We won't see him again."

———

We pulled up to the hotel. Cruz insisted that she come up to the room with me. She made sure I understood her interest wasn't personal, it was strictly part of the security protocol. I tried to act casual but her presence would complicate things. I needed my gun. I tried to think of a ploy to keep Cruz distracted while I retrieved *La Malinche* from the bathroom.

After Cruz determined no Corsican gangsters were waiting for me, I sheepishly asked if she could wait outside while I took care of some 'business' in the bathroom. It had been an eventful night and the stress wreaked havoc on my guts, or at least that's what I told Cruz. She agreed and posted up outside on the landing.

As she walked out Cruz said, "Better be careful smoking in there, you'll lose your deposit."

"What are you talking about? I didn't smoke in the room."

"Sure smells like it."

Cruz was right. Burnt tobacco lingered. Not strong, but definitely present. It smelt inviting, nostalgic even. A very distinct scent. Not the typical American char. Not the slightly sweet odor of the export-grade Marlboros you get down in Mexico. The room smelled Iraqi. It smelled like hot-burning Turkish tobacco. Then it hit me. The room smelled like Miamis. I tried to swallow down a hard adrenaline spike. Was this normal 'back-from-Iraq' paranoia or the real deal? I didn't trust myself to make that call.

La Malinche was still in the bathroom stash spot, right where I left her. I waited a couple of minutes, flushed the toilet, and washed my hands. I wrapped the pistol in some skivvy shirts and stuffed it into my overnight bag.

"You doing OK in there?" Cruz asked, her voice barely dampened by the cheap drywall.

"All good," I said. "Give me one sec."

I scanned the room to make sure I hadn't left anything behind. Car keys? Check. Both prepaid cellphones? Check. Pistol? Check. Wallet? Check. I hit the lights and locked the door behind me.

———

The drive to the FBI safehouse went by too fast. I dreaded the impending lockdown. I tried to cheer myself up by hoping that Cruz might keep me company over the next few days, weeks, months. Unfortunately, I'd learned the hard way that hope was never a solid course of action.

Cruz's profile mesmerized me from the passenger seat. Every time a car passed in the opposite direction she squinted against the headlights. It was the same gesture she made when she was intrigued or angered by something. I imagined her feline eyes narrowing the same way during sex.

I said, "The cigarette smell in the hotel room. It was Iraqi."

"What are you talking about?" Cruz stared straight ahead as she drove.

"The smoky smell you noticed in my hotel room. It wasn't from me. And it wasn't from an American cigarette. It smelled exactly like a brand of smokes we had in Iraq. A brand called Miami. They have a very distinctive odor."

"Are you inferring that an Iraqi was in your room?"

"Someone who smokes Miamis was in there."

"Lots of people have access to that room. Management, maintenance, housekeeping. There's lots of folks with a master key."

"Yeah, I get that. But how many would have access to Iraqi smokes?"

Cruz didn't answer.

15

FBI Safehouse
Los Angeles, California – Monday, 23 June 2003

Life in the safehouse sucked. A rotating cast of FBI minions shuffled through on babysitting duty. None of my minders were particularly interesting. They rarely talked to me beyond perfunctory greetings and farewells. The poor bastards seemed to dread the gig as much as I did. Their lack of enthusiasm worked in my favor. None of the Feds bothered to search my gear that first night. *La Malinche* remained undiscovered, wrapped in a wad of dirty laundry in the bottom of my bag.

Killing time was tough. I watched shitty movies, ate shitty food, read a couple of decent paperbacks, and contemplated hoarding my daily beer allowance until I had enough bottles stashed to fuel a binge. I never pulled it off. I couldn't resist downing my allotted dose at the end of each day. The beers were a sad nighttime punctuation ritual. Empty calories without the slightest possibility of drunken oblivion.

I was allowed to call my Mom and Sis but didn't bother. They had my cell number. They could call me if they needed or wanted to. They didn't.

The idea of calling Jessica crossed my mind but I shelved it quick. Even if I'd been allowed to tell her the truth, I couldn't picture that conversation. 'Hey Jessica, sorry I can't see you this weekend. I tried to help the FBI nail a Corsican gangster and failed so now they're babysitting me at an undisclosed location.' That shit wouldn't fly.

My yard time was restricted to quick workouts at the FBI gym. It got to the point where I looked forward to the drive from the safehouse to the gym more than the actual workouts. The sun-drenched, traffic-clogged freeways were my only vista on the outside world.

Hours bled into days. The drudgery grated. I went through the motions on the free weights in an effort to numb my body. Call it submission to my new monastic lifestyle. I also tried to goad a few of the special agents into sparring with me in the gym's half-sized boxing ring. None of them accepted the challenge. Conducting Fed business with black eyes and lace cuts probably wasn't a look the Bureau wanted to promote.

Despite my efforts, the workouts didn't amount to much. By the end of the week, I could actually hear myself getting fatter. My blood felt like gravy. My hands and feet felt less coordinated. Even my vision seemed diminished. I had to laugh at the irony of surviving combat in Iraq only to slowly kill myself with trash food and a lack of real exercise.

Cruz dropped by at the end of my first week in stir. Technically, I was still a person of interest in the bank heist investigation. But I didn't know what that meant. Was I a suspect? Was I a witness? My role wasn't clear. The lack of clarity kept me off guard.

The special agent pantsuit was out. Cruz was dressed in street clothes. A loose blouse that concealed her pistol and tight jeans that set my imagination aflutter. I also clocked her sensible shoes. She looked like a denim-clad cheetah ready to run down her prey.

Cruz briefly chatted with my FBI babysitter and then pointed towards the kitchen. I grabbed a seat across from her at a small breakfast table. I felt self-conscious. I looked like hell and smelled like garbage after my week in captivity.

I tried on a grin that I thought might pass for flirty. "I take it you're back to grill me on the bank," I said. "Do I need to call my lawyer again?"

Cruz smiled too. It was the best thing I'd seen in a long time. "Nah. We can put the bank business aside for now. I just came to check in on you."

"I'm glad you did. You've been here for what, less than two minutes? This has already been the best two minutes I've had since I've been stuck in here."

My stomach tightened. I hadn't intended to breach the professional/personal boundary that fast. It just happened.

Cruz sat back in her chair, but she was still smiling. I wasn't sure what those two body language clues meant when added together. After a second, I realized I didn't care. I just wanted to soak in her presence while I had the chance.

"Safehouse life is that bad, huh?" Cruz asked.

"It's horrible," I said. "I won't bore you with the details."

"Well, hopefully it won't be for much longer."

"Do you have any news on that front? Have the Feds said anything about the case? Anything about when I might get out of here?"

"No. They've given my boss a few updates, but I haven't heard anything specific."

"How does that feel?"

"How does what feel?"

"Being the junior agent that gets kept in the dark by her bosses even when you're the one putting your ass on the line out on the streets."

"That's the gig. Our jobs are probably similar in that regard. I imagine your bosses only tell you what they think you need to hear."

"Well, yeah. I'm definitely at the bottom of the totem pole and I've done my share of operating in the dark. But doesn't it bother you? You've got the moves. You've got the smarts. You're the whole package. Don't you wish you had more of a say in the decision-making process? I've seen how you interact with your partner Lawson. I get it that he's technically the senior agent, but you obviously run the show. Doesn't it piss you off to have someone like him holding you back?"

"Where is this coming from, Jim? Are you just trying to flatter me, or is this an attempt to try and get me to divulge something about the case?"

I was glad my efforts at flattery hadn't gone unnoticed. "Probably both," I said.

Cruz leaned in and rested her arms on the breakfast table. The air between us felt warmer. Her body language made it clear she wasn't going to entertain my half-assed elicitation attempts. She retook control of our little chat.

"Let me turn that question back at you," she said. "How do you feel about what went down in Iraq? I'm not talking about the bank or any specific event. Tell me about the experience as a whole. Was it 'mission accomplished?'"

"I'm not sure how to answer that," I said. "Probably because I'm not really sure we had a mission. I mean, we did at first. We were supposed to take Baghdad and give Saddam the boot, so we did that. But after that little adventure I felt like we were just winging it. Putting out fires as they popped up, trying to keep the whole thing from going sideways. And I'm not sure we were successful on that front."

"If you had been running the show, what would you have done differently?"

I wasn't sure where Cruz was headed with this line of questioning, but I didn't care. Talking with her really had been the highlight of my sentence in safehouse captivity. I didn't want it to end. I scrambled to come up with something that would prolong our time together.

"I haven't really thought about it." A partial lie at best. "I was just trying to keep the boys alive. No one asked for our opinion, so I never voiced it. Not to anyone that mattered anyway. We just took things one day at a time."

"You say that, but you obviously have an opinion," Cruz said.

"In that case, I guess my opinion is why did we even bother? On the way up to Baghdad we had a few moments where I thought getting rid of Saddam and his crew would actually make a positive impact. But the longer we stayed and the more I dealt with Iraqis of every stripe and feather it started to feel like maybe Saddam knew something we didn't. Like, maybe as a society, Iraq isn't ready for democracy or individual liberty or any of that jazz. Because things went dark real quick. As soon as the Iraqi security forces crumbled, the folks on the street turned on each other with a quickness. It was all bad dudes and blood feuds and we were caught in the middle of it."

I'd unwittingly jumped on my soapbox. I was afraid of saying something that would turn Cruz off. She was probably only asking me these things to keep me from asking her questions. Then again, maybe she did care what I had to say. Maybe this was her way of letting me know I could talk to her about stuff. Or maybe I was deluded.

Cruz gave me a half-grin and worried eyes. "Don't let me interrupt," she said. "I want to hear the whole truth according to Jim."

I was still self-conscious after my mini-rant, but leaving Cruz hanging didn't seem like a good move.

"I'm not saying all Iraqis are bad," I said. "Or that they deserved Saddam. Although maybe they did. That's for history to decide. Some of them were exceptionally brave and determined. And, in a sense, that makes the whole thing harder to swallow. If they were all a bunch of shitbirds, I wouldn't care what happened to them. But it felt like the country might have some potential. And now, whatever promise of a better future might've existed is long gone. That reality is really fucking frustrating. Especially when it cost us good men like Steve Souza." I deliberately kept my feelings about Adila out of the conversation this time.

Cruz stayed silent. She looked genuinely concerned. As much as I thought I'd craved it, I wasn't sure I was ready to share real emotions with her. I got nervous. So, I did what I always do when I get nervous around women. I tried to make her laugh.

"Here's one little anecdote that I think sums it up," I said. "Our first night in Baghdad we jammed up two teenagers that were trying to sneak around a vehicle check point. Turns out these cats were headed for a whorehouse. One of them spoke a little bit of English. He told us the locals were convinced the Marines would hunt down every male Iraqi and kill them on site. These kids didn't want to die virgins, so they risked life and limb to get to the whorehouse and get laid. I respected the dedication, so we let 'em go. It seemed like the American thing to do. Probably the only hearts and minds we won during the war."

Cruz laughed. Mission accomplished. Her smile was disarming, but in a good way.

"Please tell me your Marines didn't follow them to the whorehouse," Cruz said.

"That was a genuine concern. Fortunately, we got the order to pick up and move a few minutes later so the boys never got a chance to sniff it out."

"Thank God," she said. "You guys keep us busy enough as it is without adding an international prostitution beef to the mix."

It was my turn to laugh. Cruz sat back in her chair. I was worried she was gathering herself to leave so I kept talking.

"Here's where the story gets real," I said. "The next day we got in a heavy firefight with some bad guys that were dug in near an apartment complex. I'm talking machine guns, mortars, RPGs, the whole she-bang. One of the mortar rounds fell short and landed on a shed near the apartments. A little girl was blown out of the shed. She landed in a heap out in the street. Even from a distance it was obvious she was critically wounded. Before we could try and secure a path to the wounded girl, I saw an Iraqi guy race out into the open and scoop her up. It was one of the most heroic things I'd ever seen. The bad guys tried to gun him down, but he cradled that little girl and, despite getting tagged a couple of times, he made it back to our position. It was a horror show. The little girl's nose was blown off. I could see her sinus cavities through the hole in her face. But our Corpsman got to work on her right away and, unbelievably, she lived. The guy that rescued her wasn't so lucky. He'd taken a round through the liver and died at my feet. He went from hero to corpse in less than a minute. Despite all the blood, I recognized the guy. He was one of the teenagers on his way to the whorehouse the night before. We found out later he wasn't even related to the wounded girl. Probably didn't even know her. He simply saw a kid in trouble and made the decision to help. He paid with his life. But the sad truth is that young hero was the exception not the rule. And that's why it feels like nothing we did will really make a difference. There just wasn't enough good to go around."

Cruz grabbed my hand across the table and gave it a quick squeeze. Her cellphone started ringing. She let go of my hand and stood up.

She said, "What you did over there made a difference. Sometimes it just takes a while to notice."

I flushed and looked away. Cruz answered her phone and walked out the door.

———

Cruz's visit raised my spirits, but the feeling was fleeting. Within a day I'd convinced myself that she was just being professional. The hand squeeze was nothing more than a casual sign of compassion, even if I hoped against the odds that it was something more.

By the beginning of my second week in stir, my patience had redlined. I was on the verge of dialing MacFarlane to call the whole thing off when he showed up with Li out of the blue. Both men looked anxious.

MacFarlane said, "We've got something. You up for a little road trip?"

Fuck yeah, I was. Anything to get me out of the safehouse. Anything to keep me from brooding over Cruz.

"You bet," I said. "I'm always ready to roll."

Li gave me the rundown. "A Marine interrogator assigned to an interagency billet at the San Ysidro border facility picked up an unusual OTM. That's the acronym they use for 'Other-than-Mexican.'"

I interrupted, "We have Marines assigned to the border?"

Li said, "Yeah, there's a couple of them. Anyway, we got a call from one about 30 minutes ago. He processed an OTM that claims to be related to Noori… the guy you knew as Fuad."

"You recognize this guy?" MacFarlane pulled a photo out of his binder. "This is the guy they nabbed at the border."

Even with the full moustache it was obvious the guy in the photo had a deformed upper lip. Like a harelip. The recognition hit me hard. It was Hog-Tie. That dude Taco and his boys snatched up the day the National Guardsman was killed.

I nodded. "I know that fucker."

———

The ride to San Ysidro took almost four hours. Traffic bottlenecked all the way through Orange County. We finally arrived at the border interrogation facility just before dark.

A clean-cut Arab guy in civvies met us at the gate. His haircut screamed Marine. He offered his hand.

"Chief Warrant Officer John Razzaz," he said. "Nice to meet you."

We did introductions and followed Razzaz inside. He led us to an observation room that looked in on the interrogation booth through a one-way mirror. Hog-Tie sat in the middle of the booth on an unpadded wooden chair. Whatever route he'd taken out of Iraq had exacted a heavy toll. He had a couple of hairless patches dotting his skull. I didn't remember that damage from the last time I saw him in Baghdad. His jeans had a slick, black sheen along the thighs and crotch, like you see on long-term homeless folks. Hog-Tie's feet were bare and dappled with weeping sores. I could damn near smell the infection through the mirror.

Razzaz gave us the backstory on Hog-Tie. He was captured earlier in the morning along an old smuggling route near Jamul. He'd picked the wrong coyotes. He probably wasn't able to pay their adjustable rates. The coyotes abandoned Hog-Tie and a few Nicaraguans in a ravine known for heavy Border Patrol surveillance. They got jammed up right away. Hog-Tie tried to make a run for it. He didn't get very far on his busted feet. The Nicaraguans fingered him as an "Osama" from the Middle East that wasn't part of their group. Border Patrol sent up the alert.

Hog-Tie had a Jordanian passport under the name 'Hani Ensour.' The passport had Namibian and Mexican entry stamps. Razzaz was convinced it was counterfeit. Razzaz was raised in Egypt and labeled Hog-Tie's dialect as 100% Iraqi. Best bet—this 'Hani' character was an Iraqi running on a high-quality, fake Jordanian passport. That meant he had some suction. Which meant he might have some info I needed.

Razzaz continued filling us in with additional details. He said he had Hani in the box for a few hours before the guy finally brought up his familial connection to Noori Shammar. Razzaz didn't recognize the name, but he found a match on an FBI list. He called his liaison at the FBI's San Diego Field Office and San Diego called MacFarlane.

When Razzaz finished getting us up to speed he turned to me. "So, Jim, you know this guy?"

"Yeah. Kind of," I said. "I don't really know much about him, but I sure as hell recognize him. We called him 'Hog-Tie.'"

Razzaz' eyebrows arched inquisitively. I hid a smile. I didn't want to air any details about his capture in front of the Feds.

"Yeah, don't ask," I said. "We had to have nicknames for everyone because these fuckers never had any real identification on them."

Razzaz smiled. He knew the score. We'd have to keep the detainee beatdown stories inside our own little sewing circle.

"My buddy's platoon snatched him during a firefight in Baghdad a couple months ago," I said. "The HUMINT Exploitation Team assigned to our Battalion interrogated him and he admitted to working for a cat named Thamir al-Tikirit. Thamir was a former Special Republican Guard brigadier who had been reassigned as the Baghdad Police Chief just before the invasion. Thamir got clipped a little while later, but I remember Staff Sergeant Kinney had a source who claimed this guy sitting here was also a member of the Special Republican Guard."

"Staff Sergeant Kinney?" Razzaz asked. "I know Kinney pretty well. By any chance, was that Steve Souza's HET that was with you guys?"

Souza's name unleashed a wave of acid in my stomach. I swallowed hard. The Feds weren't going to see me get emotional.

"Yeah. Steve's HET was with us the whole time in Baghdad," I said. "I was actually with him when he got hit."

Now it was Razzaz' turn to swallow his emotions. "Steve was a great fuckin' dude. I've known him since we were both Lance Corporals. We went through the CI/HUMINT schoolhouse together as Sergeants."

MacFarlane interjected when he realized Razzaz and I were about to go down the fallen-comrade rabbit hole. He gave Razzaz a quick overview of the Oil-for-Food/hawala angle and how this Hani Ensour might fit in. As MacFarlane spoke, I flashed back to Fuad/Noori's hideout in 'Nam. Fuad had told Souza that his cousin was coming down to guard Zahra and Adila while we took him up north to hunt down Thamir. This guy sitting here in the box was now claiming to be Fuad's cousin. Could he be the cousin Fuad mentioned? The chronology didn't seem to jive.

When MacFarlane finished his spiel, I turned back to Razzaz. "Did Hani, or whatever his name is, indicate when he left Iraq? An approximate date maybe?"

Razzaz shook his head. "No. He's very deliberate in not talking dates. It appears he had some counter-interrogation training. He doesn't commit to timelines. He waited me out on the first couple of approaches. I think he was testing me to see what I had up my sleeve. When he mentioned his connection to Noori, it was completely out of the blue. It wasn't a reply to any of my lines of questioning. It was him making a move."

"Are you going to take another run at him?" I asked.

"Yeah, that's the plan. He's been cooling his heels in here for hours which he probably knows is irregular. That said, maybe now he's ready to chat for a bit. But like I said, this isn't homeboy's first rodeo. I wouldn't get your hopes up."

We strategized. Razzaz went back into the booth with an expanded list of questions to weave into the interrogation. How long was Hani in custody after Taco's boys rolled him? Was he the one Fuad asked to come down to 'Nam to stand guard over Zahra and Adila? What was his plan if he'd been able to get into the US free and clear?

It was shaping up to be a long night. I settled into a government chair and watched through the mirror as Razzaz and Hani sparred in slow, deliberate Arabic. Razzaz impressed me. He kept Hani engaged through the night. It looked exhausting from outside the glass. I couldn't imagine how taxing it had to be for the guy in the box.

Six hours later, Razzaz wrapped the interrogation. Hani was a tough customer. Always on guard, always deliberate in his responses. Hani's story for being in Fuad/Noori's neighborhood the night he got rolled by Taco's platoon still didn't synch. Hani stuck to the same story he gave in Baghdad, the one where he and the other gunmen were going door-to-door looking for two children of former regime officials who'd been kidnapped and were being held for ransom. The whole thing sounded bogus.

Even through his initial responses in Arabic, it sounded like Hani was working from a script. Razzaz agreed. There were a few subtle things in Hani's kidnap rescue tale that made it seem like he was trying to recall a fictional narrative. Specifically, he spent a lot of time recounting what Razzaz called 'housekeeping.' Hani recounted actions and events that had no bearing on the actual story. Razzaz said it was a common stalling technique when perps are trying to recall what they're supposed to say. I saw

Razzaz make little tic marks with his pencil as Hani stumbled through his account. I was reminded of another one of Uncle Mitch's maxims—time is the interrogator's friend.' Even the best criminals fuck up if you can keep 'em talking long enough.

Hani eventually cracked, just a bit. He stated that he was released two days after Taco's boys detained him. He also claimed that he never went south to 'Nam to watch over Zahra and Adila. He didn't even know Zahra and Adila had gone south. Unlike the kidnap for ransom bullshit, Hani's story about getting released rang true. Bad guys like Hani frequently got cut loose those first few weeks in Baghdad. There wasn't enough jail space to hold them. Also, if Hani kicked free two days after getting detained, that likely ruled him out as the cousin Fuad charged with watching over Zahra and Adila in 'Nam. The timelines clashed, which meant he might be telling the truth about not going to 'Nam. But it was impossible to determine either way. For all we knew, Hani could've been the one that murdered Zahra and abducted Adila. The more I mulled over the possibilities the more I realized none of it really mattered in the long run. Zahra was dead, Adila was missing, and Hani was sitting in a detention cell in California. Even if he copped to Zahra's murder and Adila's abduction, he wasn't in a place to help us much on extant leads.

MacFarlane eventually ran out of patience. The FBI didn't give a shit about Hani's Iraq adventures. What Hani did or didn't do in Baghdad had little bearing on the Feds' present case. MacFarlane redirected Razzaz to press Hani on his plans and connections here in America. As it turned out, Razzaz didn't have to press hard. As soon as Razzaz stepped back in the booth, Hani's whole demeanor changed. He started talking. In an even more surprising development, Hani claimed to have a bead on

Colombani. He shut up again after dropping that bombshell. Hani played the asylum card.

Razzaz signaled a break. We reconvened in the observation room. The Immigration and Customs Enforcement duty agent popped in. He'd just got off the phone with his supervisor. ICE and the Marshals were ready to chip in some extra manpower to ratchet up the Colombani manhunt if Hani provided a location. MacFarlane left with the ICE agent to call his supervisor in LA.

Half an hour later MacFarlane walked back into the observation room. He looked jazzed.

"We have a plan," MacFarlane said. "I just got off the phone with my boss up in LA. He made some calls back to the boys in Langley. They're willing to let us take a shot on this one. Long story short, CIA will let us use one of their asylum quotas… at least provisionally. We're cleared hot to offer Hani asylum in exchange for details on Colombani, the bearer bonds, the *hawala* index, and anything else we can squeeze out of him."

Razzaz spoke up. "Are you sure we want to offer this guy asylum? I don't have all the details yet, but he's definitely done some dirt. He's not the type to just flip a switch and become a law-abiding citizen."

MacFarlane's eyes sparkled. "That's the beauty of it," he said. "Even if Hani upholds his side of the bargain we can still decide to revoke his asylum. CIA did it to six Iraqis they ran against Saddam back in '98. Those six got uppity, so Langley and Justice coordinated to hit all six with a slew of federal charges. Espionage beefs, wire fraud, the works. Those indictments violated the terms of their provisional asylum. If Hani gets too big for his britches, we'll do the same. I'll make him go away for good."

This was a good sign. The G-men I'd known weren't usually ones for bending the rules or strong-arming shitheads like Hani. MacFarlane's willingness to 'get creative' in Hani's case proved that he was committed. MacFarlane could taste the blood in the water. It felt like the FBI's institutional momentum was something I might be able to leverage in the future. I doubted CIA had actually greenlit an asylum quota. That didn't seem like something Langley would agree to after a single phone call. In fact, I started to doubt whether anyone in the FBI had even contacted CIA. But whatever fuckery MacFarlane and his bosses were up to, I felt it just might lure some bigger fish to the hook.

MacFarlane and Li generated some placeholder paperwork that outlined the terms of Hani's 'asylum.' Razzaz verbally translated the documents into Arabic. Hani gave the documents a quick once-over and signed on the dotted line. Maybe it was my ever-creeping paranoia, but I thought Hani seemed a little too blasé about the lifeline he'd just been thrown. Maybe it was just Iraqi fatalism. Maybe he knew a stack of papers on US Government letterhead didn't mean much in the real world. Maybe Hani knew he'd always be a patsy.

———

With the paperwork out of the way Hani started talking again. Elements of his story meshed with what Fuad had told me and Souza that night in Baghdad. Thamir was Hani's commanding officer back in the Special Republican Guard days. In late 2002, Thamir put Hani in contact with some of Colombani's people in Damascus. Hani acted as a courier in those final months before the invasion, running Oil-for-Food skim to Colombani's crew in Syria. For a cut of the skim, the Syrian Connection transferred the funds through their *hawaladars* to multiple locations worldwide, including bagmen here in the US. After Thamir was killed, Hani leveraged his Colombani connections to get out of Iraq. He crossed illegally into Syria and linked up with Colombani's crew in Damascus. They got him the Jordanian passport and passage on a commercial freighter to Walvis Bay, Namibia and then on to Mazatlan, Mexico. In exchange for the passage, Hani was on the hook to help Colombani track down the *hawala* stashes in the US. Colombani deduced that Thamir didn't always use the same *hawaladars*. That meant some of the Oil-for-Food cash might still be floating around outside of Colombani's orbit. That wouldn't cut it. Colombani wouldn't settle for some of the cash. He wanted it all. Hani told Colombani that Noori/Fuad had sent a copy of the *hawala* index to his son Jawad in LA.

When Razzaz translated that last bit of information I felt my chest go tight. "That fucker got Jawad killed," I said. I pointed at Hani through the one-way mirror. "He sold out his own fucking blood!"

MacFarland looked annoyed. "Jawad's murder isn't the priority right now," he said. "If we can help LAPD clear it, then great. But we're not sacrificing Hani in the process. At least not until he gives up the Iraqi networks here in the US."

Razzaz nodded and returned to the interrogation booth. Hani further admitted to enticing Colombani with leads on the bearer bonds that were stolen from the bank in Baghdad. Hani claimed that he didn't know who actually had the bonds, but he thought mentioning the paper would make him appear more useful to Colombani and maybe keep him alive long enough to make his final escape. Hani quickly added that he was sure Colombani would kill him after he provided him with the leads, but that he agreed to help because he wanted out of Iraq. Now he was agreeing to betray Colombani to stay in the US.

The complexity and improbability of Hani's tale didn't faze me. By this point I'd become numb to all the wild-ass conspiracies and international intrigue. All I wanted now was revenge for

Souza and a location on Adila. The missing link that Hani hadn't discussed was Izzat.

I signaled Razzaz to take another break. Razzaz gave Hani his first cigarette of the day and walked back into the observation room.

I said, "I need you to ask him if he knows a *Mukhabarat* officer named Izzat al-Zaidon. It's a *nom de guerre* but I'm betting he knows who I'm talking about. In fact, you can pull Izzat's picture from one of the Be-On-the-Look-Out notices we received in Baghdad. You have access to those databases, right?"

"Yeah. I can pull the BOLO," Razzaz replied.

MacFarlane gave me a 'don't waste our time' look, but didn't say anything. I followed Razzaz into an attached office and he pulled up his classified computer. After a quick search we found the BOLO with Izzat's photo. Razzaz printed out a copy.

Hani claimed he didn't know Izzat. He didn't flinch a beat when Razzaz showed him Izzat's photo. Hani's expression stayed pathologically neutral. I didn't buy it.

I told MacFarlane and Li that I needed Razzaz to do one more thing. MacFarlane looked pissed. I could tell he thought I was slow rolling the FBI's priorities with the Izzat business. I gave MacFarlane a 'hook a brother up' gesture. I was ready to beg if need be. MacFarlane relented. Maybe he felt like he owed me after the fuck up at The Huston Hotel. I signaled Razzaz again.

I said, "Can you have Hani take off his shirt. I need to see the back of his shoulders."

Razzaz had Hani drop his shirt and turn around. There it was. The scar on his right scapula. Still purple. A bullet wound. From my gun.

I told Razzaz, MacFarlane, and Li about tagging one of the heist men in the shoulder during the bank robbery in Baghdad. MacFarlane was skeptical. Iraq was a violent place.

Lots of guys could've taken a round to the shoulder. I laid out the circumstantial evidence. Hani was a courier for Thamir. Hani knew about the Oil-for-Food skim. Hani knew the bearer bonds existed, or he wouldn't have risked involving Colombani. Conclusion—Hani was one of the heist men. Izzat was one of the heist men. Hani knew Izzat. Hani might know what happened to Izzat. He might know where that fucker is right this minute.

MacFarlane and Li broke off for a quick sidebar discussion while I continued to provide Razzaz background details. MacFarlane and Li returned and said they were willing to bite. The Feds were Ok with Razzaz continuing to press Hani on Izzat, but only if it looked like Izzat was 1) still alive, and 2) made it out of Iraq.

Razzaz went back in the box. Hani was asleep in his chair. Hani looked maxed out. His head lolled at an awkward angle. Razzaz woke him up and started grinding on the Izzat angle. Hani stuck to his guns. He didn't know Izzat. He didn't recognize Izzat's photo. Razzaz made a couple of last-ditch deflections and obliquely worked the conversation back towards Izzat. No dice. Hani didn't budge. Razzaz hit a wall.

———

It was almost daybreak by the time Razzaz wrapped the interrogation. Hani was stashed in an isolation cell while I huddled with Razzaz and the Feds. Hani's next window for contacting Colombani's crew was set for noon. MacFarlane decided to have Hani make contact while Li started working to secure a warrant for the phone number Hani gave up for Colombani's cut-out here in California. The Feds broke off to make calls up the chain of command. Razzaz instructed the detention facility folks to let

Hani shower and get some sleep. We needed him in control of his mental faculties.

Despite the sleepless night, Razzaz and I were wired. He suggested we go grab some breakfast. Technically, I wasn't supposed to leave MacFarland and Li as I was still in protective custody. But both men would be busy working the phones for the next couple hours. If we didn't stay gone too long, they'd never even know I'd left. Razzaz slipped me out a side-entrance and we boogied. I rode with him to a diner a few miles away from the detention facility. We tucked in to some *huevos rancheros* and ran out of small talk after a couple bites.

Razzaz swallowed a long pull of coffee and said, "Tell me about the night Souza got hit."

I gave him the full story. I included details about the fleeing Iraqi police motorbike from my after-action debrief with the snipers. I told Razzaz I was convinced that Izzat executed Thamir. I told Razzaz that Izzat fed Fuad a tip about Thamir's hideout at the factory to lure him back to Baghdad. I also admitted that I was convinced Izzat had detonated the explosive device that killed Souza and Fuad.

Razzaz nodded in agreement. "As far as Hani's case is concerned, I'll be out of the mix after this morning," he said. "But if we get any other Iraqis coming through the border, you can be damn sure I'll press for info on this Izzat fucker. From what you've said so far, I wouldn't be surprised if Izzat also fled Iraq. And if he did, I'd say there's a chance he might try and follow the money all the way back here to the Golden State."

"We should be so lucky," I said.

"Yeah, I'm not saying it's likely, but Izzat seems heavily invested in the Oil-for-Food skim operation. Add in the fact he might've smoked one of his own guys for the bonds and the sheer amount of effort he put in to prevent Fuad from disclosing the *hawala* index, and it's certainly possible he could pop up on our side of the border."

"If he does, I promise you I'll kill him myself," I said. "Fuck the Feds, fuck NCIS, fuck ICE, fuck the cops. If I get eyes on Izzat, I'm gonna punch his ticket."

Razzaz smiled. "I'm going to pretend I never heard you say any of that. Just on the off chance you actually get the opportunity to follow through."

16

FBI Safehouse
Los Angeles, California – Tuesday, 24 June 2003

The Feds drove me back to the safehouse. I'd done my part to assist with Hani and now they wanted to put me on ice. I didn't dig the prospect of hanging out with FBI babysitters again while MacFarlane and Li ran the Hani operation. I wanted in on the action. Li tried to console me. He said there was still a possibility they might be able to use me. He wasn't convincing. I was too exposed. Colombani knew I was bait. The Feds wouldn't risk putting me back in play and, even if they did, Colombani's crew wouldn't bite.

Despite my benchwarmer status, I did my best to figure the score from what little info I had. MacFarlane and Li inadvertently disclosed a few tasty details on the drive home. I feigned sleep while both agents fielded numerous phone calls and jabbered back and forth with each other. MacFarlane confirmed over the phone that Hani had successfully contacted Colombani's cut-out in LA. The meet was set for later that night. Colombani's contact gave Hani directions to an office park in Irvine off Interstate 5. Hani was instructed to park in a designated lot where Colombani's guy would pick him up.

The Feds talked through all the potential problems associated with rolling surveillance and overwatch. They had no idea where Colombani's man might take Hani. The possibilities were endless. Keeping tabs on Hani once he was in another car would be difficult. The bad guys would no doubt shake Hani down right away, so that limited the scope of possible tracking devices the Feds could employ. The op was high-risk. Pins and needles all the way.

I thought through the scenario. Keeping bad guys boxed in was one thing in Iraq, where you could manhandle the civilian population. It was a tougher sell here in the civil rights bastion of coastal California. 9/11 was already a distant memory. There was no appetite for police state shenanigans. The citizenry wouldn't put up with any heavy-handed bullshit.

I didn't envy the Feds' options. There seemed to be an unknowable range of potential obstacles and complications. By the time MacFarlane and Li dropped me off at the safehouse, I figured the odds of nailing Colombani were three-to-one against.

It was mid-afternoon when I shut myself into the safehouse bedroom. Almost 48 hours with no sleep had me spinning. I racked out hard. What felt like 30 seconds later, there was a knock at the door. One of the safehouse minders walked in with a phone. He said I had a call.

I put the phone to my ear and mumbled, "Hello?"

Cruz' voice shot back through the speaker. "Jim. It's Cruz," she said. "I'm calling to let you know we closed the bank heist investigation. You're in the clear. I figured you deserved to hear it from me."

Scratching the bank off my list of worries was a welcome development. The relief was palpable. I felt 50 pounds lighter.

I said, "I tried to tell you and Lawson that you guys were barking up the wrong tree."

Cruz snickered. "Ha! Is that how you remember it? If you'd actually cooperated we could've cleared you weeks ago. But you did help out on the Colombani thing. So you get credit for that."

"Does that mean I've convinced you I'm one of the good guys?"

"Let's not get ahead of ourselves."

Her tone sounded legitimately playful. I dug it. I played it cool.

"Speaking of Colombani," I said. "Did the Feds brief you up on what's going down tonight?"

"My SAC, the Special Agent in Charge, got a call from MacFarlane about an hour ago. I was out on another thing and haven't had time to get up to speed."

"Why don't you swing by here and keep me company. I'll fill you in on the details."

"How do you know what's going down?" Cruz asked. Her tone carried a hint of suspicion and maybe even worry. "They aren't putting you back in play, are they?"

"Unfortunately, no," I said. "But I may have overheard some things on the drive back from the border earlier today."

"Probably best if you forget what you heard. And no, I can't swing by. I have to head over to your hotel. Local PD got a call that someone was trying to break into one of the rooms last night. We're not even sure if it was your room that was targeted but the cops that responded to the call noted the manager had security tapes so I'm going to check it out."

"The cops just now told you about it?"

"We didn't want to advertise the fact that you were involved so the PD didn't know to notify us or the FBI. But like I said, it could just be a routine burglary. We don't know for sure that your room was targeted."

I flashed back to the Iraqi cigarette smell in the hotel room. "Be careful, Angela. Remember when you took me by the hotel to gather my gear and I said it smelled like Iraqi cigarettes? I wasn't trippin'. I'm convinced someone had been in there. And whoever that someone might have been, they smoke Miami cigarettes, which is not a good sign."

"Yeah, so you said. But I'm a big girl. I can take care of myself."

———

I passed out again. It was a deep trip into nightmare land. Little girls with severed noses and bloated corpses with their fingers sawed off. Dogs munching bodies. Fire-puckered skin the consistency of fried chicken. The dream seemed to last hours. I felt movement.

MacFarlane shook me awake. He was grinning. His waddle stretched wide. Li stood in the doorway on his cellphone.

I yawned hard and damn near dislocated my jaw. "What's up?" I asked. "How'd it go with Hani?"

MacFarlane said, "That's what we're here to talk about."

Li pocketed his cellphone and shut the door. He gave MacFarlane a quick nod. MacFarlane pulled a chair up next to my bed and started talking before I could throw off the covers.

"We nabbed one of Colombani's cut-outs last night," MacFarlane said.

MacFarlane stared at me like he needed my permission to continue with his story. I gave in. "What about Colombani?" I asked.

"He's still in the wind. Probably in Mexico. But there are some new developments."

Macfarlane launched into a rundown on the Hani op. Colombani's cutout picked Hani up at the parking lot in Irvine. As expected, someone in the car stripped Hani and threw his clothes out in the street. They drove around for hours, the full counter-surveillance boogie. They took Hani to a house in Torrance. Another vehicle drove past the house and parked up the street. It might've been the switch car that would take Hani to the meet with Colombani. Hani got spooked. He ran out a side door and sprint-hobbled as fast as he could on his torn-up feet in nothing but a t-shirt and boxers. The Feds moved in. They pulled Hani to safety and secured the house. There were two suspected Colombani associates in the crib. A scuffle ensured. The Feds dropped one of the guys. He was at Harbor Medical Center in critical condition. The other guy surrendered. The driver of the suspected switch car took off on foot and escaped. Local PD put the neighborhood in lockdown. No reports on the runner yet, but the initial search of the house turned up some interesting leads. There were dossiers on several Iraqi nationals. One of which was a woman.

MacFarlane pulled out a manila file folder with an 8x10 photo print. "Do you recognize this woman?"

The photograph looked like a close-in surveillance shot. It didn't look like it was taken in Iraq. The background lighting looked too soft. The pavement under the woman's feet looked decidedly un-Iraqi. The woman in the photo was walking along what looked like a pier.

My sleep-fried synapses clicked into action. The jawline, the cheekbones, the eyes, the hair. I could've sworn I caught a whiff of citrus through the photo. It was Adila. Her face had occupied my thoughts long enough to induce instant recognition. I took a couple of breaths to check myself.

"Yeah. That's Adila," I said. "She's Fuad's daughter. Actually, I don't know for a fact she's his daughter. Fuad, or Noori, or whatever his name is, introduced that woman to me as his daughter 'Adila.' She's the one that went missing from the farmhouse where her mother Zahra's body was found. Is she alive?"

"We don't know for sure," MacFarlane said. "But we have reason to believe that she might be. We're still going through all the documents seized from the house. Most of the dossier materials were in Arabic and French. We had an agent on scene from the surveillance team that read through the French stuff and it looks like Adila might be in Mexico. Or at least Colombani thinks she is."

Li's cellphone rang. He answered and motioned for MacFarlane to follow him into the hall. Both men disappeared behind the door.

In his haste to follow Li, MacFarlane left the dossier on my bed. I rifled through it. My French sucked but I was able to decipher a few proper nouns. One name stuck out. F/V *LA CHANGUANOSA*. A Spanish name, not French. Next to it was a date time group written in the European format. A handwritten note in the margin said 'Ensenada.' I tried to focus. Another anaconda yawn made my eyes tear up. I heard the doorknob turning. I closed the file. I placed the dossier back where I'd found it and lay down on the bed.

MacFarlane and Li came back in. MacFarlane's smile was gone. Both men looked anxious.

"We have to go," MacFarlane said.

"Wait… what about me?" I asked. "You just told me you think Colombani left the country, right? Do I still need to stay here?"

Li took one for the team. "Yes. Until we can get this sorted. Sorry, Jim, it's for your protection. Get some rest and we'll be in touch."

MacFarlane noticed the file on the bed. He snatched it up and hustled out the door with Li in trace. Neither Fed looked back. The hunt was in full swing.

———

Sleep wasn't in the cards. I fixated on the notes from the dossier. 'F/V' was an abbreviation for 'fishing vessel.' 'LA CHANGUANOSA.' Cool name for a boat. The *Changuanosa* were a group of desert raiders that terrorized Los Angeles back in the day. It seemed almost too fitting. The fates were mocking me. The date time group translated to this Saturday at 8am. The obvious conclusion—Adila was scheduled to arrive in Ensenada at 8am Saturday on a fishing boat called *'LA CHANGUANOSA.'* From what little i knew of Mexican smuggling ops, the pieces fit. *LA CHANGUANOSA* likely rendezvoused with whatever deep water ship carried Adila halfway across the globe. The Mexicans didn't monitor international shipping lanes with the same gusto as their Yankee counterparts. Adila could slide onto the fishing boat's manifest and slip into Mexico unnoticed.

If the FBI drew the same conclusion, how would they play it down in Mexico? Could the Feds get our Navy or Coast Guard to intercept *LA CHANGUANOSA* at sea? Would the Mexican authorities be willing to do so? Would the FBI risk coordinating with Mexican law enforcement to try and ambush Colombani's crew at the port in Ensenada? There was a long list of variables no matter which way you cut it. Part of me hoped Colombani's intel was wrong even if that meant Adila was still stuck in Iraq. I didn't like her chances in Mexico.

I finally dozed off for a couple of hours and woke to my cellphone dancing across the nightstand. It was Cruz. She was on her way over to the safehouse. She had something to show me.

Twenty minutes later, Cruz arrived. My FBI minders made themselves scarce. Cruz helped herself to coffee and took a seat next to me at the dinner table. No boss-lady pantsuit today. She wore her tight blue jeans and a loose flannel that concealed the Sig Sauer on her hip. Despite the summer heat, the flannel, and the hot coffee, Cruz didn't show the slightest hint of discomfort.

Her skin smelled warm and earthy. Her scent a ripe basil. I found myself inhaling a little too heavily. I tried to play it off by holding my coffee cup up to my lips with both hands, a mom-on-Christmas-morning pose.

Cruz gave me a weird look and pulled out a laptop. She fired up the computer and opened a video file. She swung around the table, so we were both facing the laptop. I welcomed the proximity.

"This is what I pulled from your hotel in Venice last night," Cruz said.

She pressed play and the second-story landing of my ragged-ass Venice digs came into view. Cruz identified my room as the second door on the landing. She fast-forwarded a bit until a human-sized shadow came into focus on the periphery. Cruz slowed the video and the shadow came into detail. The shadow gave way to reveal a man. Dark complexion. Burly moustache. Heavy five o'clock shadow. The man approached the room next to mine. He glanced back towards the camera and Cruz hit pause.

Cruz said, "You recognize this guy?"

Instant cold sweat. I moved my face close to the screen to be sure, but I already knew who it was. Even with the security camera's mediocre resolution the scar was a dead giveaway.

"Yeah, I know him."

———

I spent the next hour with Cruz going over everything I knew about the man known as Izzat al-Zaidon. I added my own editorials about what I'd do to Izzat given the chance. Cruz didn't feed into my tough-guy schtick. She was all business on this visit. She kept grinding for details. By the time Cruz relented I'd gone over everything at least twice.

Cruz finished up some notes, sat back in her chair, and stretched. I sat perfectly still. My blood fucking boiled. The thought of Izzat walking free in California sickened me. My mind drifted along some dangerous currents.

I had an epiphany. Izzat being in California might actually be a good thing. I'd have never gotten my hands on him if he'd stayed in Iraq. But he was on my turf now. I could give the bastard a proper welcome.

I said, "OK, my turn. Why did Izzat break into the room next to mine? You think he'd already been in my room that night I smelled the Iraqi cigarettes?"

Cruz nodded. "I'm starting to think it's a possibility."

"But if he didn't find anything in my room, why bother with the room next door?"

"He might've thought you rented more than one room as a security precaution. It's possible he would've broken into other rooms if the hotel guest hadn't spotted him and called the cops."

"Did he break into my car?"

"Not that we can tell."

"Any leads on where this asshole is now?"

"We shot-gunned his photo and description out far and wide. But if he's skilled enough to get out of Iraq and sneak into the US, he's not gonna be easy to find."

"Yeah, about that," I said. "If Izzat is supposed to be such an ace spy, how he'd get caught trying to break into a fleabag hotel? That seems improbable."

"My guess is he's operating solo. He doesn't have any resources in this country, no one he can trust, no one inside the law he can liaise with. He's racing with, or maybe against Colombani to track down the bonds and the *hawala* index. He probably thought the hotel was worth the risk if it provided him any legit leads."

"So, what's the play?" I asked. "How do we jam this fucker?"

Cruz chuckled. "First, there is no 'we.' You're out of the game. But NCIS will continue to work with the FBI and local law enforcement to track him down."

"So, I'm supposed to just rot away here in the safehouse while you guys take your sweet time 'coordinating' Izzat's capture? Fuck that. Put me in, coach. Let's run another tethered goat. Put the word out on the streets that I still have the bonds. Let me show my face in public and draw this bastard out of the shadows."

"That's not how it works. You're already burned. Besides, it's not my call anyway."

I tried for one last charm offensive. "But the bosses will listen to you. You're not a mouth-breather like Lawson. Even these stick-up-their-ass FBI people respect you. If we come up with a plan, I'm convinced you can sell it."

Cruz's grin melted. She looked annoyed. "You know, Jim, there's a point where the macho Marine bullshit grates on my nerves. Especially when it turns into you trying to tell me how to do my job."

I threw up my hands in a mock surrender gesture. "OK. But there are some other things in play that I bet the Feds haven't told you yet."

Cruz dead-eyed me. I dead-eyed back. She shrugged.

"Colombani has intel that Fuad's daughter Adila is arriving in Ensenada Saturday morning," I said. "On a fishing boat."

"How do you know this?"

I gave Cruz the debrief on the Hani op as I'd heard it from MacFarlane. I admitted to scoping the dossier he left on the bed. Cruz tried to not to show it, but she was interested. Her eyes did that lioness-on-the-prowl, narrowing thing. I could tell she was running through the mental calculus of what all this could mean for her efforts.

Cruz' phone rang and she excused herself to take the call in the kitchenette. A minute later she peeked her head around the wall and said she had to go. She turned for the door.

I said, "Anytime you want a real gunslinger in the mix give me a shout. You know where to find me." It was a Hail Mary. A ridiculous, desperate plea to be put back in the game.

Cruz didn't even acknowledge my bullshit with a backwards glance.

17

FBI Safehouse
Los Angeles, California – Wednesday, 25 June 2003

I managed a couple hours of sleep after Cruz left. It was late afternoon by the time I rejoined the land of the living. My sleep cycle was fucked. My head felt like it was wrapped in wet cotton. The dregs of my concussion still percolated from time to time. Today it felt like my brain trauma had decided to incite a riot inside my skull. I stumbled out into the living room as one of my FBI minders walked in the door. He told me to pack my gear. My safehouse days were over.

MacFarlane and Li were waiting for me at the FBI's Wilshire office. They both looked like shit. I tried to account for their whereabouts over the past few nights and realized they probably hadn't slept in ages. Li ushered me into the same ground floor conference room they used for our first interview.

Li said, "NCIS brought us up to speed on Izzat. Is there anything else you can tell us about him? Anything you forgot to tell Special Agent Cruz?"

"Nah," I said. "I told her the same stuff I told you guys. I can't think of anything else."

"OK. Here's where we stand," Li said. "All indicators point to Colombani being back in Mexico. We think his crew here in California is pretty much neutralized. The two guys at the house in Torrance are off the board for good. The suspected switch-car driver and the woman from the hotel are still in the wind, but we don't see them making any more moves on this side of the border while their boss is in Mexico. That goes for any of Colombani's other henchmen we don't know about here in LA. His crew pulled a lot of heat over the past week and there's nothing definitive tying you to the bonds or the index. That makes it extremely unlikely they'd waste time and effort to hunt you down. The same goes for Izzat. What little intel we've been able to cobble together on Izzat suggests he's on some sort of rogue, solo op out here. It's likely he'll follow the rest of the players down to Mexico. Again, all of this is based on assessments, not hard facts. But what I'm getting at is we think it's safe to cut you loose. Unless of course you still want protection?"

"Thanks for your concern, but I'm ready to get back to my life," I said. "I sure as hell don't want to spend another day at the safehouse. Besides, I need to get back to 29 Palms. My battalion is scheduled to return soon and I've got tons of work waiting for me."

MacFarlane said, "Heading back to 29 Palms would be a good idea. Keep clear of LA for a while. We'll be in contact and let you know if there are any developments that necessitate brining you back under protection."

"Sounds good," I said. "I appreciate you keeping me in the loop when you can. But now that we have that settled, what's up with you guys? What's the play?"

MacFarlane grinned. "That's not something we can discuss with you now that you're out of the mix. But don't worry, we have a plan."

I nodded and gave MacFarlane an 'aw shucks' shrug. I didn't need to know the details of their plan. Because I had one of my own.

———

The Feds were cool enough to have my car brought up from the hotel in Venice. After I signed some more paperwork, I was free to go. I hit the 10-East as rush hour died out. Li didn't specify when my temporary leave would expire, but MacFarland was right—getting out of LA seemed like the right call. I had a three-to-four hour drive to 29 Palms, so it gave me time to think. Even though the Feds wouldn't tell me, I was convinced they had something brewing down in Ensenada. They were either coordinating to have *LA CHANGUANOSA* interdicted at sea, or they were going to set a trap in Ensenada to roll up any bad guys waiting for Adila's arrival. I was betting on the latter. If they took Adila off the boat while it was still at sea, they might not get a chance to flush out Colombani, Izzat, or any of the other players. If the Feds were willing to use me as bait, they wouldn't think twice about using Adila as the same. The Mexican authorities probably didn't give a shit either way. They'd go along with whatever the Feds wanted as long as they were properly incentivized. I racked my brain for any other info that might lead me to a different conclusion. I couldn't come up with anything. Ensenada was the most likely play.

I started fading about an hour into the drive. My body couldn't decide whether it was time to sleep or kick into high gear. I spaced out behind the wheel a few times and pulled off at the first available exit. A garish Indian Casino done up in neon and faux adobe beckoned. I parked and wandered inside. Strangely enough, the sensory explosion of flashing lights, jackpot sirens, and coin rattle helped clear my head. I decided to grab dinner at a sports bar tucked into the casino's back forty. I munched a burger and ruminated on Ensenada. MacFarlane and Li seemed convinced that Izzat would follow Colombani down there. That seemed like a desperate move, but desperation was probably all Izzat had left at this point.

I couldn't shake the fury invoked by the idea of Izzat walking free in Mexico. I wasn't convinced the Feds or their Mexican counterparts had the moves to bring him in. If the *Mukhabarat* had Mexican players like Rudolpho Santana on the books, an experienced officer like Izzat likely had a lot of room to maneuver down there. My mind kept replaying images—the burning bodies at the bank, Zahra's corpse at the farmhouse, Souza's funeral. I wanted a drink to douse the mental horror show, but I was afraid it would blunt my rage. I wanted my hackles up. I wanted to keep that hateful, ulcer-inducing edge. I wanted Izzat dead. I wanted that fucker's soul.

There were a couple of folks I could call to help me slip back into the game. One guy in particular had suction in Old Mexico. He had the juice to make things happen. My mind blazed with the possibilities of taking the fight across the border.

By the end of my meal, I had mapped out a course of action. It was time to go on the offensive. I was going to Ensenada.

———

My first call was to Randall. He didn't seem surprised to hear my voice. He seemed even less surprised when I told him I needed to talk to him about something that shouldn't be discussed over the phone. He told me to come on up to his place. Joshua Tree was an hour away. I told him I'd be there in 45 minutes.

Randall's gate opened as I approached. I parked the Impala in his prefab garage. Randall waved me over to the house. We posted up at the bar where Randall had a rack of Hi-Life waiting.

Randall said, "Does Easy know you're here?"

"Nah," I said. "This is one of those situations where I figure it's best if he can maintain some plausible deniability. Technically, he's still my lawyer, but I want to try and keep him distanced as much as possible. At least for now."

Randall face contorted into a death's head grin. "I see. You want to keep Easy out of the mix, but you don't have any issue with pulling ol' Randall smack dab in the middle of it… whatever 'it' happens to be?"

Unconsciously, I imitated Randall's crazy countenance. "Randall, I hope you don't take offense, but I had you pegged as a man with a gunfighter's heart. The kinda guy that puts himself in danger just to test himself. The kinda guy that values justice over the law. Am I on target?"

Randall's grin vanished and his voice dropped a notch. "I certainly was that man… for a long time. Whether I still am remains to be seen, I guess. It's been a stretch since I've tested myself in the way you mean."

We'd stumbled into an uneasy silence. The conversation had turned too deep too fast. Men are shitty communicators. Marines are even worse. We were in uncomfortable territory. Randall sensed it and shifted awkwardly on his barstool. It was odd to see a man like Randall make such an indeliberate gesture.

Randall recovered quickly and his voice returned to its normal cowboy register. "So give me the lowdown, young buck. What kind of mess did the greenhorn Lieutenant get himself into this time?"

"You remember that Iraqi girl, Adila?" I asked. "I mentioned her when I was last out here with Easy? She's the daughter of that Iraqi Intelligence officer, Fuad. Looks like she's coming into Ensenada Saturday morning. The Feds are betting her arrival will flush out some bad dudes, including the asshole that killed Steve Souza. Steve's killer is a bastard named Izzat that I ran into a couple of times back in the sandbox. Somehow, he made it out of Iraq and now he's chased the money all the way here. I aim to dump that fucker. I'll roll solo if I have to, but some backup would be nice."

Randall dropped the butt of his Lucky into an empty Hi-Life bottle and fired up another smoke. "Tell me more. What's the Fed op look like?"

"Well, that's just it," I said. "I don't really know the details. I copped a quick look at one of their files while my handlers were out of the room. The file included Adila's arrival information, including the name and arrival time of the boat she's supposed to sail in on. It's possible the Feds could've coordinated with the Navy, Coast Guard, or other Mexican authorities to intercept the boat at sea, but I don't think that's their play. The way I see it, if they try and take her at sea, there's a good chance the bad guys waiting for her in Ensenada would get tipped off by their people in Mexican law enforcement or maybe even by one of the crew on the fishing boat. One of the bad actors is a dude named Santana that works in the Mexican shipping industry, so there's a good chance he's got someone on the payroll who can track all of this. I'm banking on the fact that the Feds assume the same. They really, really, really want to get their hands on the guys looking for Adila, so I'm confident they'll use her as bait to draw 'em to the port."

Randall stared me down hard looking for signs of equivocation. "Say it goes down the way you think. What's *your* plan?"

"The Feds think Izzat's already in Mexico," I said. "My plan is to find him before they do and clip him."

"That's sounds pretty ambitious. How in the hell you plan on finding a lone Iraqi in the wilds of Baja?"

"I have a friend down there who can help."

Randall's gaze turned suspicious, "Before you say anything else, let me throw this out there. Mexico is a lawless place, but even so, they don't take kindly to *gringos* murdering folks on their patch. A young *guero* like you hunting around, asking sensitive questions, that shit is gonna attract the wrong kinds of attention. If you get locals involved, and specifically I mean this *friend* of yours, you're even more exposed. Think long and hard about how much you trust this person."

"I have been thinking about it," I said. "I trust him. Rogelio is a man who understands revenge. I saved his woman from a rough situation years ago and helped him find the men responsible for threatening her. So, in that sense he'll feel obligated to return the favor. Plus, he's an outlaw. He's semi-retired but still runs in the right circles. That Mexican shipping official Santana helped the *Mukhabarat* evade import sanctions back in the '90s. If Izzat is in Mexico, he's likely been in contact with Santana. Rogelio can find Santana, which in turn helps us find Izzat."

Randall fired up his third Lucky and cracked another beer. "You said help 'us' find Izzat. I'm still waiting to hear exactly how you think I come into play."

"I just need extra eyes for surveillance," I said. "I'm not asking you to kill anyone."

"Good, because I haven't killed any Mexicans since 1987. I'd like to keep it that way. That said, if I had me a chance to bag an Iraqi… well, that's a different story. I still hold some grudges from '91. You shoulda seen what those bastards did to some of the Kuwaiti women we came across."

"Well, I'm hoping it doesn't come to that. Besides, I want to do Izzat myself."

Randall's demon grin resurfaced. "I wouldn't want to rob you of the closure." Randall made air quotes when he said 'closure,' like such things didn't really exist outside the wizardly realm of the head-shrinkers. He was probably right.

We never shook hands on it or made any verbal agreement, but from that moment on I knew Randall was in. We got busy on the details. Randall told me to leave the Impala in his garage. Having just come off a stint as a Fed lackey, there was a good chance they'd have the Impala BOLO'd at the border. Feds might have even tagged the Chevy with some tracking devices. Either way, it would be best to leave it here, even if that meant Feds snooping around the ranch. Randall said he'd hide his arsenal of ghost guns just in case. Randall had a mid-80s Toyota T-100 he'd let me borrow. In keeping with Randall's dedication to anonymity, the old Toyota pickup wasn't registered in his name. Something about an ex-girlfriend who owed him big time. If the cops contacted her, she'd know to confirm the truck as a loaner. It was part of a long-standing agreement between Randall and his ex. The Toyota would blend in better down south.

Randall ran through a checklist of other precautions. It was detailed to the point where I knew he'd done this sort of thing before. One of the questions centered on creating alibis. Or at least the illusion of an alibi. Something that could create reasonable doubt. Randall asked if there was anyone who could alibi me on this side of the border while we were down in Mexico. I had an idea on someone who might fit the bill.

––––––––

The phone rang at least ten times. I could picture Jessica scoping the incoming number and debating whether to answer my call. I heard a click and thought it was going to voicemail.

After a second or two of silence, Jessica's voice came through. "Hey," she said.

"Hi, Jessica." I realized I'd dialed her number before I'd worked out exactly what I was going to say. "Uh, hey sorry I haven't called in a while. It's been a crazy few days."

"Few days? I haven't heard from you in weeks," Jessica said.

She was pissed. But she'd kept track of when I last called. That was a good sign. She was still interested.

"Yeah, I know," I said. "My schedule hasn't really been my own lately. I was hoping maybe I could explain in person."

Jessica exhaled. A lifetime of disappointment in men filtered through the phone's receiver.

"When?" Jessica asked.

"I was actually going to be down your way tomorrow."

"When tomorrow?"

"Uh… tomorrow morning. Can I take you to breakfast?"

Silence. I could see her weighing the potential letdown of keeping me in her life.

"I have a showing at one," she said.

"Great. What if I swing by around ten?"

18

Off Highway 62
Joshua Tree, California – Thursday, 26 June 2003

The alarm buzzed at 4:30am. The previous night's planning session with Randall kept me relatively sober. I rolled out of the rack without a hangover. It was a nice change to the routine. I was ready to rocknroll. I needed the early start. To maintain the fiction I'd relayed to MacFarlane and Li, I needed to get out to 29 Palms this morning to make an appearance at the Regiment.

Traffic was nonexistent on Highway 62. I made it to the base in 30 minutes flat. No hassles at the gate this time despite the fact I was driving a truck with no Department of Defense decal.

The same Staff Sergeant I'd talked to last time was back behind the Regimental Duty desk. I guess with most of the crew off at war, the Marines left behind were pulling day-on/stay-on duty shifts. I had the Staff Sergeant confirm that I still had time left on my temporary duty orders. Apparently, no one from the FBI had called my chain of command yet to let them know I was no longer on the Feds' clock. Sometimes bureaucracy can be a blessing. The temp orders would allow me some freedom. Neither the Corps nor the Feds would be keeping close tabs on me. With Mommy and Daddy distracted, little Jimmy could play outside with minimal adult supervision.

I swung by the Battalion headquarters. The building looked deserted. 'Skeleton crew' might be too generous a label. The Battalion Duty Officer was a Sergeant that looked like he'd just started shaving. He confirmed there were no new updates regarding the Battalion's return schedule. Armed with that info, I jumped back in Randall's truck and sped west. I called Easy from the road and told him to expect some calls from me over the next couple of days. I told him not to answer, just let them go to voicemail. I asked him to call me back and leave me a couple voicemails as well. Like we were playing phone tag. Easy suspected I was on some sort of outlaw trip, but he also knew better than to ask for details. He agreed to play along. I hung up and checked the time. My watch showed 7am. I hit the gas. I needed to be in Carlsbad in three hours.

———

No kimono this time. No preprandial sex either. Jessica was fully dressed and anxious to get out of the house. I took her to breakfast at a café in the village. This time it seemed like she didn't care about being seen with me in public. She gave off complicated vibes. My small talk failed. By the second cup of coffee, we hit a wall.

I played clueless to give her an opening. "What's wrong Jessica? Do you not want me here?"

Jessica winced. "What are we doing Jim? I don't hear from you for weeks and now you're taking me to breakfast? What's your angle?"

"I'm not playing angles," I said. "I like you. You're fun, beautiful, smart. I like spending time with you. That's not weird, is it?"

She sighed again. A long one like she gave me over the phone. The gesture felt borne of heavy repetition over the years.

"But where does this go?" she asked. "I needed to get laid. You were willing. And with the exception of that first night, very able. But what now? Do you really see yourself dating a women 15 years older?"

"I hadn't really thought about it," I said. "I mean, we don't really know each other yet. But that doesn't mean I don't want to get to know you better."

Jessica looked up over my head, like she was trying to remember her script. "I don't know if that's a good idea, Jim. We kinda fell into a routine before you disappeared. And if I'm being honest with myself, I liked that routine. It felt good. But that's what I'm worried about. I'm tired of finding good things just to lose them again. Not to mention I still haven't explained any of this to Rachel. I've never pretended to be mom of the year, but sneaking a guy young enough to be her brother in and out of the house isn't setting a great example."

"Well, I don't know what to say on the Rachel front," I said. "I'm not a parent so I have no business weighing in there. But I like you and I want to keep seeing you. If you're cool with that."

The hard lines around her eyes disappeared. I couldn't tell if it was resignation or endearment. Jessica reached across the table and cupped my hand with hers. Then she abruptly excused herself to use the lady's room.

I settled the bill and we got back in Randall's truck. Breakfast hadn't solved anything, but I felt we'd shelved the big, relationship-altering decisions for now. It was a minor reprieve. I didn't want to rock the boat any more than I had to.

Jessica looked around the dusty cab of the truck like she just now realized I was driving a different vehicle. "What happened to your car?"

"A friend's borrowing it," I said. "Actually, I needed this truck, so we swapped."

"Why did you need the truck? Where're you headed?"

This wasn't exactly how I envisioned giving Jessica the sales pitch, but it was now or never.

"So, as it turns out, I have to head down to Mexico for a couple of days," I said.

Jessica rolled her eyes. "Who's the lucky girl?"

"Nah, it's not like that. It's a work thing. Or at least it's work-related."

She gave me a 'I knew you were playing angles' look. "Jim, I don't know much about you or the military or any of that stuff, but I'm not a complete fucking idiot. Marines don't go off by themselves to Mexico for quote/unquote 'work stuff.' I'd rather you just not say anything if you're going to lie to me."

I tried to navigate the minefield. "I'm not lying. Look, I don't know how to tell you this. Or I guess, I don't know how much of this I can tell you. It's for your own safety."

Now I really sounded like an asshole.

Jessica closed her eyes and shook her head. "Please, Jim. Just stop. Stop talking. Take me home."

"Jessica, I'm not lying to you," I said. "There's some shit I got wrapped around in Iraq that, through a series of events you wouldn't believe even if I could tell you, has now spilled over into Mexico. I'm going down there to sort some of it out."

"You're going to Mexico alone to deal with Iraq stuff? Do you know how fucking crazy that sounds Jim?"

"It does. I totally agree. If I was in your shoes I'd think the same thing. Although, one minor point of clarification, I'm not going alone."

Jessica pinched the bridge of her nose. It was the same exasperated gesture Cruz gave me from time to time. The universal female signal for 'I don't know why I bother.

"Who are you going down there with?" she asked.

"A friend. It's best if I leave it at that."

"What's her name?"

"She's actually a he, but I can't tell you his name."

"Why do I still get the feeling there's a woman involved? You can tell me if there is Jim, it's not like we're married. I think I deserve to know."

"Technically, yes… there is a woman involved. Well, she might be involved. That remains to be seen. But she's not the main reason I'm going down there."

We pulled up to Jessica's house. She was still staring down at the floorboard. I'd already dug my own grave. Now it was time to start scraping the bedrock.

"So, Jessica, while I'm down in Mexico. I was kinda hoping you could make a couple of calls from my cell phone. You don't have to talk to anyone, just call the number I give you and hang up when it goes to voicemail. Just over the weekend. I should be back by Sunday."

"Fuck you, Jim."

Part Three

Old Mexico

19

La Ballena, San Miguel
Baja California, Mexico – Thursday, 26 June 2003

The second person on my call list was Rogelio, my Mexican connect. But the number I had for Rogelio had long been disconnected. I'd have to catch him in person. Fortunately, I knew exactly where he'd be.

Rogelio's joint was called *La Ballena*. The restaurant/bar sat on bluff overlooking the Pacific in a fishing village a few clicks north of Ensenada. It was 8pm by the time I got there.

Randall was scheduled to meet me in *La Ballena's* parking lot in an hour. He didn't want to come inside. Randall was rightly paranoid about Rogelio laying eyes on him unless it was absolutely necessary. It was all for the better. I needed some time to talk to Rogelio alone. What I had in mind was a big ask.

Rogelio and I had a complicated past. He was a semi-reformed pirate who'd taken some heavy scores back in the 80s. About ten years ago he parlayed some of his illegal profits into the bar to carve out his own niche in Baja's recession-proof tourist industry.

The first time I walked into *La Ballena* I met Ro's on again/off again girlfriend Ximena. She tended bar and flirted with customers as part of her schtick. I was young, naïve, and totally smitten. It never dawned on me that Ximena's flirtations were simply part of the act. I flirted back.

I stayed at *La Ballena* until closing that first night. I ginned up some liquid courage and followed Ximena out to the parking lot, hellbent on professing my love for her. As fate would have it, a couple of *gringo* bikers from some no-name Arizona club decided they also wanted Ximena's attention. One of the bikers cornered her near the dumpster and got handsy. He tried to slip his hand into Ximena's skirt. I raced over and sucker punched him from behind. I dropped the asshole, but damn near broke my hand in the process. The other biker came at me with a knife and would've sliced me good had my leather jacket not saved the day. As I bobbed and weaved to avoid getting stuck, Ximena ran back inside the bar. The biker I'd dropped regained his feet and joined his buddy. The pair blocked my only path out of the lot. I was about to be well and truly fucked. Until a mean-looking bastard roared out of the bar with a machete, looking for all the world like a man prepared to go full Rwanda.

The machete guy turned out to be Rogelio. He chased the *gringos* back to their bikes where one of them pulled a pistol he'd stashed under the saddle. At first the pistol failed to dissuade Ro from closing on his prey. But Ximena screamed from the bar, begging Ro not to get shot. Ro finally relented. The bikers seized the break in the action to speed off into the night. Ro turned back towards the bar, ready to chop me up. Ximena intervened before Ro could let his blade eat. She explained that I'd fought the bikers on her behalf. Ro stared at me. His eyes flamed hate. He vibed homicidal. I sensed Ro was debating whether or not to kill me out of simple convenience. Then, after what seemed like a full minute stare-down, Ro gave me a quick nod and turned away. He threw his arm over Ximena and walked back inside the bar

The next morning, I was grabbing breakfast at a roadside taco stand near Rosarito when I noticed two bikes with Arizona plates parked in the lot of the motel next door. I waited a couple of hours until the owners appeared. Sure enough, it was the two asshole bikers from the night before. I jotted down the license plates and drove straight back to *La Ballena*. I caught Ro alone as he prepped the bar for the lunch trade. I told him I had the plates of the two *pendejos* that tried to fuck with his girl the previous night. He clocked me like I was trying to set him up. But then his mood shifted just as suddenly as it had the night before. Ro's murderous eyes softened. For whatever reason, in that instant Ro decided I was on the level. He bought me lunch. He spotted me beers. He thanked me for the information and told me I was always welcome back at *La Ballena*.

A month later I was on my way to Tucson to see a girl. Just past the Arizona border I spotted a missing persons billboard along the highway. The billboard promised a cash reward for information leading to the location of two missing men. The names underneath meant nothing to me, but the photos of the missing white trash bikers were unmistakable. I knew for certain no one would ever cash that reward.

So, what began as a near fatal introduction to Rogelio's world evolved into something approaching a legitimate friendship. I visited *La Ballena* every time I was in Mexico. Ro always made time for me. Of course, I still crushed hard on Ximena, which could have made things awkward, but she was always gracious enough to never manipulate my feelings or play me against Ro like a meaner-spirited woman might have.

Over the years, I fell into a comfortable rhythm with Ro and Ximena. I always made it a point to bring lots of heavy-tipping *gringos* through the joint. The regular rotation included a couple of college girls I brought down from San Diego that Ro thought were good for business. Ro always comped me food and drinks. Our quasi-transactional relationship developed into something more personal. Ro and I became buddies. At least to the degree that a Mexican pirate and wet-behind-the-ears college kid can be *compadres*.

Now, as I stood in *La Ballena's* parking lot again, I admitted to myself that despite our shared past, my trust in Rogelio was still conditional. I wouldn't trust him with my sister, but I'd trust him to back me in a gunfight. He was that kind of friend. I hoped I wouldn't have to put that trust to the test over the next few days, but if there was anyone in Baja could help me get a bead on Izzat, it was Ro.

———

I smoked my last cig in the truck and walked inside the bar. I couldn't risk losing *La Malinche* if the Toyota got jacked, so I tucked the pistol into my belt. The pistol's receiver grated my lower back. My gait felt off, like I was walking with a hip replacement.

Despite the relatively early hour, *La Ballena* was hopping. Tito & Tarantula blasted over the stadium PA that Rogelio had rigged to the in-house sound system. A dangerous mix of tequila-soaked *vaqueros* and their age-inappropriate girlfriends littered the joint. I elbowed my way to the bar. I spotted Ximena. She poured mezcal into a row of shot glasses with a grace that emphasized her sex-kitten allure. She looked up and saw me smiling at her.

"*Oye Guapa!*" I yelled over the sound system.

"Jimmy!" Ximena slammed the mezcal bottle back in the well and ran up to me on her vertigo-inducing platform heels.

Ximena pulled me across the bar and kissed me on the lips. "It's been forever! I can't remember the last time you were here. Where have you been?"

"Until about a month ago, I was in Iraq," I said.

"Ay-aye-aye. Jimmy, I'm glad I did not know this. I would have been too worried."

"It's all good *mi amor*, I made it back with all my parts," I said.

I blushed as Ximena gave me an approving once-over. Her eyes lingered on one 'part' a little longer than I was comfortable with. But it felt nice that she still noticed.

Ximena and I bullshitted at the bar for a couple minutes until a gaggle of irate patrons demanded the mezcal shots she'd abandoned. She sent the hostess to go find Rogelio. A barely legal waitress set me up at a two-top near the window overlooking the ocean. I sipped a Pacifico and stared towards the pink lights of *Puerto Ensenada*. The lights bothered me. The sodium glare reminded me of the fluorescent overhead lighting in the FBI's interview room.

Rogelio strolled up to my table, looking piratical as ever. Pearl-snap shirt, black-leather pants, rattlesnake boots. Ro was one of maybe two people I'd ever met that could've pulled off an eye patch.

"Que onda guey?" Rogelio pulled me off the chair and into an *abrazo*. Like Ximena, Rogelio favored some lift in his footwear. Dude was probably 5'9" in real life, but the heels on his snake boots put him almost eye-level with me.

I slapped his shoulders and pulled back from the man-hug. I didn't want him to feel the butt of *La Malinche* poking through my shirttail.

"Trying to stay out of trouble, my man," I said. "It's good to see you, Brother."

"Likewise, 'mano. What brings you down San Miguel way… *guey?*"

"Business. Not pleasure."

"Jimmy has *business* in Ensenada? But you are still an officer of Marines, no? What possible business could you have in Ensenada?"

"It's a long story," I said. "I owe a friend."

"This friend is a woman, yes? Ha! The Jimmy I know would only turn outlaw for a woman."

"Who said anything about turning outlaw?"

"Please, 'mano. The only *gringos* with business in Ensenada are outlaws and people who work on cruise ships. And I can't picture you in one of those white *marinero* uniforms."

"Well, you got me there, *jefe*, no cruise ships in my future."

"Listen, Jimmy. Maybe you should forget this business, huh? Things are not like they used to be. The violence is different now. Too much money at stake. The killing is out of control. Even here in Baja. *Cuidado, 'mano.*"

"That's what I wanted to talk to you about," I said.

"I don't like the sound of this, Jimmy. You walk into my bar with that *cuetta* stuffed in your jeans and you want to talk to me about violence? This can't be good."

I blushed. How the fuck did he know I had the pistol? "I didn't mean any disrespect, Brother. You know I wouldn't come into your place strapped unless I had no alternative."

"No worries, 'mano." Rogelio gestured to the crowd. "Half of these *pendejos* carry any given night. They've got nothing to lose. But you do. Remember that."

Rogelio's apprehension was starting to make me nervous. I cut to the chase. "Do you know a guy named Rudolfo Santana? He's some sort of shipping official. I think he works out of Mazatlán."

Rogelio gave me the big eye. "What business could you possibly have with a man like Rudolfo Santana?"

I gave Rogelio the whole story. Almost the whole story. I left Randall's name out of the mix for now. But I made sure Ro knew why I needed to find Izzat. When I finished, Rogelio flagged the waitress and told her to set us up with another round in his office. I followed him through the crowd of wannabe *sicarios* and their teenage *hynas* into a small room behind the bar. Rogelio closed the heavy, reinforced door and the noise from the bar fell to a hum.

Ro held a swig of beer in his mouth, like he needed to rinse before he spoke again. "If I can find this Izzat, what do you plan to do?"

"I plan to kill him, Ro," I said. "He killed my buddy, so he's gotta go. It's as simple as that."

Rogelio clucked deep in his throat. He sounded like a rooster warming up for his morning crow. "It is never as simple as that, a*migo*. If, as you suggest, this Izzat is assisted by a man like Rudolfo Santana, then he is moving in the *most* dangerous circles. Furthermore, if he is working either with or against a man like Colombani, then the danger is ten-fold. I know Anton Colombani. I did business with him years ago, in my previous life. The man is a savage. Corsicans make my countrymen look… how do you say in *Ingles,* 'circumspect?' Colombani is a man of animal rage."

"I don't really care about Colombani," I said. "The Feds want him bad and I'll do my best to stay out of their way. I want Izzat. If Izzat's working with Colombani, then so be it. If I have to tangle with Colombani to get to Izzat then that's what I have to do."

"Revenge doesn't suit you, *'mano.* You *Yanquis* always win in the long run because you don't fall victim to your passions. Leave the revenge to Latin peoples. We can't escape it. Revenge is in our DNA. But you don't have to play that game."

Ro's words induced a flashback. I could still picture him with the machete in his hand. A madman with murder in his eyes.

"This is different, Ro," I said. "I can't let this one go. If Izzat is here, I'm gonna take him off the board for keeps."

Rogelio finished his drink and stared at his hands. He popped his outsized knuckles. He looked back up with sad eyes.

"I wish you felt differently, *'mano*," Ro said. "And I know you are man enough not to bring it up, but I still remember. I owe you for saving Ximena from those fucking *putos*. So of course I will help you."

I was touched by Rogelio's concern. Had we not both been such macho assholes we might've even hugged. Instead, Ro insisted we do a shot of mezcal to commemorate the evening. I promised him it wouldn't be my last night in *La Ballena*. After everything had a chance to blow over, I'd be back and we'd celebrate.

We hashed out some coordination measures. I assured Ro this wasn't a solo trip. I told him I had a friend backing my play, but that it was probably best for all involved if he didn't meet this friend unless it became necessary. Ro agreed. He also told me not to bother buying a Mexican cell phone. We couldn't risk broadcasting our business into the ether. We'd communicate exclusively in person.

I agreed to come back to *La Ballena* at noon tomorrow to check in. I gave Ro another *abrazo* and exited his office. Back in the maelstrom of the bar, I caught Ximena's attention. I blew her a kiss and walked towards the exit. The *vaqueros* huddled around the bar clocked my gesture. Their faces read 'who the fuck is this Casper flirting with Ximena?' The locals eyeballed me hard. I pushed through the exit door without looking back.

———

Randall's Isuzu Trooper was already tucked into the far end of the parking lot. He flashed his headlights once to acknowledge that he'd seen me. I pointed to the Toyota and gave him the 'follow me' sign. We drove to a motel off the highway and rented adjoining rooms. It was one of those 'pay cash in advance and don't bother with ID' type of joints.

After we checked in and stashed our weapons, Randall walked into my room and took a seat. He looked like a scarecrow, all arms and legs folded into the low rattan chair. I briefed him on the meet with Rogelio. We had over 14 hours until our first check in at *La Ballena*. Randall said he'd get up early and start reconnoitering the marina and some of the access routes off the highway. I confirmed that I'd do the same.

Randall said, "I reckon that if your boy Izzat is here, he's going to stick close to the port. A guy like that would want to minimize his exposure, so going to ground near the target area makes sense."

"I agree," I said. "What should I be looking for tomorrow during the recon?"

"First off, we need to know the roads and topography in excruciating detail in case we have to move in a hurry. Anything that might jam us up needs to be mapped out. Construction zones, police checkpoints, local traffic conditions, anything of that sort. Also, we need a backup comm plan. As the saying goes, 'no comm, no op.' Our walkie-talkies have limited range, so we need to map out a couple of payphones and call windows we can use if we get separated. Finally, we need to look for any indications that our FBI friends are in play. Look for American SUVs from the consulate up in Tijuana. The consulate usually uses Chevy Suburbans and Ford Expeditions. They might use other, lower-profile fed-sleds as well. Keep an eye out for anything with US or out-of-state Mexican plates."

I looked down at my notes. The surveillance checklist Randall had just laid on me filled an entire notebook page. Tomorrow was going to be a busy day.

Randall dropped a kit bag on the bed. "We also need to pack this stuff. I've got the radios, spotting scopes, first aid kits, ammo… pretty much everything we'll need."

I scoped the gear. We could've rolled into Baghdad with Randall's stash. I hoped it would suffice for Baja.

20

Downtown Ensenada
Baja California, Mexico – Friday, 27 June 2003

Randall and I hit the streets early. As a couple of *gringos* with California plates, we had to limit our rolling surveillance to single passes. The city was relatively calm for a Friday morning. Normal workaday stuff. No overt signs of an increased police presence. I didn't spot any obvious G-rides. I had to pull over every 20 minutes to write down all the other stuff Randall had tasked me with. By 11am, I had a detailed outline of my zone of responsibility. Checkpoints, construction sites, payphones… everything was mapped out.

I got back to the motel before Randall. The cantina next door boasted flashy ads for a tasty Mexican lager. A couple of ice-cold *pistos* would've hit the spot. I talked myself out of the beer and ordered Fish tacos and a Pepsi. It wasn't until after I finished the second taco that I felt a slight pang of regret. I hoped and prayed my gut could handle the chow. Chasing bad guys with a case of the Montezuma's would be a nightmare. Hopefully the bacteria from the few street meals I'd managed back in Baghdad would keep the Mexican bugs in check.

Randall pulled in half an hour later and waved to me from across the parking lot. I followed him into his room and we briefed each other on what we'd seen that morning. The southern zone Randall had staked out was busier, more chaotic. Lots of tourists meant more traffic and more cops. Tangling with bad guys anywhere near the marina district was going to be a messy affair even under the best of circumstances.

I left Randall at the motel to go check in with Rogelio. Ximena shacked up with Ro in a stilted apartment that hung over the backside of the bar. Ro opened the door before I could knock. He was still wearing the same *pistolero*-cum-pirate garb from last night. I walked in and saw Ximena curled up on the bed. Sound asleep in nothing but a baggy t-shirt. Her proper Latina curves on full display. I diverted my eyes before Ro could clock me peepin' his girl.

Ro' handed me a cup of coffee. "No sightings of Izzat yet. But I expect to hear back from a couple of contacts within the hour."

"No worries," I said. "I didn't expect any hits this quick. Thanks again for doing this, 'Ro."

"I'm not sure you'll be thanking me later." Rogelio drained his coffee. The sad eyes from last night returned. "It's not too late to walk away."

"I'm not walking on this one, Ro. I already told you that."

Rogelio sighed and raised his hands in resignation. Ro's cell phone buzzed and shimmied across the breakfast table. He answered and broke into a rapid-fire exchange with the caller. My Spanish was decent, but I still couldn't comprehend the machinegun cadence of 'Ro's *Norteño* dialect. Rogelio took down a few notes and hung up. He handed me a slip of paper with an address near Playa Tijuana. Our first real lead. We agreed to link up later that night at a bar in Playa called *El Tiburon Negro*.

———

Randall was chowing down in the cantina when I returned. His caloric intake seemed improbable for a man with such a wiry build. Randall shook his head as I approached, a signal to not talk about anything within earshot of the bartender or other patrons. He swallowed a last shard of tortilla and we walked back to his room.

As far as leads go, the address Ro gave me was thin. Maybe anemic. But it was still worth checking out. One of Rudolfo Santana's known associates was spotted at a house in Playa Tijuana. The house wasn't for rent. The family that lived there disappeared in a flash and Santana's guy moved in. According to Ro, Santana usually focused his criminal activity further south. Baja wasn't his normal stomping ground. So, if one of his people posted up in a house in Playa, there was a good chance he was hosting someone outside his normal orbit. Conceptually, Izzat fit the profile. A known *Mukhabarat* officer leaning on a known *Mukhabarat* asset for a safehouse hookup. It was enough to get me interested.

Randall did a map recon of the address Ro gave me using a dated tri-fold road atlas. He picked out primary and secondary approaches and surveillance positions. There really wasn't much of a plan beyond setting up on the house. If I spotted Izzat, I'd try to wait until he was indoors, preferably alone. I'd clip him and we'd bounce back to the US. Simple in theory. Fucking insane in practice. I could tell the *ad hoc* approach grated on Randall, but we didn't have any real alternatives. We packed up and drove north along the beach-frontage trails to avoid the *Federale* checkpoints that littered the highway. Even with all the weapons secreted in their hiding spots, we couldn't risk avoidable encounters with the Mexican fuzz.

The target house was located on the eastern side of the highway. The neighborhood hovered between shanty and working class. In terms of maintaining a low profile, Izzat couldn't have asked for a better location. Unlike the expat condos and *gringo* timeshares that dotted the beach, this neighborhood vibed 'mind your own business.' Most of the homes were small, boxy digs arrayed haphazardly along a series of curved service roads. The slapdash layout of the dwellings had me worried that the address wouldn't match what was listed in the road atlas.

I needed to get eyes on the crib. I hit up Randall on the handheld to let him know I was going to make a pass. He acknowledged and drove up to his designated overwatch position on a hill under a giant radio antenna that lorded over the neighborhood.

Rolling through the *barrio* was sketchy. A *guero* in a truck with California tags attracted the wrong kind of attention. The sun was still high overhead. The midday heat transformed the road dust into a pseudo-psychedelic mirage. The hot earth, ramshackle cribs, and mind-fuck visuals gave me strong Iraq vibes. Even the sweet decomp scent of the burning garbage hit like Baghdad. I took *La Malinche* out of her hiding place behind the glove compartment and tucked the pistol under my thigh. My very own blue steel security blanket.

Fortunately, the neighborhood stayed quit. The target house looked deserted. No vehicles or tire tracks in the dirt driveway. No lights or noise from inside. I drove slow and made mental notes. The house had barred windows and a security screen on the door. Other than that, the crib looked wide open. I circled around on a parallel street to scope the backyard. A single window and a rusted chain link fence. No real security features and still no signs of recent habitation.

Randall's voice squeaked through the radio, "I've got a car headed up my way. Looks like a civilian, but I can't risk getting cornered up here. I don't have a cover story for why I'm sitting up on this hill. I need to move."

"Roger that," I said. "Let me know where you're headed."

"Meet me at that taco stand we passed right before exiting the highway," Randall said. "That's a good spot for a couple of *gringos* to pass the time."

I checked my watch. I still had a couple of hours until my scheduled meet with Ro at *El Tiburon Negro*. I told Randall I'd meet him at the taco stand.

The proprietor of the taco shack sized us up. I could sympathize with his reservations. Randall's *bandido*-turned-scarecrow look coupled with my shitty Marine haircut set us apart from the normal tourist clientele. His wife was more receptive. She fussed over us and whipped up some excellent chow. She let us linger. Her husband knew better than to try and give us the boot so long as his wife wanted us there.

Clock it—almost two hours at the taco stand. I needed to move. My next meeting with Rogelio was approaching fast.

I paid our tab and drove over the highway to the beach. I spotted the long, narrow profile of *El Tiburon Negro* on the main drag and found some street parking that looked more or less legal. The normal coterie of street urchins that ran the parked car protection racket must have had the day off. I hit up Randall on the handheld and told him I was headed to the bar. He said he'd cruise the drag and find parking on the north end.

It was five minutes after six when I walked into the bar. The joint was shady, literally and figuratively. No windows, no natural light. Both the ventilation and lighting were minimal, trending towards nonexistent. The name made sense. From the inside, the room aped the contours of a shark's body. The joint reeked of ammonia and something metallic. I pictured the staff sweeping out puddles of blood with industrial cleanser every night after closing.

Rogelio was waiting for me at the back of the barroom. The interior was so dark it took me a few seconds to spot him. He waved me over. His silhouette looked menacing in the blue light that leaked out from a neon agave plant on the wall. Ro was alone at his end of the bar. That made sense. Whatever info he had for me was best kept out of earshot of the locals.

Rogelio leaned in. "I don't have any updates on Izzat." His voice sounded different. The confidence of the pirate replaced by something more like concern. Maybe even fear.

I frowned and shrugged. "No worries. You didn't need to drive up here to tell me that, 'mano.'"

Rogelio continued, "There's more. Santana is in Ensenada. He was seen early this morning with a man matching Colombani's description. Also, my sources in the Federal Police report that several carloads of American officials arrived last night from the Consulate in Tijuana. This thing at the marina tomorrow, with your Iraqi girlfriend… I fear it is actually going to happen."

"She's not my girlfriend, but thanks for the update," I said. "This is good news, Ro. If Colombani, Santana, *and* the Feds are there, Izzat has to be close."

Ro's face creased. "That's what I'm worried about, Jim. I'm concerned you're about to do something stupid that will fuck up your life forever. Maybe even get you killed."

"This isn't a suicide trip, Ro," I said. "If I get the chance to dump Izzat and get away clean, I'll take it. If not, I'll let it ride."

"You've never struck me as the type to let anything ride, Jimmy. You didn't let it ride that night when Ximena was in danger. I'm damn certain you didn't let it ride while you were off invading Iraq with your Marines. And I'm abso-fucking-lutely convinced you're not going to let it ride if you get a shot at this man who killed your friend."

Ro told me to stay in the bar for ten minutes after he left. I nursed a beer and counted the seconds. At ten minutes on the dot, I dropped some cash on a coaster and hightailed it out of there.

Even though it was evening, the ambient light outside felt an order of magnitude brighter than the cave I'd just emerged from. It took me a few seconds and a couple of hard blinks to adjust my eyes. Eventually, I spotted Randall's Isuzu down the road. My brief stay in *El Tiburon Negro* made me extra paranoid so I spent a few minutes wandering around, checking for tails. Once I had convinced myself I was clean, I ambled over to Randall's ride.

I hopped in the passenger seat and gave Randall the update from Ro. We strategized. None of the options looked appealing. We needed to find Izzat before Adila's boat pulled in tomorrow. The odds of pulling off an assassination caper after the Feds were in place seemed pretty damn slim.

Back to surveillance. I left the Toyota near the taco shack and we took Randall's Isuzu up to the lookout by the antenna. Randall had some long-range optics but no night-vision goggles. We had to rely on what little ambient light poured out of the *barrio.* Making a positive ID from this distance was out of the question, but we'd be able to spot vehicles.

We chain smoked and talked shit. Randall regaled me with sea stories from back in the day. Filipina hookers two at a time in Olongapo. Outrunning the shore patrol in Oki. All the good shit the old-breed Marines used as reenlistment fodder. I pinged him on Central America. He gave me a 'my lips are sealed' signal.

I changed topics. "What about DESERT STORM? Tell me about the Rags you blasted in Khafji.'

Randall gave me the straight dope. He told me he lit up a couple Iraqis that got separated from their patrol. One of the guys was still alive when Randall got to him. Randall let the poor bastard hold two in the head. He said he still had the guy's cartridge belt back at his compound in J-Tree. Randall's nonchalance made me feel like I was talking to Ox twenty-plus years in the future. It was comforting to know that no matter how much the Corps changed over the decades, Marines like Randall and Ox remained.

Randall started to ask me something but paused mid-sentence. He pointed out the windshield. "Vehicle," he said. "It's moving towards the house."

I squinted hard to pick up the headlights. Sure enough, two beams flickered through clouds of dust. The red glow of the brake lights blossomed as the vehicle stopped in front of the target house. The darkness ruled out a make/model ID, but I pegged it as an SUV of some sort. The headlights went black. The occupant or occupants were smart enough to turn off the interior lights. I couldn't make out how many were in the vehicle. A shadow moved from the vehicle towards the house before disappearing into the front porch. The vehicle kept its lights off and U-turned on the access road. The driver stopped for a beat, turned the lights back on, and drove back towards the highway.

I said, "Can you tail 'em?"

Randall side-eyed me. "Of course. What are you going to do?"

"I'm gonna check out the house on foot," I said. "I want to know who got out of that vehicle. After I scope the house, I'll walk back to the Toyota and link up with you on the tail."

"If I jump on this tail, I won't be here to back you up," Randall said. "You OK with that, young buck?"

"No choice at this point. We gotta divide and conquer."

Randall stayed silent for a beat. "OK. If we get separated beyond radio range, I'll be at payphone number two at midnight. You've got the number. Call me then."

Randall let the Isuzu coast down the hill in neutral for about a hundred meters before he hit the ignition. Old habits die hard. Although I was sure the target house was out of earshot, Randall didn't want to alert the occupant to the fact that we were posted up here on the hill

I stumbled down the bluff towards the house. In the cool night air, Mexico no longer smelled like Iraq. I caught a whiff of purple sage and ocean breeze. The scent calmed me. I felt like I now had the homefield advantage. If that was Izzat down there in the house, he was in my world.

The access road was mercifully deserted. No other cars had passed since the mystery vehicle departed. No pedestrians. No dogs. Just black dirt and a few porch lights in the distance. The neighboring houses looked empty. I circled the house to clock for movement. Nothing shaking. I posted up across the street with my eyes fixed on the front door. The bedroom lights popped on. I ran through the front yard and flattened myself outside the doorframe and waited, *La Malinche* ready for action.

The light in the bedroom went dark. I held my breath as I watched the doorknob. It twisted counterclockwise. A short man stepped out onto the porch. I pistol whipped the back of his head. It was a hard shot. One he didn't see coming. Asshole didn't drop unconscious like in the movies. He fell into a crouch and tried to cover his head. A quick scramble. I got off a soccer kick. Caught him in the chin. Starched that fucker. He was laid out on his back with arms straight up in the air. The pose made him look like a backup dancer in Michael Jackson's *Thriller* video.

Nerve sizzle radiated up from my toes. My foot felt broken. I flexed my toes and tried not to swear too loud. The toes responded. I was lucky—no fracture. Note to self—wear proper boots next time.

My victim started moaning. He listed to his side as if invisible hands were rolling him onto a stretcher. I pulled out my penlight and studied his face. It wasn't Izzat. This dude was Mexican and way younger. I rifled his pockets and found a wallet and a phone. I stashed the goods and limped for the road. I stopped at the edge of the yard and contemplated going back to grease the guy. I nixed that idea. A pistol shot would draw out the neighbors. Plus, I didn't want to kill anyone I couldn't positively ID. This dude was almost certainly jungled up with Izzat and Santana's lot, but guilt by association didn't always merit a death sentence.

My foot throbbed like a sonofabitch. I hobbled as fast I could without aggravating it any further. I finally made it back to the Toyota and tried to raise Randall on the handheld. No joy. I wagered the mystery vehicle was headed towards Ensenada. I sped south and prayed for no checkpoints.

Randall came back up on the radio a few minutes later. He ID'd the mystery car as a blue, early-90s Ford Bronco. The Bronco pulled off the highway near the Hotel Calafia, a few klicks north of *La Ballena*. Randall had to stay on the highway. The Bronco crew would make him if he pulled into the hotel. Randall said he'd circle back and pick up the tail again if the Bronco moved out. He reminded me again of the payphone in case we got separated for good.

I passed the sign for the Hotel Calafia. Just beyond the hotel was a dirt turnout that skirted a cliff overlooking the ocean. The skeletal remains of an ancient school bus stood sentry at the edge of the cliff. The Bronco sat idling, half-hidden next to the bus. I pulled into the hotel lot and drove a lazy circle around the driveway. The Bronco's cab was still blacked out. No way to ID the driver or count the passengers. Parking here seemed off-script. I wondered if the guy I tuned up back at the house in Playa had found another phone and called to warn the Bronco crew.

The Bronco drove past the turnout just as I merged back onto the highway. I radioed Randall to let him know I would speed ahead and cover the next exit. He confirmed he was headed southbound again and would try to pick up the tail. Our two-car rotating surveillance wouldn't work for long. There were too many exits to cover and not enough traffic to hide us. The next exit revealed two options. West toward the beach. East toward the desert. I gambled on West. I waited a beat before rolling towards the coast. No taillights. The Bronco vanished. I lost the tail.

I radioed Randall and told him to keep heading south. We'd rally in the *La Ballena* parking lot. I needed to talk with Rogelio again. Time was running short.

———

La Ballena was packed. It felt a touch more sinister than your normal Friday night fiesta. I walked through the front doors and felt like I'd stuck my head in a reggae blast furnace. The bassline hit so hard I was worried my heart would start palpitating in time with the sixteenth notes. I was still limping from punting that *puto's* skull. I looked sketchy. The crowd sized me up. I needed to find Ro *rapidamente*.

It took me a few minutes to spot Ximena in the sea of cowboy hats. I finally caught her attention and she gestured to the door behind the bar. Rogelio opened the door to his office and waved me in. The security door shut with a satisfying vacuum sound. The bass lingered but it was more vibration than noise inside Ro's little sanctuary.

I gave Ro a rundown. I threw the wallet on the desk. "You know this guy?"

Ro pulled out a driver's license and squinted. "Fake name, but yeah, I know this *maricon*. His name is Luis. Fucker used to be a *Federale*. He got bounced for raping a woman in custody."

"A fucking rapist? Maybe I shoulda smoked him up at the house. Does he work for Santana?"

"Possibly," Ro said. "Luis is local. Knows the area. Knows the players. He would be the kind of guy Santana could use while operating up here in unfamiliar territory. Colombani wouldn't trust him though. Anton doesn't work with ex-cops no matter how far outside the law they've strayed."

"Do you know where Luis—" A vibration in my pocket cut me off. The cellphone I swiped from Luis was ringing. I showed it to Ro.

"This is Luis' phone," I said. "Will you answer it? Just pretend you're someone who found the phone."

Ro made a 'slow down' gesture with both hands. "Jimmy, let's hold up a second—"

"Please Ro. It's gonna go to voicemail soon."

Ro flipped open the phone and answered in a voice a shade lighter than his natural baritone. I could hear rapid fire Spanish through the speaker. Whoever was calling was pissed. I wondered if it might be Luis. Enough time had passed. He could've recovered from the soccer kick and rallied to the warpath. Ro's eyes narrowed in disgust. The voice on the other end signed off with a final string of expletives and the phone fell silent.

I said, "Was that Luis?"

"No. It was one of Luis' colleagues. Apparently, they got a call from Luis up in Tijuana. He was in the emergency room."

"He's lucky he's not in the grave," I said. "If I knew that asshole was a rapist, I'd have twisted his cap all the way back."

"Probably best that you didn't," Ro said. "Save your bullets for the man you really want. Trust me, you don't want to make murder a habit." Ro's words sounded confessional.

"Speaking of the man I really want, now that we have a phone number for one of his associates, you think we can use me as bait to lure these assholes?"

Ro paused again as he mentally tallied the facts at hand. "It is highly unlikely a man like Izzat would expose himself this close to an operation."

"Agreed," I said. "I don't think Izzat would break cover over a shitbird like Luis. But if I can get my hands on some of his local *compadres*, I might get a line on him."

"What were you planning? Turning my bar into your own personal Guantanamo Bay? Use the beer taps and bar rags to waterboard these men until they give up Izzat?"

"I wouldn't waste beer on these fucks."

Ro smiled but was not amused. "You should dump the phone and forget about this."

"Please, Ro. I'm begging you, Brother. I'm almost out of time. Adila's boat is scheduled to arrive in less than eight hours. I gotta find Izzat before then or there'll be too much heat."

The sadness flooded back into Ro's eyes. I felt like a dick. He didn't owe me for helping Ximena all those years ago. But he felt like he did. And now I was asking him to do things that put us all at risk. Worse yet, I knew he would do them.

Ro sighed. "I will have Ximena call them back and tell them that we have the man who attacked Luis here in the parking lot."

"We can do it somewhere else, Ro," I said. "I don't want to put you, Ximena, or the bar at risk."

"No. We'll do it here," Ro said. "I can keep things under control here. Don't worry, Ximena and I will stay anonymous. They won't know it's our bar. This is just a spot we picked to make the exchange. And if they do make the connection, so be it. You aren't my only *amigo,* Jimmy Wilde." Ro tapped a desk drawer and pulled out two chrome-plated .45s and a custom-tooled *bandolero.* The kit upped Ro's pirate swagger another notch, which I didn't think was possible.

Ro called in Ximena and briefed her on the situation. She was game. In fact, I got the impression she actually relished the opportunity. I started to wonder if maybe Ximena and Ro had a history with these goons I didn't know about. Given that *La Ballena* was a haven for all manner of rough trade, it wouldn't have surprised me if Luis' crew had stumbled through here in the past.

We walked to a payphone outside the bar. Ro waved away a skinny *vaquero* who'd just dropped coins in the slot. The kid started to say something but held his tongue when he peeped Ro's .45s. Ximena grabbed the phone and dialed. Someone answered. She launched into an Oscar-worthy monologue. She spoke the same blast-beat Spanish as Rogelio. I didn't pick up the whole story but the gist ran something like this—they were holding a guy who had wandered into *La Ballena,* gotten shitfaced, and started bragging about rolling some tiny Mex dude up in Playa Tijuana. Ximena's boyfriend blackjacked the sucker, found the phone in his pocket, and was now willing to trade up for a finder's fee.

It seemed like an improbable tale. Maybe the bad guys thought so too, but didn't have any other leads to work from. The voice on the other end agreed on a price for the finder's fee. Ximena gave him the meet location. *La Ballena* closed at two. She told the mystery man to meet in the parking lot at 3am.

Ximena hung up and smiled. She was rightfully proud of her performance. Ro had been in the life long enough to know that these types of meets rarely went smooth. He seemed anxious to get it over with, although with Ro you never really knew what he was feeling. He was also laser focused. I sensed this must have been his natural state back in the pirate days before he became the slightly-less-scary bar owner I'd always known. Ro's intensity was both calming and a little bit terrifying. I was just glad he was on my side.

Randall's Isuzu pulled in on the far side of the parking lot. I walked over and gave him a rundown on the situation. For some reason I found myself trying to pitch Randall on the plan like I was selling him a used car, 'Hey, it's going to be a long, sleepless night, but we might actually get our hands on someone who could lead us to Izzat!'

There was also the fact that Randall would now have to meet Rogelio. He wouldn't be able to stay anonymous if we were all gonna do some dirt together. I acknowledged that we were about to cross a serious redline. Our actions down Old Mexico way had been pretty benign up to this point. But if Luis' friends showed up, shit would get very real, very fast. Randall didn't complain. He flashed his crooked smile. He knew all along we'd end up getting dirty. I had a sneaking suspicion that Randall was actually happy that things were turning heavy. He excelled at this kind of shit. When it came right down to it Randall was a simple man. He was a gunfighter who'd been without a gun and without a fight for far too long. Randall missed the juice.

————

The hours crept. I fought exhaustion and second-guessed all the decisions that led me to this point. My mind raced ahead to what would happen after the pending parking-lot showdown. Even if everything worked perfectly and I found Izzat, how would I deal with Cruz and the Feds once I got home? No doubt they'd tried to check up on me by now. No doubt they harbored serious suspicions about my whereabouts. I wondered if Jessica left those hang-up calls on Easy's voicemail like I'd begged her to do. I also wondered about my Marine chain of command. If they discovered I was down in Mexico mixing it up with the criminal set, I'd be in deep shit… maybe even brig bound.

I had a few moments of self-doubt where I dreaded the whole adventure would fail. Either the Feds or the Marine Corps would catch me in a lie and I'd be hosed. Then I thought about Izzat again and got angry. Souza deserved the effort. Maybe Adila would survive too. Regardless of whatever schemes Fuad had perpetrated over the years, it seemed unjust for his entire family to get wiped out. Adila's survival felt necessary. In the end, I wanted Iraq to mean something. I didn't want to be sitting in *La Ballena* thirty years from now second-guessing the sacrifice. Besides, I was already here, heeled with an illegal ghost gun, waiting to ambush some Mexican cartel-types with a retired *pistolero* and a pirate for my backup. If nothing else, this trip was shaping up to be the most memorable Baja romp of my life. I hoped it wouldn't be my last.

Ro and Ximena closed the bar at two sharp. By 2:15 they'd hustled everyone out of the parking lot. A couple of drunk *hombres* tried to linger in a beater pick-up, but Ro whispered something to the driver and they hotfooted it out of there like they were being chased.

Now it was time for a little show and tell. I introduced Randall to Rogelio and Ximena. I wasn't sure how they'd take to each other, but the initial impressions looked favorable. Quick handshakes and nods. Nothing said out loud. Game recognized game.

Randall set up a few traffic cones in 50-meter intervals arcing away from the bar towards the highway. Long-distance shots at night would be a sketchy proposition at best, but having a few range markers might help. Satisfied he could still see the cone out at 200 meters, Randall slung his rifle and crawled up on the roof. If things got really out of control he might have to kill his first Mexicans in 16 years. I prayed it didn't come to that. I already had Ro and Ximena way out on a limb and they sure as hell didn't need the extra drama.

Ro disappeared into his office and came back out transformed. Black jeans, black hoodie, and a black sequined Luchador mask. I tried not to laugh. Ximena didn't even try. Ro flipped us off, but he was laughing too. The mask was necessary. He was going to have to get up close and personal. Getting ID'd by these clowns would be problematic. If any of Luis' buddies made Ro or Ximena we would have to kill the whole lot. If not, my friends would be looking over their shoulders for a long time. Maybe forever. Mexico occasionally forgives, but never forgets.

What the plan for dealing with Luis' friends lacked in feasibility, it made up for in simplicity. Without overthinking it, we'd determined to simply roll the bastards by force and transport them out to the desert for a little 'interrogation' session. The hard part would be keeping everyone alive during the takedown. But if by some miracle we managed that feat, I was fairly confident that we could transport them to the desert while they were still breathing. If that happened, we had a good shot at getting some answers. I was fully prepared to keep asking harder and harder until they gave up Izzat. If those 'asks' included some additional physical coercion, then so be it. In our modern, enlightened age, there's a consensus amongst the elite and media castes that torture doesn't work. People who think that are flat out wrong. If push came to shove, I'd admit that torture didn't *always* work... but most of the failures were simply operator error.

At 3:05 Randall spotted some headlights out by the highway. It looked like a vehicle had parked on the shoulder. I could just barely make out the faint outline of an SUV. Or maybe a light-body pickup. Whatever it was, it wasn't moving.

Seven minutes later, I heard more vehicle noises on the exit ramp. This one sounded like a truck. Finally, the outline of the blue Bronco appeared at the end of the lot. I flashed the headlights of the Toyota to signal the driver. The Bronco crept forward. The driver kept the lights off. I felt my chest go tight as the truck got closer. Shit was about to pop off.

The Bronco slow-rolled past the 50 meter cone. Engine noises blared. Rogelio raced up behind the Bronco in a truck I'd never seen before. The driver of the Bronco didn't see Ro's truck until it was too late. The Bronco was boxed in. I hi-beamed the Bronco, jumped out, and drew down on the driver's window. I made out three silhouettes. Two rifle barrels pointed up towards the roof.

I screamed at the driver to turn off the ignition. Ro shouted the same commands in Spanish as he closed on the Bronco from the rear. The driver slowly stuck his hands out the window. Before he opened the door, I heard tires squealing in the distance. A pickup truck barreled towards us. A guy stood tall in the pickup bed. Even in the dark I could tell he'd shouldered a rifle. Fuck me. A second trail vehicle made perfect sense. I would've used one too if I was the bad guys. I should've anticipated this.

Randall picked up the slack—a rifle shot cracked overhead and the windshield of the backup truck transformed into an abstract painting. The pickup swerved and crashed into the parking lot's perimeter fence. The guy in the pickup bed got launched over the guardrail. I caught a glimpse of the dude rag-dolling out onto the black beach below.

The driver of the Bronco tried to gun it. I dumped a couple rounds into the grill. Ro zapped the rear tires with his dual .45s. The Bronco fishtailed and stalled. I ran up behind the passenger window and shouted at the occupants to toss their weapons. Ro ran up on the driver's side and made a similar demand. The passenger's face flashed fear. He knew we had them dead to rights. He complied. The passenger dropped his AK on the deck and showed empty hands through the window. I heard footsteps behind me and turned to see Randall closing on the backup truck tangled in the fence. Within seconds he had the driver zip-tied and kneeling. The driver's forehead leaked blood all over the sand. He'd dinged his melon on impact. If Randall had been aiming for his dome, that poor bastard wouldn't have any head left to ding. The guy that was thrown from the truck bed was nowhere to be seen. Randall peeked over the perimeter fence. It was a good 60-foot drop to the beach. Fuck him, even if the rifleman survived, he was out of the game. Crab meat wrapped in denim.

We worked quick. Both of the bad guys' vehicles were banged up but still operational. Ro and Ximena split up and drove the Bronco and Ro's truck away from the bar. They ditched both wrecks at a small turnout about half a mile down the highway. Sparks from the Bronco's shot-up rims were visible as Ro gently coaxed the SUV down the road. The sight of Ro in his Luchador mask sliding down the road in the blown-out Bronco was so absurd that I actually laughed out loud. The farcical image reinforced the old maxim that sometimes even the shittiest of plans came together when you moved with enough speed and violence.

Randall and I zip-tied our four new prisoners and loaded them into the back of the Toyota. Randall had them lie flat so he could keep them under his boots while he perched behind the cab. With our human cargo secured, I took the wheel and we raced down the road to pick up Ro and Ximena at the turnout.

We dropped Ximena back at *La Ballena.* She had a plan to clean up the scene while we took our captives out to the desert. I had no doubt Ximena would be ready with a credible story if anyone reported the gunshots. She was a great actress and an expert at getting men to believe her. She'd have the cops chasing ghosts if they actually bothered to investigate.

I drove east. Ro directed me along a series of back roads. There was zero traffic at this time of the morning. When we were well outside the city limits, Ro directed me up a fire break that led into the foothills. At the top of one of the smaller hills was a rusty fence behind an ancient cattle guard. Ro motioned for me to park. I quickly surveyed the scene. The place vibed ghost ranch. No one would hear our 'interrogation' out here in the dust.

I helped Randall unload the Mexicans. Ro frog-marched them a few paces from the truck and had them kneel in the dirt. The prisoners were swaddled in nuevo-chic cartel duds. Garish shirts and designer jeans that cost more than drugs. The fashion choices were suspect, but I dug the contrast between the kitsch and the criminal. The absurdist style was enhanced by the anger in their eyes. Call it 'Hate Couture.'

Ro didn't bother asking for any names. He launched straight into a barrage of machinegun Spanish. He told the men we were looking for Izzat. The name didn't seem to register. I handed Ro a photo of Izzat. Ro held a penlight under the photo and asked again if they knew the Iraqi.

The driver of the Bronco grew some balls and started sassing in a weird dialect that sounded only partially Spanish. Ro shook his head and shot the guy next to the driver. One round, dead center in the breadbasket. The impact of the .45 round folded the man backward like a human lawn chair.

It took my eyes a few seconds to recover from the muzzle flash, but when I regained my night vision, I saw that Ro had everyone's attention. The Bronco crew's eyes bugged out of their skulls. The anger was gone. I smelled piss, fear, and a few other primal scents that can't be named. Even Randall looked shocked, which had to be an alien feeling for a man of his experience.

The gut-shot man didn't scream. He just lay on his back, blinked hard, and made a few clipped, gurgling noises. In the beam of Ro's penlight, I could see smoke rising out of the hole in the man's stomach. The combo scent of blood and gunpowder induced Iraq flashbacks. Mr. Gut Shot definitely had a bad case of the Cordite Blues. I forced myself to breathe slow and steady until I was back in the moment. It was hard to take in. Here I was in Baja, with Randall and Ro, torturing Mexicans for information on a rogue Iraqi intelligence officer. This was definitely not how I envisioned spending my post-Iraq leave.

Ro gave the men a few beats to recover their wits before he started back in with the questions. I thought I caught a glimpse of recognition in Ro's eyes as he bore down on the Bronco driver. The driver shuffled on his knees. His eyes darted back and forth, like he was calculating his odds of survival and, despite rechecking his math, couldn't accept the answer. Ro made a spectacle of brass-checking his .45s. The driver took note. He finally got his shit together long enough to spit out some words. Ro listened intently and wrote something down in a notebook.

Ro translated for me and Randall. "This guy is from down south. He works for Santana. He knows Izzat but not by that name. He says Izzat has been in Mexico for about a week. That house up in Playa Tijuana is where they had him stashed until two nights ago. Izzat is down in Ensenada with Santana now. He gave me the address where they're staying."

Randall chuckled. "Well, that was sure as hell easier than I thought. I like your interrogation style, *amigo*. Pretty damn effective, if you ask me."

Ro held up the notebook with the address. "I don't want to celebrate just yet. All of this could be bullshit. Men will tell you all sorts of crazy things when you shoot their friends."

The Bronco driver started shuffling on his knees again. His back-and-forth rocking reminded me of the guys we jammed up in Iraq. It was an unconscious attempt to get the blood recirculating through cuffed wrists and bound ankles. It was the same dance worldwide. The Baghdad Shuffle was alive and well here in the wilds of Baja.

Ro motioned to the driver with his chin. "So yes, it's definitely possible this guy is trying to lead us astray, but I told him I'd track down his family if he's lying. He knows he's gambling with their lives if he tries to fuck with us. He also knows that's a risky wager with a guy like me. Still, I'm not convinced. I recognize this street address. It's in a tourist area of Ensenada. It's not the kind of place I would imagine men like Santana or Izzat would stay. We don't have enough time to properly verify the location. The boat still arrives in four hours, yes?"

I realized Ro directed that last question to me. I checked my watch. "Uh… yeah, that's right."

A couple of thoughts hopscotched around my skull. "Hey Ro, if these guys have a phone number for Izzat or Santana would that help us?"

As soon as the words left my mouth, I realized I'd just called Ro by his name in front of the prisoners. I started to apologize but Ro cut me off.

Ro said, "Maybe if we had more time. I know people who can track phones. But no one who can do so in the next four hours."

Randall stared me down. "We've more than worn out our welcome down here. I recommend we check this address. If Izzat's there, we'll figure out a way to hit him. But if he's not, it's high time we got back across the border. *Comprende amgio?*"

I coughed on the lingering fugue of gun smoke. "Yeah, that sounds reasonable."

Ro nodded. "I agree. That is probably your best option at this point."

I pointed to the three men still on their knees. "What do we do with these guys?"

Three more shots. Ro hit the first two men right between the eyes. The third guy was able to get to his feet before he caught a round in the back. Ro stood over him and pumped another two rounds into the base of his skull. Ro looked over to the first guy he'd shot in the stomach. The man's mouth tried to form words, but nothing came out. One final muzzle flash turned his lights out for good. The crack of the last shot reverberated across the hills for what seemed like a full minute.

Rogelio walked back to the Toyota and sat in the passenger's seat. I looked at Randall. Randall shrugged and hopped into the bed of the truck with a motion that induced some heavy deja vu. I half expected to hear Ox telling the platoon to mount up. Iraq and Mexico were all the same ballgame now. Ro holstered his .45 and pointed down the hill. I aimed the truck towards the lights of Ensenada and hit the gas.

21

Downtown Ensenada
Baja California – Saturday, 28 June 2003

Rogelio was right. The address the Bronco driver gave up for Izzat and Santana didn't fit the bill. It was a modest *casita* on Hidalgo Avenue a couple blocks from the Marina. We made a pass. No lookouts posted. At least none that we could spot in the hazy predawn. Ro had me take a left before we hit the waterfront. He wanted to get a look at the back of the *casita* from the next street over.

Randall tapped the rear window and nonchalantly pointed across the street. A primer gray pickup with an M60 machinegun mounted to the roll bar was parked under a mango tree. I could see the word 'MARINA' stenciled in darker gray across the driver's door.

I choked back a 'What the fuck?'

Rogelio's eyes widened and his nostrils flared, like he was mustering as many senses as possible to assess the situation. "It's a raid. Mexican Marines. They're moving on Santana. Keep driving and stay cool."

I looked in the rear view just in time to see Randall slink out of sight as he pressed himself flat against the truck bed. I chanced another quick look at the gun truck. The driver and gunner stared back through black motocross face-shields and Kevlar helmets.

I'd seen that look a thousand times in Iraq. It was pure death mask. The Mexican Marines didn't plan on taking any prisoners today. It was going to be a 'call the meat wagon and forget the paperwork' gig. I diverted my eyes and kept driving.

Ro said, "We might be able to watch this go down from up the street. Take the next left."

I parked in front of some apartments a couple blocks up from the *casita*. Within seconds three trucks like the one we saw under the mango tree converged on the tiny house. Gunned-up Mexican Marines in black tactical gear dismounted and fanned out across the perimeter of the front yard. A muffled pop echoed down the street. A thin wisp of smoke rose from somewhere near the front door of the target house. Staccato rifle fire followed. No more than five or six short bursts. A couple of pistol shots peppered the mix for good measure.

Federale patrol cars rolled into blocking positions along the avenue. Lights flashing, no sirens. One of the cars on the next block pulled over a ratty Honda civic. The Honda driver looked like a local caught in the wrong place at the wrong time. If we lingered, we'd get jammed up too.

Ro whipped around in his seat. "*Chinga la Ma…* Cops setting up a perimeter. Jimmy, we gotta move. U-turn here. I'll get us back to the highway." Ro's face contorted as if he was performing some sort of mental-math calculation.

I cut over to Avenida Reforma. We drove south. No cop cars ahead. We'd moved just in time to escape the roadblocks. Pure luck. Even with Rogelio's considerable suction in this part of the world, it would have been tough to talk our way out if we got jammed. Two armed *gringos* and a semi-reformed Mexican pirate hanging out at the scene of a government raid would never be dismissed as coincidence. We didn't have the *plata* to bribe our way out of this mess.

We hit a red light at a four-way intersection a couple blocks short of the highway. I debated running the light but chickened out and stopped just short of the paint. A motorcycle sped past us on the right and narrowly avoided a delivery truck turning on a green arrow. The bike fishtailed violently. The rider recovered momentarily but had to break hard to avoid the guardrail. The bike lost traction and slid out from under the rider. The rider rolled across the intersection with his arms pulled tight to his chest. The bike skidded to a stop in the crosswalk. The engine whined. The throttle was pinned against the asphalt.

I drove through the red light and pulled up to the rider. Ro started to say something, but I didn't listen. I jumped out of the truck. The rider got to his feet and started rolling his head back and forth like a boxer shaking off a punch. He wore a large full-face helmet that made his body seem conspicuously skinny and withered.

I tried to get the rider's attention, "*Estas bien?*"

The rider pulled up his scratched plastic eye visor and looked back at me. I was close enough to him that even in the dim light I could see the scar. It was Izzat. He turned and ran to the bike. I hesitated. I reached for *La Malinche* and fumbled the draw. Izzat pulled the bike upright, mounted, and goosed the throttle. I regained control of the pistol and tried to draw a bead on the bike. Too late. Izzat was already halfway to the onramp.

I sprinted back to the truck. Ro and Randall gave me hard 'What the Fuck?' stares. I hit the gas. I maxed the Toyota and almost lost control as we swung onto the highway.

Ro yelled. "Jimmy! What the hell is going on Jimmy!"

I had a hard time getting the words out. "It's him Ro! It's fucking him! Izzat!"

"What the hell are you saying, *'Mano?'*"

"That fucker on the bike. It's Izzat. He must've escaped during the raid."

Randall's head poked through the small sliding window between the cab and the truck bed. "What's going on gentlemen? Why are we in hot pursuit?"

I kept shouting. "It's him! It's Izzat! On the bike. I saw his face. It's him!"

Randall shot a 'are you fucking with me?' look back through the window.

We hauled ass northbound. Still too early for any real traffic. I weaved past a couple of tractor trailers and caught sight of Izzat a few hundred meters ahead. Izzat's comically large helmet turned back over his shoulder. He saw us. He accelerated so fast it looked like we were driving in reverse.

Randall and Rogelio stayed silent. I sensed they didn't believe me. The look in their eyes said, 'Maybe the lack of sleep and 24/7 stress has Jim chasing ghosts.' In a sense they were right. Izzat was a ghost. A ghost I planned on chasing straight to hell.

I lost sight of Izzat as the highway rolled back to the west near Punta Morro. As the road swept back to the north, Ro pointed through the windshield. Izzat was dead ahead. A semi was trying to pass another 18-wheeler in the right lane. The two lumbering vehicles formed an inadvertent roadblock. Izzat downshifted and weaved lane-to-lane looking for an opening. The delay gave us valuable seconds to catch up. Izzat finally swung to the shoulder and goosed it. I followed in trace, praying that the tires would survive the minefield of road debris scattered along the edge of the asphalt.

Just north of El Sauzal, Izzat leaned hard into a clover offramp. We were close enough I could hear the bike shudder. This didn't seem like a good place for him to try and lose us.

I yelled, "Where's he headed, Ro?"

Ro's eyes darted back and forth. "The coastal access road," he said. "That's the only thing that makes sense. He's trying to avoid the police checkpoints to the north."

I followed Izzat through the offramp. The Toyota's tires squealed; the chassis bucked. We damn near smacked the jersey barriers. I recovered in time to see Izzat turn again. He rocketed through a warren of residential streets. A T-intersection loomed. Izzat punched straight through into a farmer's field. His bike speed-wobbled as the street suspension tried to absorb the dirt clods. I stayed in full pursuit. We hit the field way too fast. Randall let out a rebel yell as we caught air. He channeled his inner bull rider and managed to stay upright in the truck bed with only one hand on the roll bar. Izzat banked back towards the beach access road. The bike sent up a rooster tail of dirt and crops. The Toyota shuddered again as we bounced onto the asphalt. Randall white-knuckled it and somehow managed to stay upright.

Ro shouted, "We're almost back to *La Ballena*. We can take him here!"

Izzat turned towards the ocean again. It was a desperate move. He didn't know the area. He obviously hadn't recon'd the area like Randall and I had. Now he'd have to cut back across the access road or he'd sail off the cliffs. The access road gave us the speed advantage. I pulled up almost even with Izzat. Ro waved frantically at something ahead. I saw it. The dirt trail converged with the access road. I smiled. The timing was perfect. Izzat cut hard to beat us back to the road. I clipped his back tire. The bike waffled and flipped end-over-end. I heard Randall let out an uncharacteristically concerned, 'Holy shit!' as Izzat cartwheeled over the truck.

I skidded to a stop and hit the ground running. Izzat was lying on his back, a denim and leather-clad ragdoll. His femur was shattered. The bone punctured his pantleg midway up his thigh. His chest heaved. I used my foot to push the visor back on his helmet. We made eye contact. A heavy realization caused my arms and legs to tingle. My future would be defined by this moment. Despite the gravity of the showdown, I didn't feel compelled to ceremony. I stuck the barrel of *La Malinche* through the visor gap in Izzat's helmet. He stared back at me over the barrel, his face twisted in shock. I don't think he recognized me. For a split second I debated on whether to say something even though I wasn't sure Izzat would understand any English in his current condition. But Randall was right: *La Malinche* translated my rage better than words ever could. I pulled the trigger.

Greasy smoke wafted out of Izzat's helmet. The mist tinged red with blood and tissue. The usual cordite tang of gun smoke was replaced with a different scent. Izzat's shattered skull smelled like Miami cigarettes and revenge.

Randall and Ro walked up beside me. Ro pointed back down the road to the south. It was light enough to make out the figure of a man walking our way. Probably a local that was coming to see what the fuss was all about. We needed to get gone.

I patted down Izzat's corpse. He had a cellphone that was banged up from the crash but still looked operational. I pocketed the phone and rifled through his other pockets. He had a few pesos and some small denomination US bills. No gun. No other pocket litter of any intelligence value.

Randall and I heaved Izzat's body into the bed of the truck and we drove north about half a mile. Ro pointed to a pullout and directed me to park near the cliff that fell away to the beach. Randall helped me drag Izzat's body to the edge of the cliff. I looked down at the gray ocean below. The tide was up. With any luck the body might get pulled back to deeper water for a few days. We propped Izzat on the precipice.

I looked over at Randall and gave a mock toast. "For Steve."

Randall echoed. "For Steve."

I kicked Izzat's body over the cliff. The corpse bounced off the rock face a few times before splashing in the shallows. Ro whistled from the truck. A car had pulled up back near the scene of the crash. A couple of locals examined the wrecked motorcycle. It was time to go.

———

A few minutes later, we pulled into the parking lot of *La Ballena*. Ximena walked out of the apartment as we unloaded the Toyota. She had an expectant look on her face. Ro gave her a little gesture that signaled, 'we'll talk about it later.' Ximena said she'd grab us coffee and walked back up the stairs into the apartment.

Randall shagged his Isuzu. It was time to hit the road. None of us knew what to say.

Randall broke the silence, "Gentlemen, this was the most fun I've had in years."

The comment caught Ro off guard, but only for a second. My pirate friend broke into a pirate smile.

"Glad to be of service, *amigo*," Ro said. "Come back and see us anytime. You are always welcome at *La Ballena*. Drinks on me."

Randall gave Rogelio a fist bump and then turned to me. "Well, young buck, it's time we parted ways. Stick to the plan and I'll see ya when I see ya. No rush on the truck. I won't need her for a while."

"Got it," I said. "And thanks, Randall. For everything. This was a big ask. I owe you. I haven't forgotten about our arrangement. I'll drop off the first delivery here soon."

"*Adios, pistoleros,*" Randall said. He cruised out of the parking lot and hit the highway. I reckoned even with a detour through Mexicali he'd be back in Joshua Tree by supper time.

Ximena walked up with coffees. "He left without his *café*."

I chuckled. "I don't think Randall is gonna need any caffeine. This morning's activities will keep him juiced for a good long while."

Ximena forced eye contact with both me and Ro. "And what exactly did these activities include?"

Ro coughed reflexively. "I'll tell you all about it later, *mi amor.* For now, give Jimmy his coffee so he can be on his way."

Ximena handed me the coffee and planted a kiss on the corner of my mouth. She whispered something in Spanish that I couldn't translate, but her inflection made me feel all warm and fuzzy inside. I quickly looked away and saw Ro side-eyeing me. Even with all we'd been through together, or perhaps because of all we'd been through together, Ro still scared me. I didn't want Ximena's casual display of affection to flip one of Ro's internal switches. Dealing with Iraqis and Mexican bandits was one thing. Dealing with an unhinged Rogelio would be quite another.

To diffuse the situation, I quickly turned to Ro with my arms held wide. "Thanks for everything, *hermano,*" I said. "You are a true friend. And, if you'll allow me to say so in front of your woman, a bad motherfucker to boot."

Ro smiled again. More assassin than pirate this time. He managed to look scary and endearing at the same time.

"I'm glad it worked out Jimmy… at least so far."

I opened my mouth, but Ro cut me off.

Ro's voice dropped to the bottom of his baritone range. "I can handle any fallout down here, but you need to take care up in *el norte.* Your government will catch wind of what happened. You know they will, Jimmy. They'll look at you hard. Don't give them any... how do you say, 'ammunition,' to fuck with you. What happened here has to stay here. Take all this to the grave, *'mano.*"

"I will, my friend," I said. "That's a promise."

I slid into the cab of the Toyota and hid *La Malinche* and Izzat's cell phone in the hollowed-out A/C vent behind the glove compartment. I gave Ro and Ximena a nod through the window and drove north. Ro stood with his arms crossed over his .45 chest rig with Ximena leaning against him. She blew me a kiss that I caught in the rearview mirror.

22

San Ysidro Border Crossing
US/Mexico Border – Saturday, 28 June 2003

The Tijuana traffic was mercifully light. I made the border in good time. The border agent waved me through with barely a word. Any news of the action down south hadn't yet made it up this way. At least not in Yankee channels. Once I crossed back into the US, I hit the 5 North and lit up a dart. The smoke soothed. My shoulders finally relaxed. The relief hit like a drug. I tried not to get too comfortable. It was still too early in the game to celebrate.

The drive north gave me time to dwell on everything that had happened. I was a little surprised that icing Izzat didn't dredge up any of the expected feelings of revulsion or self-doubt, or any of that other bullshit the pros like to talk about. I thought about Souza. I kept picturing his devastated wife and kid standing by his coffin, but the rage I'd felt at the funeral was gone. I'd killed the man who killed my friend. That made me feel better. Obviously, it didn't do shit for Steve's family, and it never would. But I understood that wasn't the point. Ultimately, dropping Izzat wasn't about them. It was about me. Killing is a personal business. And business had been good this weekend.

My thoughts also drifted back to Adila. I waded through the possibilities. Did she make it to Ensenada? Was she in protective custody? Would I ever see her again? None of the logical conclusions seemed promising. The Mexican raid on Santana's house that we'd witnessed just a few hours earlier led me to believe that the marina operation was compromised. But even as I tried to parse out the likely pitfalls of Adila's situation, I couldn't bring myself to reject all hope for her future. For reasons I couldn't explain, Adila's survival seemed necessary to justify all the other sacrifices. I yearned for proof that she was alive. My gut told me she was.

Steve and Adila. They were all I thought about on my drive back to the world. I should've thought harder on my own situation. I should've used that time to try and figure out some angles with the Feds, with NCIS. I should've called Easy and let him help me navigate a softer landing. But I didn't do any of that.

———

I pulled into Jessica's house around breakfast time. She answered the door in the same green kimono she wore our first morning together. I tried to hug her, but she pulled away and left me in the foyer. I watched her disappear into the kitchen.

Jessica came back with my cellphone. "Here." She dropped the phone in my hands.

"Thanks, Jessica," I said. "I mean it. Thanks."

"I made the calls like you asked," she said. "I still don't know what you're up to, but whatever it is, I don't think it worked. That damn thing has been ringing off the hook."

I opened the phone. The log showed a bunch of missed calls over the past 48 hours. A couple from Easy as per our plan. Most of them from Cruz.

Jessica looked exhausted. "So? What now?"

I gambled. "Is too much to ask for me to take a shower?"

Jessica made a little 'humph' noise and walked to a hallway closet. She threw me a towel.

"Use my shower upstairs," she said. "Rachel might be home any minute."

The shower felt good. Too good. The pent-up tension of the past two days melted and I damn near fell asleep standing up. Jessica's voice yanked me back to reality. She was calling my name. I felt a surge of excitement. I thought she was going to join me in the shower. I finished rinsing and turned off the water so I could hear better.

Jessica's voice was closer now. "Jim!"

"I'm in the shower."

"You have visitors."

Visitors? What the fuck? I toweled off quick and threw on my jeans. I couldn't find my t-shirt. I walked downstairs bare-chested. Jessica was holding the front door open. Cruz was standing in the doorway, looking every bit the pistol-packing goddess. MacFarlane and Li flanked her. That was not a good sign. My stomach churned.

Cruz stared me down hard. For a brief second, her glance dropped down to my waist and then back up to eye level. Jessica watched Cruz watch me. Both women's eyes narrowed.

"Get dressed, Jim," Cruz said. "You need to come with us."

I looked at Jessica and mouthed 'I'm sorry.' She tossed me the missing t-shirt. Jessica looked back at Cruz. The women stared at each other. Total silence. As if on cue, they both turned their gaze back on me. I knew right then I'd permanently fucked up any possible future with Jessica. The realization didn't feel as disappointing as I thought it would. It felt preordained. Par for the course.

———

The Feds drove me back to San Diego. I rode in the backseat next to Cruz. She didn't look at me once during the half-hour trip. No one talked. My initial spike of panic subsided. Whatever the Feds had up their sleeve was beyond my ability to control. I relaxed. I dozed. It was a nap of the guilty. The rest of the resigned.

We parked under a nondescript office building on the outskirts of the city. Definitely a government job. The joint looked weekend empty. Li ushered me into a conference room. I wasn't cuffed. No one offered coffee or water. Mixed signals all around.

A bearded guy walked in before we sat. He looked familiar. I flipped through the mental rolodex. Bingo—Iraq. I met this dude in Baghdad. He was 'Brent' from CIA.

I said, "Hey, Brent."

"Take a seat Jim." Brent replied. He sounded like an American Roger Moore. Brent was Mr. Cool incarnate.

We settled around a modular conference table. I tried to gauge faces. Everyone except Brent looked sleep deprived. I felt a telekinetic transfer of exhaustion from Cruz and broke into a lion's yawn.

I shook off the mental fatigue and tried to concentrate. After what had just gone down in Mexico I needed to stay on guard. I studied the room again. One thing stood out—none of the Feds had notepads. I got a 'this meeting is off the books' vibe. It felt like the silent treatment was orchestrated to get me to speak first. I obliged.

"What's up, team?" I asked. "Do I need to call my lawyer?" I kept my eyes on MacFarlane. He always seemed eager to hear his own voice.

MacFarlane opened his mouth, but Brent beat him to the punch.

Brent said, "No lawyers today, Jim."

"OK. So what did you want to talk about?"

Brent said, "I want to talk about the man you know as Izzat al-Zaidon."

"What about him?"

"Where is he, Jim?"

My peripheral vision narrowed. The conference room turned trash compactor. The air felt squeezed and I started to panic.

I bore down hard and shook the butterflies. I jumped to conclusions. If the Feds had already made me for greasing Izzat, I'd be wearing bracelets. I sure as fuck wasn't about to start copping to anything now.

I said, "Why would I know where Izzat is?"

MacFarlane couldn't help himself; he showed his first card. "We know you were in Mexico the past two days, Jim. Tell us about Izzat."

Brent frowned. I could tell he was displeased MacFarlane was playing the 'we know all' approach before I'd said anything of note. I looked over at Cruz. She avoided eye contact. That sour tinge of panic started to bubble in my gut.

I turned my attention back to MacFarlane, Li, and Brent. "Look, Gentlemen, I don't know what you want me to say."

MacFarlane and Li glanced at each other; the insider eyes I'd seen them make during our earlier interviews. It was a signal to either explain or withhold certain information. I didn't know which it was in this case, but it didn't matter. Brent didn't give them a chance to finish their little Kabuki dance.

Brent said, "You get a pass on this one, Jim. Whatever happened in Mexico can stay in Mexico. But I need to know what you know."

Interesting that Brent said 'I need to know' and not 'we need to know.' I needed to stall to figure the angle. Ro's advice about taking everything to the grave lodged in my brainstem.

I said, "Let me get this straight Brent... or whatever your real name is. You want me to talk about 'stuff' that may or may not have happened down in Mexico, that I may or may not have been involved in, without my lawyer, solely because you, a spook I've met twice in my life, tells me I get a pass? Even while I'm sitting here surrounded by Federal law enforcement officers? What would you do if you were in my position, Brent?"

Li said, "This is not a custodial interrogation, Jim. We haven't read you your rights. This is an investigation. A time-sensitive one. We aren't charging you with anything, but we need you to start talking. Izzat is still our best lead on the *hawala* index and the bonds."

I looked at Cruz. I tried to look as pathetic as possible. I played the 'I'm just a dumb grunt and I don't know what the big bad Feds want with me' angle. She didn't buy it, but she did give me the slightest of nods. The gesture read 'you can trust them.'

Time to deflect. I needed to take these hounds off the scent for a beat. Give 'em something else to gnaw on for a spell.

I said, "Can we back up for a second? Shouldn't you guys be in Ensenada? Wasn't Adila's boat scheduled to arrive this morning?"

MacFarlane struggled to check his surprise. "How do you know about the boat?"

His reaction indicated Cruz hadn't dimed me out to the Feds for peepin' their dossier on the sly. God, what a woman. I owed her big. I needed to cop to reading the file without letting the Feds know I'd already admitted as much to Cruz. I decided to offer a bit of truth to keep their attention off the bigger lies I didn't want to own.

I said, "I took a peek at that file you left on my bed in the safehouse."

MacFarlane's surprise changed to embarrassment. He looked to Li for a lifeline. Li obliged.

"Tell us what you think you saw in the file," Li said.

Brent bristled. He was pissed. He didn't have time to rehash old news. He dropped a bomb on me. He jumped the line. The Feds would have to wait.

Brent said, "Adila's dead, Jim. She never made it out of Iraq. She was gunned down near Basra a few days after her parents were killed."

That familiar, adrenalized sourness shot up through my throat. I choked it down. My brain clouded. Brent's take didn't jive. I needed answers.

"What the fuck do you mean she's dead?" I asked. "I saw a photo of Adila in that file. I could tell by the background setting that she wasn't in Iraq. She had to have made it out. What about the boat in Ensenada?"

The room stayed silent. Heavy eyes all around. Except for Brent. He still looked pissed. Mr. Unflappable was starting to flap. I locked eyes with him, telepathically pleading for him to tell me he was wrong about Adila's death.

Brent asked the Feds if he could talk to me alone. It was actually more of a demand than an ask, but artfully presented given that Brent's hackles were up. MacFarlane started to protest but Li shut him down. Li signaled MacFarlane to follow him outside. It seemed as though the power dynamic between Li and MacFarlane had shifted since I saw them last. Li was running the show now.

I looked up at Cruz. She was already at the door. Her look said she was done with this case. And done with me. Permanently, if she could help it. I didn't blame her.

The Feds left. It was just me and Brent. I kicked back in the chair.

Brent said, "That whole boat thing was a story we fed to the right people to get the bad guys to expose themselves. It worked. The Mexicans popped Adolfo Santana this morning in Ensenada. Although I'm guessing you already knew that. But they didn't get everyone. Colombani didn't take the bait. He flew out of Tijuana yesterday morning before we could get the Mexicans onboard. Both Santana and Colombani still have contacts operating on both sides of the border. Those are the people I need to find. And I need to find them fast, before they go back underground."

I stayed silent. Brent's face clouded. He projected a manic intensity. I was his only target now. He was locked on and losing patience with my mute act.

"Fuck the FBI," Brent said. "We're way beyond law enforcement now. Fuck this 'I need to talk to my lawyer bullshit,' this is you and me. Tell me what you know. Start with Izzat.

I wanted to believe Brent. He and his boys were the ones that raced me back to the Country Club that night I got blown up at the factory. Plus, Brent was a player in the Fuad family drama. In that sense I felt like he was personally invested. Still, Brent was a spook. Even if I trusted him to keep me out of the Feds' crosshairs, I had other people to consider. If it was just my ass on the line, I'd be more willing to trust Brent with the skinny on Izzat and everything else that went down south of the border. But Randall, Rogelio, and even Ximena were involved now. I couldn't bring myself to come clean unless I knew Brent would keep them out of the fray.

I tried to find the right words to keep it cordial. "Look, Brent... I don't know what to tell—"

"Fuck that." Brent cut me off. He leaned forward in his chair. His old, practiced aloofness that he tossed around Iraq was nowhere to be found. His new intensity roiled the air between us.

Brent locked me up again with his eyes. "I don't care what went down the past couple of days in Mexico. I don't care about any of your friends that may have been involved. All I care about is finding Izzat and his connections on this side of the world. The FBI wants the *hawala* network and the bonds. Good for them. If we find Izzat and they can make some arrests, all the better. But that's not my priority. I have other things in play I can't tell you about, but believe me when I tell you that time is of the essence."

Brent seemed sincere. Asking the Feds to give us the room didn't seem rehearsed. But I was still paranoid. I scanned the ceiling and walls looking for mics and cameras. I realized that even if the room was wired, I'd never be able to spot the surveillance gear. Thoughts bounced around my gray matter like bb pellets in a matchbox. I finally rested on 'fuck it,' if this was all some sort of elaborate trick to get me to incriminate myself, Easy would get me out of it on the back end with his lawyer kung fu. I still had faith in his abilities to outmaneuver the Feds. Also, I rationalized, perhaps naively, that giving CIA an assist might help smooth over my legal troubles down the road.

I said, "What if I had a cellphone that used to belong to Izzat?"

Brent leaned across the table. "Where is it?"

"It's in the truck. But listen… I have it hidden next to an illegal pistol. If the Feds find the gun, I'm fucked."

"Don't worry about it. MacFarlane is having that truck towed down here as we speak. Tell me where the phone and gun are stashed. I'll retrieve them before any of their people get access. No one with a badge will be the wiser."

I let out a long exhale. "The gun and phone are stashed in a hollowed-out compartment behind the glove box. Part of the A/C vent was removed and there's a hard plastic catch that releases the covering. If you feel around behind the glove compartment, you'll find it."

"Done," Brent said. "Now about Izzat. Where can I find him?"

"You're going to have to wait for high tide."

———

I was alone in the conference room for nearly an hour. At one point I considered getting up and walking out. I nixed that idea. I wouldn't make it far. I was too fucking tired. The far corner of the room looked dark and inviting. A small oasis of shadow that could shield me from the tyranny of the overhead fluorescent lighting. I curled up on the thin, hi-tread carpet and passed out. It was my most unburdened sleep in recent memory.

Li gently kicked me awake. I had no idea how long I'd been out. It took me a few seconds to realize where I was.

"What's going on?" I asked.

"You're fee to go," Li said. "The truck is parked outside. We contacted your chain of command and they terminated your temp-duty orders. Technically you're still on leave until 0800 tomorrow morning. You need to get back up to 29 Palms and check in."

"Uh… yeah, OK." I couldn't muster any other words.

Li turned to walk me out of the building. I realized MacFarlane had disappeared. I figured this might be the only time I'd get a chance to talk to Li without his colleague present.

"Hey, can you tell me any more about what happened to Adila?" I asked. "Was Brent just fucking with me or is she really gone?"

Li sighed. I could tell he knew more but was deciding how much he could share. "Sorry Jim, but as far as I know Brent is telling the truth. Adila's dead. CIA came to us about her a while back, maybe a day or two after you first mentioned her. They claimed she was killed but that the *Mukhabarat's* contacts in Mexico and California likely didn't know she was dead. Brent's boys came up with the fishing-boat ploy. We agreed to it because it was our best shot at capturing people who could provide intel on the *hawalas* and the missing bonds. CIA needed our help to get the Mexicans to play ball and take down the bad guys operating in Mexico. Of course, we wanted Santana alive but that didn't happen. He was killed this morning in the raid. If I'm being honest, the Mexican Marines were probably under orders to make sure he never walked out of there. I'm guessing he had too much dirt on other Mexican officials and they couldn't risk him talking in custody. Especially now that we were involved. But that aside, like Brent said, Colombani left the country before we could get the Mexican authorities on target. So now we're left trying to sweep up all the loose ends. There's a chance we can still salvage this whole effort and identify some of the money men operating here in the States. That's why we brought you in."

"Yeah, about that," I said. "I'm still not saying I was in Mexico, but how can you be so certain I was?"

Li chuckled, but he wasn't amused. "Don't press your luck, Jim. You squeaked by on this one. Brent told us you gave him Izzat's phone. We should be able to pull some leads off it. That buys you a reprieve, but it's conditional. You need to stand down. Don't tempt fate. Go back to 29 Palms, be a good Marine, keep your mouth shut, and leave all this behind."

I knew Li's parting shot was more warning than advice. The Feds would still be watching me. Brent may have used some Agency voodoo to keep me out of jail this time, but he wouldn't stick around to cover for me. It felt like a genuine stay of execution. Surprisingly, I didn't feel the same sense of euphoria

I'd experienced dodging close calls in combat. I just felt numb. All I wanted now was more sleep.

The Toyota was parked outside in an empty lot. The keys were in the ignition. I acted like I was retrieving something from the glovebox and opened the secret stash vent. I ran my fingers across the empty space where Izzat's cell phone had been. Hopefully Brent or the Feds could pull some useful data from it. I couldn't give them Izzat, but the phone felt like a nice consolation prize. Maybe they'd trace some of the numbers in the call log to expose additional bad guys. Maybe they could lean on that first batch of villains to identify their bosses. Maybe they could keep working up the chain. It seemed plausible. Izzat was a trained operator, but he was in a hurry when we caught up with him. I doubt he'd had time to zero out his phone before I punched his ticket. I stuck my hand deeper in the compartment until my fingers brushed steel. *La Malinche* was still there. Thanks, Brent. Maybe there were still a few trustworthy spooks after all.

As I exited the lot, Cruz pulled up alone in her G-ride. She lowered her window. Despite my fatigue, I still felt the butterflies in my stomach. First Jessica, then Adila, now Angela. I was about to permanently lose three women in one day. The fact that none of them were ever mine to lose in the first place didn't make it any easier.

"Hey, Angela."

"Do you realize how lucky you are, Jim?"

"You're the second person to tell me that in the past half hour."

"It's true," Cruz said. "Brent, or whatever his name is, pulled out all the stops on this one. I've never seen the FBI back off like this."

"So, what exactly do they think I did?"

"Nice try, Jim. I'd recommend you count your blessing and forget all this."

"I hear ya, but some things are harder to forget than others."

Cruz did that thing with her eyes—the unconscious narrowing. She titled her head through the window. "What are you saying, Jim?"

I realized this would probably be the last time I ever spoke to her. I tried to wrangle a smile. It didn't work.

I said, "Well… I was hoping I wouldn't have to forget you."

For a split second, Cruz' face softened, but she caught herself. "Bye, Jim."

23

Marine Corps Air-Ground Combat Center
29 Palms, California – Thursday, 28 August 2003

The Battalion was finally coming home today. Three months behind schedule. I wanted to ensure the homecoming ran smooth, so I rolled out the rack extra early. Randall was already up. He had the coffee brewing. I'd crashed at his spread pretty regularly over the past month. Per our arrangement, I'd picked up some stuff Randall needed for his gunsmithing projects. I had to go to Arizona yesterday to get the gear, so it was late by the time I arrived. When I returned, we got to drinking and talking about Mexico. Randall asked if there had been any updates from the Feds and whether or not I'd seen Cruz again. Reluctantly I admitted that it was no dice on either count. He asked if I thought the Feds still had me under surveillance. I hadn't noticed any physical tails in almost two weeks. I assumed I'd slipped off their priority list. Honestly, I didn't really care if they were still surveilling me. Let 'em watch. I was determined to walk the line, to hold tight to the straight and narrow. I told Randall my outlaw days were over. He smiled that crooked smile and gave me a 'that's what you think' laugh.

The late-night talks with Randall got me thinking about the big picture. I didn't have many answers, but it felt like maybe I had an outline. A skeleton on which to hang the flesh of the past, present, and future. Maybe it was a futile attempt. Maybe I was still too young to know what any of it meant. But I felt compelled to try and give my past some shape. Maybe even slap a little direction on my future.

After the drama in Mexico, I tried to convince myself that I'd entered a new phase. From here on out everything would be divided into 'before Iraq' and 'after Iraq,' with Mexico serving as the segue. The 'before' chapter closed the second my bullet entered Izzat's skull. At least, that's what I kept telling myself. But that left the 'after' chapters, which gave me plenty to worry about. The future lurked hard, especially now that my separation papers were approved. I'd be a civilian after a few more paychecks. Some days, that realization was scarier than the ghosts of Souza, Fuad, Zahra, Adila, and Izzat combined.

I left Randall's at the crack of dawn. Despite the *de riguer* hangover, the drive to 29 Palms was pleasant. The not-yet-oppressive hi-desert air felt strangely inviting. I blasted Little Richard through the Impala's tape deck to goose the mood. The Radio Baghdad vibes felt good. By the time I reached the base, I felt genuinely happy. No bad shit to sour my spirits.

The receiving area for the Battalion was set up in a parking lot. The place was packed with anxious families and hand-drawn welcome-home signs. I usually despised these types of obligatory, heartwarming scenes. But this one felt different. It felt right. The Marines deserved a proper homecoming. Fuck the parades and speeches. I'd done everything in my limited powers to ensure there would be no extraneous bullshit. The plan was this—turn in weapons and get the boys reunited with their loved ones as fast as possible. The Old Man had approved 30 days block leave for those that wanted to take it.

The first bus carrying the Marines home from March Air Force Base rolled into view. The homecoming crowd buzzed with anticipation. Iraq had left me with a complicated relationship when it came to crowds. It was good to be around people who were engaged in normal, friendly day-to-day stuff. But the fear of someone targeting such a gathering lingered. This crowd felt different. I dare say my heart *was* genuinely warmed. No coppery fear, no adrenalized tension, just friends and family desperate for a reunion. It was about as wholesome a scene you could ever imagine that involved Marines. Of course, the true toll of the deployment wouldn't shake out for months or even years—the fractured marriages, fizzled friendships, the important moments missed. All that shit would linger for generations. But right now, in this moment, those were all worries for another day.

The homecoming plan worked. All the administrative stuff got sorted and the Marines kicked out on leave in relatively short order. The parking lot cleared out quick. There were only a few stragglers left behind.

Majors Miller and McSorley shuffled over to chat. Both men were surrounded by their wives and a gaggle of kids. McSorley was Irish Catholic and had an improbable tally of offspring for a man in his mid-30s. I counted at least six. His kids hung from his waist at weird angles. The youngins seemed hellbent on never again letting dad escape their grip.

I welcomed my bosses back and gave polite waves to the family hangers-on. Miller asked if everything was good with the re-deployment training schedule. I told him it was under control. I told him not to worry about it. I sincerely hoped both men could drop their packs for a few days and enjoy their leave. More importantly, I wanted both of them to get some fucking sleep. They looked mummified. I remember both majors looking bad before I left. Now they looked almost alien with their rawhide cheeks and loose-fitting cammies.

Perhaps because they were unsure how to navigate the homecoming ritual, both Miller and McSorley kept talking to me for much longer than I thought necessary. Eventually, the wives got impatient. They'd shared their husbands long enough. These women had real world shit to contend with. Naptimes, dinner prep, and probably a dozen other tasks that I would never guess. Miller's wife cut him off mid-sentence and said it was time to go home. The wives yanked their husbands out of there quick.

I hung back waiting for a chance to talk to the Old Man. I had a few duty rosters he needed to sign. Also, I wanted to gauge him to see if he had been read-in to the 'extracurricular activities' I'd participated in since getting back to the World. I had no clue what, if anything, NCIS or the FBI had told him.

The Old Man was busy talking to the Adjutant. I didn't want to disturb him, so I wandered off. I saw Ox sitting on his sea bag next to one of the buses.

"Welcome home, Ox," I said.

"Hey, Sir. How have things been back here in the World?"

"I was actually going to ask you how things were back in the Sandbox after I left. Why don't you go first."

"Well, Sir, it was pretty much more of the same," Ox said. "We left Baghdad not long after you redeployed. We went down south to deal with those Shi'a assholes. By the time we got there, Uncle Sam had pretty much worn out the welcome. But hey, get this. I did bag me a couple of genuine Iranians down there. And one Sudanese if you can believe that? I still don't know why or how that poor bastard got involved."

"Ha! Good for you, Ox," I said. "What did that bring your final tally to?"

"Aw shit, Sir, I don't know. Somewhere around 25, I guess?"

Ox knew exactly how many dudes he'd plugged, but I didn't want to put him on the spot. "Damn impressive, Ox," I said.

"I'll get ahold of the Ops diaries and get all the details for your award write up."

"Shit, Sir, I don't care about no fucking medals. I just want to go back. I had the time of my life over there."

"I don't doubt it, Ox." The thought of Ox back in Iraq was much more comforting than the idea of him separating from the Corps, getting bored, and going back to Iowa to knock over banks with RPGs.

It dawned on me mid-conversation that Ox might not have anywhere to go now that he was back in the World. I probed the topic a bit and Ox finally convinced me he was waiting on a ride from a buddy, not a taxi. Satisfied that Ox wasn't about to go on a solo crime spree, I bid him farewell.

I hustled back to the Battalion headquarters. The Old Man was in his office. I got him to sign off on the duty rosters. I studied his face for any sign he might be savvy to my recent adventures. I couldn't get a read on him. If the Old Man was hip, he did a masterful job of hiding it. He asked a couple of perfunctory questions about the upcoming training schedule and then shooed me away to make some calls. As I exited his office, I caught his reflection in the window. The Old Man fired up a massive cigar. Uncle Sam had banned smoking in Government buildings a few years back, but the Boss didn't seem to give a fuck on homecoming day. Good for him.

———

I had some other paperwork to take care of so I headed back to the Ops Office. It occurred to me I hadn't talked to my Mom and Sister in a couple weeks so I decided to shoot them an email. I found a computer, logged onto my civilian email account, and started clearing out my inbox. About ten messages down

I noticed an email from what looked like a spam account. The sender's handle was a jumble of letters and numbers. At first glance, the subject line appeared blank. I squinted and noticed a single period had been placed in the subject line. My first instinct was to delete it, but curiosity got the better of me.

I opened the email. The first line read, 'Jim—this is Adila.'

My stomach dropped. What the fuck is this? Thoughts zipped through my head faster than I could sort them. Is this the Feds? Brent and his CIA cronies? Are they trying to bait me? Or am I the bait? Reflexively, I looked behind me. The office was empty. The entire Battalion headquarters was empty. My hands shook so hard I had to sit on them. I needed a smoke. There was no one around to tell me not to. I dug out a dart and lit up right there in the Ops office.

The blue light of the computer monitor gave me tunnel vision. The email burned on the screen. It was a one-liner. A simple plea to call a number with a Los Angeles area code. No further explanation, no proof of life, no indicators of where the sender was physically located.

I thought through my options. I could notify the Feds. Notify Cruz. Try and get in touch with Brent. Or call the number.

I pulled out my latest burner phone and dialed the number. Fuck it, maybe I needed to keep the Iraq chapter open just a little bit longer. Fuck it always wins.

THE END

About The Author

Josh Bates retired from the United States Marine Corps in 2022. His service included combat tours in Iraq and Afghanistan and operational assignments across the Indo-Pacific. He lives in Kailua, Hawai'i with his family. *The Baghdad Shuffle* is his first novel.

DOUBLE‡DAGGER
— www.doubledagger.ca —

Double Dagger Books is Canada's only military-focused publisher. Conflict and warfare have shaped human history since before we began to record it. The earliest stories that we know of, passed on as oral tradition, speak of war, and more importantly, the essential elements of the human condition that are revealed under its pressure.

We are dedicated to publishing material that, while rooted in conflict, transcend the idea of "war" as merely a genre. Fiction, non-fiction, and stuff that defies categorization, we want to read it all.

Because if you want peace, study war.

www.ingramcontent.com/pod-product-compliance
Lightning Source LLC
Chambersburg PA
CBHW021039310726
48969CB00006B/1724